THREE TIMES TO FREEDOM

THE MACBEAN CHRONICLES

J.D. CARR

———

Text copyright © 2015 by J.D. Carr

ISBN-13: 978-1508748410

ISBN-10: 1508748411

I gratefully acknowledge the support given to me by my family and friends during the creation of "Three Times to Freedom," the first volume of The MacBean Chronicles; and a special thanks to my cousin, who helped me in time of need and introduced me to the world.

J.D. Carr

"We will go to the sun of freedom or to the death; if we die, our cause will continue living."

Augusto Cesar Sandino

CONTENTS

FOREWARD

The early spring storm blew in from the northeast covering the New England hills with 18 inches of heavy wet snow. Schools were closed and Hardy MacBean listened for cars coming down Salem Street. He had just finished packing a snowball when he heard the muffled wobbling sound of tires churning through the deep snow. A dark grey Plymouth sedan came in to view as he wound up and let the snowball fly. He observed the arc of his missile as it sailed through the snow filled air and held his breath in disbelief as it passed through the driver's open window.

"Shit!" Hardy exclaimed as the snowball pasted the driver squarely on the side of his face. He heard a man shout out, "Son of a bitch!" His heartbeat quickened as he watched the brake lights flash and the car slide across the road, plowing into a snow bank. Turning away, he ran as fast as he could toward the back yard of his house, stumbling and falling head first into a snowdrift. Winded, he picked himself up, sputtering, gasping for air and continued to run, looking for a place to hide.

Hardy woke in a sweat. Feeling the jet slow, he looked down on endless fields of green stretching to the east with the morning sunrise lighting up the sky.

"Hell of a dream," he thought. He had all but forgotten about that day so long ago.

Part One

THE BEGINNING

Chapter 1

The Ides of March arrived with a massive snowstorm blanketing the Northeast. Mary MacBean felt a terrible cramping grip her stomach. Exactly six months pregnant, she was taken by surprise when her water broke in a torrent onto the white tiled kitchen floor.

"What in hell?" she thought. "My baby is coming too soon."

She walked toward the bathroom, pausing to lean against the living room couch, gripping her stomach with both hands, wondering what she should do with her children asleep upstairs and her husband hundreds of miles away. The birth was happening all too quickly, and then he came without much warning. She hardly felt his birth, catching him as he fell into her hands. He couldn't weigh more than two pounds she thought. She looked him over from head to toe. His baldhead gleamed, and his disproportionately large ribcage stretched the skin of his puny frame as he let out a long piercing cry.

"What am I to do?" she exclaimed to herself.

She walked in slow motion, as if in a dream while she carried her son to the kitchen. Laying him down on the stainless steel countertop, she opened a large drawer full of sewing supplies and removed a heavy pair of scissors along with a length of thick twine. She tied off the umbilical cord in two places and watched as the cord stopped pulsing. Holding the scissors in her left hand she whispered softly, "God," before cutting the cord between the ties. She looked down upon his face, and slowly wrapped him in a white cotton towel with the initials MMM monogrammed in dark blue.

3

"You stay warm while I figure out what to do," she said, leaning over and kissing him. She looked out the kitchen window, reflecting on the phone call she received from her mother and father the day before as they prepared to fly out of Boston, saying they would be home in time for the baby's birth. She looked out at the snow swirling onto the porch and thought about the drive to the hospital and decided that her son's best chance for survival would be to take the train and avoid the unplowed roads. She lay him down on the living room couch, wrapped the towel with the half finished baby blanket and called up to the children.

"Gillies, Eliza, hurry, get dressed, you have a new baby brother and we need to get him to the hospital! Now!"

The children ran down the stairs and watched as their mother frantically grabbed coats and boots from the closet. They each inspected their new baby brother who lay nestled amongst pillows making gasping noises in between long, woeful fits of crying. Mary buttoned the children's coats over their pajamas and put on their boots. Bundled up, they left the house in single file with Mary leading the pack, cradling her baby, with her footsteps making a pathway to an old 1940 Chevy pickup. With Gillies and Eliza holding hands on the bench seat, she drove slowly in second gear toward the station with her baby tucked inside her coat.

"Mommy," Gillies asked, "what are we going to call him?"

Eliza looked perplexed, not understanding the question. She snuggled closer to her mother.

"What a disaster, what a storm," Mary said, looking ahead into the blinding snow as the wipers slapped against the ice building up on the windshield.

"We'll call him Hardy, your little brother is a hardy soul."

The five-mile drive to the station seemed to take forever as Mary gripped the wheel tightly with one hand and held her baby with the other, hoping that she would make the 8 a.m. Boston and Maine passenger service.

Pulling into the station with less than a minute to spare, Mary parked the truck, jerked open the door and stepped into the deep snow. Clutching Hardy with one hand, she held the driver's door open as Eliza and Gillies climbed down from the seat.

"Gillies, take my hand and take your sister's hand."

She clasped Gillies hand and they all trudged through the snow, sliding across a sheet of ice below the elevated departure deck as the train rumbled in from the north.

They arrived in Boston's North Station at 10:03, and with the help of a conductor who carried Eliza, they ran through the station out to Causeway Street with Gillies trailing and yelling above the screeching brakes of the incoming trains, "Wait, Mommy, wait!"

The conductor hailed a yellow cab and safely stowed Mary and her children in the back seat, shutting the door and wishing them well. They reached Fruit Street and the entrance to Massachusetts General Hospital after what seemed like an eternity riding through Boston's unplowed streets. When Mary walked into the hospital, the nurse quickly weighed Hardy at two pounds three ounces and called up the maternity ward requesting an incubator for immediate use.

Mary MacBean held her children's hands as she looked through a large plate glass window into a brightly lit room. She watched as four nurses, all wearing masks, attended to a dozen incubators. One of them carried Hardy to the window and showed Mary a tag attached to his left foot with MacBean written in black ink. A doctor on call stood next to Mary as tears rolled down her face.

"Mrs. MacBean," he said, putting his arm around her shoulders, "I can only imagine how difficult your day has been. Your son is alive and safe because of you. It is quite a miracle really. Now it's time for us to give you an exam and don't worry, we will look after your very special little boy."

Mary watched as the nurse began to feed Hardy with an eyedropper, filled with the breast milk she had pumped when she arrived at the hospital. He was hungry and eagerly consumed the milk as soon as it hit his lips. The doctor walked Mary across the hall to a private room with two beds.

"Let's have a look," he said.

She was exhausted and grateful to have a room with her children and grateful that Hardy was safe.

"Hello, hello operator?" Mary asked, "I'd like to place a call to Washington please, Lincoln 2200. Yes, I'll wait, thank you."

"Central Intelligence Agency, how may I help you?" the operator answered with a crisp New England accent.

"This is Mrs. William MacBean. May I speak with William MacBean please?"

"I will pass you through; please hold, "she replied.

A woman answered with a pronounced Southern drawl.

"Office of Policy Coordination, this is Miss Clara Winston. How may I help you?"

"This is Mrs. MacBean calling; may I speak with my husband?"

"I'm sorry, but Mr. MacBean is away on assignment. May I take a message?"

Mary felt her emotions swell and did her best to contain her disappointment.

"Why yes," she said in a tired and wavering voice, "Please tell William our son was born this morning at 7:27, we are at Massachusetts General, room 429."

"Of course, Mrs. MacBean, I'll ring him up right away," Clara said with heightened purpose.

Mary cradled the phone, holding on to the only connection she felt she had with her husband. Hanging up, she curled into a ball and fell sound asleep.

Clara Winston dialed the Waldorf-Astoria in New York. William MacBean along with five of his agents was setting up hidden microphones and recording equipment for a conference that had been secretly sponsored by the Communist Information Bureau. The 800 guests expected to gather included prominent U.S. and European literary and artistic figures that believed the conference was designed as a call for peace with the Soviet Union. Americans Arthur Miller and Norman Mailer joined with delegates from Europe to denounce the policies of the U.S. government. A majority of those in attendance believed that a third world war was imminent and the underlying purpose was eventual world domination by the United States and its Western Allies. MacBean had been given orders to record and identify prominent speakers, as well as known foreign agents. As a CIA operative, he had recently been appointed assistant director of the newly created Office of Policy Coordination. The OPC included representatives of the State Department, Defense Department and the CIA. Considered the covert action branch of the Central Intelligence Agency, OPC concentrated on propaganda, economic warfare and preventive direct action. This included sabotage, demolition, evacuation measures and subversion against hostile states, including assistance to underground resistance groups and anti-communist elements in threatened countries of the free world.

Chapter 2

On Wednesday, January 14, 1942, the United States and Great Britain agreed to have the U.S. Joint Chiefs of Staff and the British Chiefs of Staff work together to advise leaders of both nations on military policy during the war. This was accomplished during the Arcadia Conference, where President Franklin D. Roosevelt and British Prime Minister Winston Churchill met to discuss a unified Anglo-American war strategy. The U.S. service heads of the army, navy and air force and their British counterparts were merged into one office, with the Combined Staff Planners and the Combined Secretariat offering administrative support. Toward the end of the conference, President Roosevelt arranged for a private meeting with Winston Churchill. They discussed the disarray that Roosevelt found existing within the United States intelligence community, and his wish to eventually bring all of the intelligence departments within the executive branch. Roosevelt believed the executive departments, along with the U.S. Army and Navy, each with separate code-breaking departments, had no overall direction, control or coordination. It was during this meeting that Churchill offered the assistance of the British Secret Service MI6, and the loan of one of its officers.

"Franklin," Churchill said, "If we are to win this war, we will need to press every bright young man and woman we have into the intelligence service. We must discover what the enemy is thinking before they even know it themselves. We must out guess them at every turn. This is not the end of all wars, simply the beginning of wars that will produce death and destruction far greater than we can now conjure in our collective imagination."

"My dear Winston," Roosevelt replied, "The signatories of the Tripartite Pact have increased to eight and, no pun intended, this leaves us a bit behind the eight ball. We have a great deal of ground to cover, and we must hope Joe Stalin can sustain us from the east, because Japan has upped the ante. The immediacy of world war is upon us. God help us survive this axis of evil."

That afternoon Roosevelt signed executive order 9066 authorizing the incarceration of all Japanese Americans into newly constructed internment camps

.

On his return to Britain, Churchill dialed up MI6 Chief Stewart Menzies. In June 1942, Lieutenant Commander William MacBean was commissioned as the MI6 Liaison Officer to the newly formed United States Office of Strategic Services. He received orders to fly by military transport to Washington, D.C., and report to Colonel William J. Donovan.

MacBean was met by Donovan's driver at the newly constructed ultramodern Washington National Airport and was driven to 2430 E Street NW. Colonel Donovan, who had been appointed to head up the Office of Strategic Services the previous month, stood up from his desk as MacBean walked through the door.

"Good afternoon, Commander MacBean, welcome to the OSS," Donovan exclaimed, "We've been expecting you."

"Thank you very much, Colonel Donovan, I'm very pleased to be at your service," MacBean replied in a crisp Scottish accent.

"Did you have a good flight?" Donovan asked.

"Yes sir, a bit of a headwind."

"I hope you don't pull rank on me," Donovan quipped, breaking the ice and pointing out the disparity.

"I wouldn't think of it sir," MacBean laughed, "I am at your command."

"We will get along just fine MacBean!" Donovan exclaimed.

They immediately got down to business, discussing the development of the MI6 espionage and resistance movement in Europe and how Donovan wanted to bring together the various United States Government intelligence agencies and create a counter espionage branch within the OSS, modeled on the organization of British Counter Espionage. They also discussed combining the U.S. Army and Navy code-breaking departments with British military intelligence in the immediate effort to crack Axis ciphers.

At the age of 22, MacBean graduated from Trinity College, Cambridge with a Ph.D. in mathematics. He was fluent in English, French, German, Russian and Spanish. Immediately following his graduation, he enlisted with the British Royal Navy. After taking a series of exams he was assigned to the British Secret Intelligence Service and stationed at the Government Code and Cipher School at Bletchley Park, Buckinghamshire. Here he used his math and linguistics background to advance the military's development in the cryptanalysis of secret code.

The British military developed a secret intelligence division in June 1941 under the code name "Ultra." The designation was adopted for wartime signals intelligence, obtained by breaking high-level encrypted enemy radio and teleprinter communications at Bletchley Park. Under Donovan's command, MacBean would implement the X-2 Counter Espionage Branch and work within the OSS in concert with Ultra until the OSS dissolution by President Truman in 1945.

William met his future wife, Mary, the day he landed in America. They married in the fall of 1942 and by the wars end Mary had given birth to both a boy and a girl. William's initial plan at the end of the war was to return to the United Kingdom with his young family, resign his commission and accept a teaching position in the mathematics department at Trinity College. At the same time he received an offer to join the faculty at Trinity, President Truman personally asked him to oversee the liquidation of the OSS, preserving its clandestine intelligence capabilities and creating a new intelligence organization known as the Strategic Services Unit (SSU) within the War Department. Truman trusted MacBean and believed that he could successfully facilitate the transition with little oversight. William and Mary agreed that Trinity could wait and William accepted Truman's offer.

Chapter 3

MacBean secured two adjoining suites at the Waldorf-Astoria that were strategically located next to the conference hall. He watched as his agents set up four Ampex 300 magnetic tape recorders. The 300 was a modified improvement of the 200A model and it took up half the space. It was considerably more portable and could be wheeled about by one agent. Two agents ran wire to a dozen hidden microphones in three suites that were about to be occupied by the Soviet delegation, while the others placed microphones throughout the conference hall. As they were making the final connections and testing the equipment, the phone began to ring. William knew there could only be one person who would be calling.

"Hello, Clara, MacBean here," he said without letting Clara get the first word in.

"Oh, Mr. MacBean," Clara said sounding out of breath, "your wife just called and your son was born this morning!"

"What did you say, Clara? Slow down!"

"I said that your wife called and you have a new baby boy!"

"I thought that's what you said" MacBean's voice trailed off, "how could that be? He wasn't supposed to come until late June," he muttered to himself.

"I don't know, sir, but your wife and children are at Massachusetts General Hospital."

"Okay, Clara, please call Mrs. MacBean and tell her that I will catch the very next train to Boston, and tell her I hope to be there by tonight."

"Yes, sir," Clara said with relief. "I'll do so right away."

MacBean hung up the phone and looked around the room as the men completed their work.

"Listen up," MacBean said as the news of his son's birth began to sink in, "When you're finished testing the equipment, I want you to ring up room service and order enough food and drink for the rest of the day and into the night. I don't want you to move until the conference has ended, and then I want you to continue monitoring the Soviet delegation until they pack up and leave. I'll see you all back in Washington for translation."

MacBean grabbed his coat and bag, left the hotel and hailed a cab for Grand Central Station. When he arrived, the Colonial Express had just pulled in from Washington, D.C. "Lucky break" he thought, as he climbed aboard and found a seat in the club car. He ordered a glass of scotch whiskey and settled in for the five-hour ride. In the dimming afternoon light, he looked out the window at a fresh blanket of snow as the train clipped along the tracks toward New Haven. He closed his eyes and leaned his head back, thinking about his wife and how they had met.

Chapter 4

At the end of William MacBean's first day in Washington, Colonel Donovan announced that he had spoken with his wife and they had both agreed that until William could be situated they would enjoy having him stay with them at their Georgetown home. He also mentioned that his son David was home on furlough and would also be staying over for a few nights.

"I think David has made plans to entertain some of his friends and you might enjoy meeting them, help you settle in over here."

"Thank you very much for your offer," William said. "I'll take you up on that. I always enjoy meeting new people."

"Alright then, let me get my coat and hat and we're off!" Donovan exclaimed.

The ride to the Donovan home gave William his first look at Washington, D.C. When they reached Georgetown, he found the homes made from brick with ornate palladium style windows similar to the houses in Buckinghamshire.

"Our house was built pre-revolutionary war by a British Loyalist who fled to Canada. I thought you might find that of interest. And here we are! Home at last!"

"Welcome, Commander MacBean!" David Donovan exclaimed as he met them at the door. "Very good of you to join us. Please let me show you to your room. What may I get you to drink?"

"Tea will be quite fine, thank you," said MacBean as he climbed the front hall stairs to the second floor. David showed him to a room overlooking a small garden and reflecting pool.

"Your bath is in here," David said, opening the door to the bathroom. "I'll have your tea up in a moment. Take a load off your feet and relax. We have a few guests coming over for dinner at seven," he said closing the door.

A few minutes later a silver teapot and tray arrived along with milk, sugar, a china cup with saucer and Carr's Table Water Biscuits. Thanking the maid, William closed the door and poured his tea. After a long day, a hot cup of tea proved to be just what he needed. He sat on his bed, swung his legs up and laid his back against the headboard. He read some briefs that Colonel Donovan had given him, closed his eyes and fell

up, William?   Are you awake?" David questioned

akened from a foggy dream of hunting grouse with his

r on the Culloden plain, not far from where his great,

, Gillies MacBean, was slain by the British.

, I'm awake," William exclaimed, feeling somewhat

short nap.

sts will be arriving shortly, so I thought I would warn

"Right, thanks, I'll be down soon," William said.

He ran a shower, long enough to fully wake up, toweled off and thought about what he should wear. He chose his only pair of brown leather shoes, a pair of khaki slacks, his summer tweed and a plaid tie. "That should do", he thought as he combed his short crop of auburn colored hair.

William descended the stairs just as the guests began to arrive. As he reached the bottom landing, the front door opened and a young woman burst into the house. William was quite startled by her explosive entrance, but more so by her beauty. She had long raven black hair, flashing green emerald eyes and skin the color of milk. William stood with his mouth slightly agape as David walked into the entrance hall and greeted his feisty friend.

"Mary! How wonderful, you made it! Father told me that The Washington Star has hired you! Is that true?" He asked with excitement.

"Why, yes, it is, David. I'm so lucky, isn't that terrific?"

"What's more terrific is that you're here and I'm sure that you'll

15

manage to write an article or two that will embarrass us all! But we'll still be very proud of you Mary!"

Giving Mary a bear hug he turned to William.

"William, I'd like to introduce you to one of my oldest and closest friends, Mary…"

"Hello, William, it's so very nice to meet you," Mary said extending her hand. David smiled as William began to speak in his thick Scottish brogue.

"The pleasure is mine, Miss, Miss," shaking Mary's hand.

"Why it's MacBean!" Mary said.

"Now, now what did ye say?" exclaimed William wondering if he had heard correctly.

"It's MacBean!" David laughed, "No, it's no joke on you William, this is Mary MacBean, the real ticket!"

"Well, I'll be damned," William said, his voice full of consternation.

"Damned about what?" asked Mary.

"Well, Mary," David quipped, "I should have introduced you and used William's full name, Lieutenant Commander William MacBean, from England!"

Mary looked at William from his head to his shoes and shrieked before she began laughing uncontrollably, sputtering between laughter.

"I guess the joke is on both of us! David, you cruel bugger!"

David and William each erupted in laughter along with Mary's.

"Come on you two, let's go out on the porch and get acquainted," David said.

"What would you like to drink Mary?" David asked.

16

"I'll have a gin and tonic, David — lots of tonic, a little gin," Mary replied.

"And you, William?" David asked.

"I'll take a scotch, please, with a wee amount of water."

Mary looked at William and thought he must be at least six foot six inches tall, about a foot taller than she was. He was slim though muscular and she found him quite attractive with his short-cropped hair, Roman nose and clear complexion.

"How long have you been in Washington, William," she asked.

"I just flew in mid day."

"Are you staying long?"

"I don't know really, my assignment here as liaison officer from British intelligence is to see how our forces can team up. You know, the war and such."

Colonel Donovan and his wife, Ruth, appeared on the porch along with a half dozen recently arrived guests.

"Well hello, Mary," they both said in unison. "We see that you've met William MacBean!"

"Fancy that," David said laughing about the chance meeting between the two MacBeans, "fancy that."

"Why yes, I have, Mr. and Mrs. Donovan, in a roundabout way that is," Mary said. "David had his joke with us, of course, and it was rather hilarious, the proverbial jokester that he is!"

David grinned, thinking about the many pranks he had played upon Mary over the years. Who could imagine two unrelated MacBeans meeting one another like this, he thought. It was a good laugh that had been handed to him on a silver platter.

"I'll take credit where credit is due" David said. "Let's formally introduce William to the whole crowd. Everyone, listen up, please, I'd like to introduce all of you to our guest, Lieutenant Commander William MacBean; no, no relative to our lovely Mary!"

The room broke out in laughter. William continued to be distracted by Mary MacBeans presence, while she darted about the porch, shaking hands and laughing along with the guests. She seemed to be a natural when socializing and William realized then that he had never in his life been so taken by any woman as he was by this Mary MacBean. After all the hand shaking, she arrived back at his side as if by magic.

"Where are you from, William?"

"My family comes from Dalcross, northeast Scotland, near Inverness. And you?"

"I'm from Westport, Massachusetts. I went to school as well as college outside of Boston. I've just been hired by *The Washington Star* to do research and they did say they would let me write an article or two."

"That's terrific," William said. "I hope you will have enough free time to have dinner with me while I'm in Washington." For just that moment he couldn't believe he had been so forward with her, but he couldn't seem to help himself.

"That would nice," Mary said. "I'll give you my number and you can ring me up. I've just arrived here myself, and I'm quite busy unpacking and getting my apartment put together. Before I forget though, if you're looking for a place to live, there is a one bedroom walk up available next door to me that is fully furnished."

"Why thank you Miss MacBean, I'll take you up on that if you don't mind."

"Of course I don't mind. I'd be glad to help out, but please call me Mary. Just ring me up and I'll arrange for the landlord to show you the apartment."

William thought about the prospects of living next door to Mary MacBean and couldn't believe his good fortune.

"When did your family arrive in America?"

"Well," Mary replied, "not to bore you, but my father is very proud of the American MacBean clan and he drummed the family's history into me when I was a little girl. And since I was his only child, he had a captive audience. My fourth great grandfather, Duncan, arrived in America in 1736 aboard the ship "Prince of Wales" along with 177 other highlanders. There were MacKay's from the Strathnaver region and members of Clan Chattan, mostly Mackintoshes from Inverness. As you may know, the MacBeans are members of the Clan Chattan Confederation."

"Yes, of course, and we still are," William replied.

"The MacBean's settled on the coast of Georgia," Mary continued, "on the banks of the Altamaha River, in a town which is now known as Darien but originally known as New Inverness. New Inverness is considered the "Plymouth Rock" of Scottish heritage in the Southeast. But I don't suppose you've ever heard of Plymouth Rock?"

"I most certainly have, Plymouth Rock and the Pilgrims," William cut in. "Massachusetts, Cape Cod Bay, isn't that right?"

"Yes, it is, in the town of Plymouth," Mary added.

"Well, go on," William said.

"In 1739, the newly landed Scots petitioned the Trustees of Georgia that no slavery be allowed in their colony. The petition was granted and remained in effect until 1749, when it was removed from the charter. In 1751, Duncan and his wife, Kathrine Mackintosh moved north to New England and settled in Westport, Massachusetts."

"A fascinating history," William said, "and to think your family left Inverness more than 200 years ago, while mine stayed and fought for freedom."

"I learned about the battle of Culloden and our Major Gillies MacBean," Mary enjoined, "but the Scots had no chance with broadswords against canon and musket! It was such a disastrous day."

Surprising each other and in unison, Mary and William broke out in the first verse of the MacBean family Gaelic lament "My Fair, Young Beloved," written by MacBean's widow soon after the battle.

> *With thy back to the wall, and thy breast to the targe,*
> *Full flashed thy claymore in the face of their charge,*
> *The blood of the boldest that barren turf stain*
> *But alas! Thine is reddest there, Gillies MacBean.*

They both laughed at their shared knowledge as Mary clapped her hands and William acknowledged Mary's keen recitation.

"The Gillies MacBean in the poem was actually my great grandfather many times over and my brother is Gillies MacBean the eighth.

"God, wait until I tell my father!" Mary exclaimed.

Ruth Donovan tapped her glass with a spoon, drawing the attention of everyone on the porch.

"I would like to make a toast to my dear husband, who in the last hour received exciting news from the War Department. His rank has been elevated to Major General!"

The entire porch erupted in applause as David began to pop the corks of a half dozen bottles of champagne.

"Major General!" Mary said with excitement, "May I have the scoop?"

"Of course Mary, the scoop is all yours and only yours!" piped William Donovan, beaming from ear to ear. In the excitement, Mary left the porch to call *The Washington Star* while William MacBean raised his glass and toasted his newly ordained boss.

"Major General, sir!"

During the following week, William MacBean moved into 129 12th Street, SE. His second story apartment looked out over a tree-lined street adjacent to Mary's apartment at 127. A small covered porch off his bedroom allowed some relief from the hot July sun, but the heat in Washington was so uncomfortable that he would submerge his sheet in cold water and lay it out over himself when he went to bed. It provided much needed relief and would always be dry in the morning.

Mary joined Eleanor Roosevelt's Press Conference Association along with 60 other women who had filled positions at newspapers left open by men that had signed up for war duty. She began to report the news from the White House with a daily column in the morning edition of *The Washington Star*. William was busy with Major General Donovan in what appeared to be a race against time. Many nights he would work until first light and then take a cab home to catch a few hours of sleep, wash up and start the process all over again. His first few weeks were spent interviewing men and women who held the necessary skills needed to run the newly formed intelligence service. 24,000 men and women would eventually serve in the OSS.

William didn't let much time pass before he began courting Mary MacBean. One Saturday evening when they had finished eating dinner in the small garden behind Mary's apartment, they moved indoors to escape the mosquitoes. Mary sat in front of a fan and began to read *And Now Tomorrow*, a *New York Times* best seller. She loved to read aloud and William enjoyed listening. She put down her book and glanced at William.

"How would you like to come home with me and meet my parents?"

"Mary I'd love to meet your parents and visit Acoaxset and the Westport River you have told me so much about. It just so happens the General said we have earned a vacation, and that I should take 10 days off, get away from this oppressive Washington heat, recharge my batteries. Taking a break now may be the only free time I'll have coming."

"Wonderful!" Mary exclaimed, "I'll call father and tell him that I'm making reservations for the Night Owl this Friday and he can pick us up Saturday morning in Providence."

William watched as Mary became animated. Laughing, she jumped up from her seat and into his arms. He never knew what to expect from Mary and loved her spontaneity.

Union Station was packed with soldiers and civilians queuing up to board the outbound trains, determined to leave the Washington heat behind. William carried their bags to Pullman Sleeper 9, cabins 4 and 5, and left a bag in each. Mary sat on her bench looking out the window.

"Why don't we grab a table in the dining car," William asked.

"That sounds marvelous, William."

They locked the cabin door and made their way back toward the rear of the train, stopping in the club car to have a celebratory toast. After consuming two gin and tonics each, they settled in the dining car and studied the menu as the train lurched and slowly moved out of the station. William ordered rib eye steaks for two along with a bottle of Chateau Laffite Rothschild. They lingered in the dining car long after they finished dinner, ordering a bottle of Remy Martin to round out the evening. As daylight faded, they left the table and began to make their way back to the cabins, visibly unsteady by the movement of the train and the effects of the alcohol. Leaning against Mary's cabin door, they kissed as William put his hands around her waist and held her tightly. The train jolted them as William opened the door and stumbled into the cabin laughing. Closing the door and continuing to kiss, they stripped off their clothes with William catching his foot in his pants leg, falling sideways into the lower bunk with Mary falling on top of him. He was overcome with Mary's beauty as he gently rolled her over, draping his arm across her shoulder. He gazed upon her nakedness lowered his mouth and sucked her nipple as the trains wheels clicked along the track, rocking them from side to side.

"William," Mary said, "I've never been naked with a man before."

"I must admit," William replied, "My first time too."

He moved his hand slowly along her body, placing his palm on her pubic bone, feeling a small cushion of hair. Aroused with passion, Mary groaned above the noise of the train's wheels, her body tensed. As he moved his legs between hers, she looked up at his muscular body.

"Please, William, please, not now, not yet," she said closing her legs, pushing him away.

"It's okay Mary," he replied, "I can wait."

"New Haven!" the conductor called out, knocking once on the cabin door "Kingston, Providence up next!"

William lay in the bunk, with Mary's head resting on his arm. After a 10-minute stop, the train began moving once more and soon was past Bridgeport and out into the country. William thought about the woman he held in his arms and nudged her, waking her. The first words from his mouth surprised him, but he knew then that he had found his mate.

"Mary, wake up," William said. "Will you marry me?"

"What?" she said, waking from her slumber, "What the heck?"

"You heard me" William said, his Scottish accent thickened with emotion. "Must I ask you again?"

"No," Mary said beginning to laugh, and repeating, "I will, I will, I will!"

Myles and Sarah MacBean arrived at the Providence Union station at quarter to eight Saturday morning as the *Night Owl* engine's brakes billowed steam and its cars screeched to a full stop. Mary and William emerged from the station holding hands, with animated conversation and smiles all around. Her father greeted them as they descended the station's steps.

"Very nice to finally meet you, William MacBean," he said reaching out his hand. "We've heard so much about you. Please meet Sarah MacBean," he said smiling.

"A new MacBean, how refreshing!" Sarah said as she shook William's hand.

"Thank you so much for your hospitality Mrs. MacBean, I am honored to meet you."

"It's wonderful to meet a MacBean with such a brogue," she said turning to face Mary, "I hope William enjoys lobster salad, your father pulled his traps the other day."

"I love lobster," William said.

As they drove through Fall River, Myles pointed out the old mills made from granite block, explaining to William the textile industry, which had thrived there for more than a hundred years, but lost much of its business before the Great Depression to the newly built mills in the south.

"A lot of the migration had to do with climate, higher humidity which was beneficial to manufacturing, closer proximity to the raw product and abundant labor. Labor is cheaper in the south. Also the families who owned these mills never updated the machinery. The successive generations of family lived off the fruit of their fathers and grandfathers hard work and milked these mills for all they were worth. And some of them wondered why they went out of business. There was also a big fire. Many mills burned to the ground. Fall River is now but a glimmer of its' historical past."

Leaving Fall River they entered Rhode Island and drove south toward Adamsville and then turned east and crossed back into Massachusetts. William looked across the West Branch of the Westport River, spotting an Osprey arcing high above, and began to understand why Mary loved Westport as much as she did. They both had similar love for wildlife and the open countryside. Myles drove onto Atlantic Avenue and stopped at a long rambling shingled home with wide-open porches that looked out over the ocean and the islands beyond.

"We're here!" Mary said with great enthusiasm.

Later, as they sat on the porch eating lobster salad, Mary pointed out the Elizabeth Islands.

"There's Cutty Hunk, the closest to us, and then behind and to the left is Martha's Vineyard. And to the left of the Vineyard is Nantucket. We'll sail to Nashawena this week. It's just off the Vineyard, and we'll swim in a special spot called Quick's Hole. I know father would love to take us out for a sail, but that can wait, because today I'm taking you to Elephant Rock beach for a swim."

William thanked the MacBeans for lunch and Mary packed swimsuits into a canvas bag.

"Let's go!" Mary exclaimed.

After a short five-minute walk to the beach clubhouse they entered a small office where Mary retrieved the keys to her family bathhouse.

"Follow me!" she said walking toward a row of bathhouses, each with a brightly painted door. "Ours is the red one," she said locking hands with William pulling him along.

The bathhouses, each built on stilts above the beach showed their age with cupped silver grey white cedar shingles worn thin from the ocean salt and years of storms barreling out of the northeast. The MacBean bathhouse No. 7 was set in the middle of a line of 15. The dimensions were larger than its neighbors, with windows to the north and south. As they undressed in the afternoon light, William dropped his pants on the floor in his attempt to hang them on a wooden peg.

"Damn it!" he said as coins fell from his pocket and disappeared through spaces between the bathhouse floorboards. About to put one leg into his bathing suit, Mary reached out and took hold of his hand.

"William," she said, slipping her arms around his waist, kissing him deeply with her tongue.

Cupping his hands under her thighs, he lifted her up, shifting his arms under her legs. With her thighs pressing against his forearms and her knees bent, he leaned her against the wall. He entered her, moving slowly at first, and then faster as Mary clasped her arms around his neck, gasping with each slap of her body against the bathhouse wall.

Chapter 5

Almost 40 weeks from the day William and Mary first made love; Mary gave birth to their son Gillies. Sixty years would pass, and on a cool blustery September day, an old man known as the town beachcomber walked up to the MacBean home on Atlantic Avenue. He approached Gillies MacBean who sat on the front porch looking out to sea at the ocean's white caps and the islands beyond. With no introduction, he began to recount how as a young boy, he would look for coins below the bathhouses at Elephant Rock.

"One day in the summer of '42, I was under your family's bathhouse," he said, "and I witnessed a young man and woman cause the foundation and the walls to tremble and shake with a love making so intense that I have never witnessed anything like it before or since." The old man chuckled, recounting how he lay on his back looking up through the spaces in the floorboards, holding three new shiny quarters in his hand. "I had a front row seat," he said. "It was quite a show."

Gillies gazed out at the Texas tower, with its revolving light. He thought about the family bathhouse that was swept away years before on the last day of August 1954, when Hurricane Carol hit the New England coast with a 15-foot storm surge and winds gusting to 135 knots. He didn't acknowledge the old man. He looked past him to the beach, watching the terns with their wings flickering high above. Not a word was spoken between them, and the old man descended the porch steps and walked off to the north. Days later, Gillies found an old picture taken of his mother and father sitting on the front porch steps dated August 22, 1942 with the caption, 'William's first visit'.

"I'll be damned," he said to himself, realizing that his birthday, May 29, 1943, was exactly 10 months later.

Chapter 6

The Colonial Express pulled into Boston's South Station. William MacBean woke from his nap, collected his bag and stepped down from the train. He hailed a cab to the hospital, where he would hold Mary in his arms and be introduced to his newborn son, William "Hardy" MacBean.

Part 2

INNOCENCE LOST

Chapter 7

The car plowed into a four-foot snowdrift and came to an abrupt stop. The door opened and a man called out.

"You little bastard, where the hell are you?"

Scrambling to pick himself up from the snow, breathing in quick short bursts, Hardy's adrenaline spiked, his ears resonated with the sound of his beating heart. He hurriedly looked around for a safe place to hide. He couldn't go into the house for fear of waking his mother who was recovering from surgery. He glanced over at the incinerator in the middle of the yard, knowing he had little time left to find a place to hide and ran to it. He removed the top and climbed in, then lowered the top over his head. The incinerator smelled of charred paper and bits of garbage that he had burned the previous day. In his crunched position, he looked out through the quarter-sized holes and waited in silence, holding his breath, barely breathing. Hoping the man would give up, he watched in horror as he approached the incinerator, following the newly made footsteps in the snow.

"What do we have here?" the man said, lifting the top off the incinerator. Hardy looked up and, as luck would have it, the first thing he saw was the police chief's badge.

"Now you get the hell out of there, young Hardy MacBean!"

Standing up, Hardy climbed out of the incinerator and into the hands the law. His face was covered with soot, as were his jacket and pants.

He knew he was in trouble when he looked up and saw the curtain move in his mother's bedroom window.

The Chief recognized Hardy from a previous visit to the police station when his mother brought him in along with Mr. Hill from Hill's Hardware. He remembered that Hardy was caught shoplifting by his mother and she brought him in to the station to teach him a lesson. They all agreed that Hardy would work in the store that afternoon to pay for his theft. But Mr. Hill insisted on paying him thirty-five cents so he could buy the rubber handle used for the end of a hockey stick, the same one he had stolen.

"You throw that snowball, Hardy?"

"Yes sir," Hardy said in a whisper.

"Whaddya do that for?"

"I dunno," his voice hardly audible.

"Mother or father home?"

"My mom is, but she just got home from the hospital and she's upstairs in bed."

"Well, you ask your mom to bring you down to the station when she's feeling up to it."

"Yes sir," Hardy replied, dreading the eventuality of the future.

With a sinking feeling in his gut, he wasn't looking forward to explaining any of it to his mother. Chief Wesley Harding walked to his car without looking back. One week later his mother drove him to the police station, where he sat in the Chief's office and received a lecture about how he should think first before doing something stupid.

"Hardy," the Chief said, "I don't want to see you back in here."

When the Chief finished speaking, he looked at Hardy and pointed to a sign above the door that said, 'THINK' in large black letters. Hardy wouldn't forget that sign for the rest of his life.

Mary wished that Hardy's father had been there. She had never been very good at giving Hardy a strong reprimand. She remembered the last time she tried to spank him with a hairbrush and how surprised she was when he took it away from her. There was little talk between them while she drove them home.

"Your father is flying in tonight." She said clearing her throat.

Hardy woke with a start, listening to the grandfather clock and the whirring gears that preceded the chime. The clock struck midnight and he heard a car pull into the drive below his bedroom window. A door opened and closed and he listened as the car backed out and drove off.

"That must be Pop," he thought. He listened to the front door open and close, and the noise of a suitcase as it slid across the wooden floor. He heard his father walk to the butler's pantry, open the liquor cabinet, with bottles clinking together and the sound of ice cubes rattling into a glass as he drifted off to sleep.

Chapter 8

William MacBean wakened from a fitful sleep. The temperature was cool compared to Guatemala and he rejoiced in the New England weather. Home from an assignment to remove and destroy communication equipment used at a CIA training camp on the Caribbean coast, he thought about the Bay of Pigs invasion and how months of instruction failed to prepare the 1,400 Cuban exiles from a swift and deadly defeat within three days. Five infantry battalions and one paratrooper battalion were now dead or captured. Kennedy was furious. He was convinced that Castro had been forewarned. When William received a message from his wife concerning Hardy's latest troubles, he had just completed his mission and was on his way back to Washington to meet with the CIA Director. The previous director, Allen Dulles, had given him the task to design and implement listening devices throughout the newly constructed headquarters at Langley and the recently appointed director, John McCone, wanted to speak with him about his progress. When he landed in Washington, he sent the director a message informing him that he was flying home to take care of urgent family business.

Hardy's brother and sister were both away at a private boarding school, and William had purposely kept Hardy at home to help Mary around the house and keep her company. It was just a matter of time before Hardy would be sent off to boarding school, but William realized that sending Hardy's brother and sister away at an early age had its problems. Hardy's brother was 10 years old and his sister 12 when they were sent away to boarding school. Although they returned for holidays, they had become distant with both him and Mary. It wasn't much different when he was sent away, although his father was a widower and was never involved in the day-to-day care of his children. He did have his brother Gillies to lean on. But much like his father, William relied on others to manage the children. Although Mary did her best, Hardy had always been a handful. He remembered the night he helped Hardy pack a suitcase and watched him as he walked out the front door into a cold night. He didn't think it would be long before Hardy would return, after all he had left dressed only in his pajamas and slippers. As the night grew on and temperatures continued to drop, William walked the neighborhood searching, calling out Hardy's name. Eventually by chance he found him curled in a blanket hidden under the branches of an ancient spruce, his lips blue, shivering uncontrollably. From that time forward, he never doubted his son's determination or commitment to any decision that he would make. With the latest run in with the local police, he knew that Hardy needed a steady hand, one he couldn't provide from hundreds of miles away. He dressed and quietly closed the door to the bedroom, hoping not to disturb Mary from her sleep. He could hear water boiling on the kitchen stove as he descended the stairs. He turned off the electric burner just as the water boiled away, saving a glass syringe from certain destruction. When Hardy was eleven years old the family veterinarian announced that someone would need to give their dog Lilly a shot twice a day and Hardy didn't hesitate to accept the responsibility. Hardy and Lilly were the same age, the best of friends and inseparable. William removed the syringe and laid it out on a towel to cool. He could hear Hardy turning the grates in the coal furnace, making ready to swap the full ash buckets for empty ones. He opened the door to the basement and called down.

"You need any help Hardy?"

"No thanks, Pop, I got it."

William descended the stairs in time to grab one end of the ash bucket and help Hardy out through the basement door.

"These buckets are way too heavy," William said as they walked out to the garage. "You trying to hurt yourself?"

"Nope."

"I saved the syringe Hardy, the pan was just about out of water. What's this I hear about Chief Harding?"

The silence from Hardy was deafening, his suddenly pale face blank of emotion. Hardy had wondered what he would say to his father when asked, but before he knew it he blurted out, "I hit the Chief in his face with a snow ball and he caught me."

"I'm sorry to hear that, Hardy. Why did you throw the snow ball from your house?"

Hardy didn't know what to say. He pictured himself perched at the top of the hill far away from his house, hidden among the tall pine trees with plenty of room for escape. He answered his father the same way he answered Chief Wesley Harding.

"I dunno."

"Well then, Hardy," William said, "if you're going to do something like that, you'll need to plan it out a whole lot better, and for God's sakes make yourself a good escape route. Don't be such a damn fool or I'll give you back to the Injuns."

Hardy cringed at his father's use of the word 'Injun'. It usually meant he was in trouble.

"Now let's finish up here and take care of Lilly. Then we'll ask your mother what she wants for breakfast."

"Okay, Pop," Hardy answered, hoping he was finished with

Chief Harding and the snow ball incident.

They returned the buckets under the furnace ash chain and Hardy climbed into the coal bin. His father watched him as he shoveled pea coal into the open auger. Hardy emerged from the bin, brushing the dust from his corduroy pants, leaving black smudges on both legs, and followed his father up the basement stairs. They entered the kitchen and found Lilly collapsed on the floor.

"Damn it, her insulin is low!" Hardy exclaimed

He quickly assembled the needle and syringe and retrieved a bottle of insulin from the refrigerator door. Holding it up to the light, tapping it to dispel the bubbles, he inserted the needle through the rubber seal and withdrew 50cc of liquid. Kneeling down, he pulled Lilly's loose skin together on her right hind leg with his thumb and forefinger, creating a raised bump of flesh. With his left hand he inserted the needle; slowly pushed the plunger, removed it, and rubbed the injection spot with his thumb.

"Good girl, Lilly, good girl," he said.

Within a minute, Lilly was up off the floor, wagging her tail and doing a dance. Hardy was always amazed how quickly she would recover.

William called up the stairs to Mary and asked her what she wanted for breakfast. With her order in, they boiled up two eggs, cooked some bacon, made some toast and climbed the stairs to her room. Although Mary was almost fully recovered from her surgery, she was quite happy to have her breakfast brought up to her bed.

"Hardy, I don't know what I'd do without you," she said looking at William. "What are you and your father going to do today?"

"We thought we'd take a walk up Holt Hill, huh, Pop?"

"Sounds like a brilliant idea," William replied.

"Well, you boys have a good time. I'll get up in a while and do some work around the house," Mary said, "thank you so much for my breakfast Hardy."

"Get your boots on and grab Lilly," William said. "And meet me in the car."

Hardy liked to walk in the woods with his father. He enjoyed listening to the sound of the wind rushing through the pine trees. Whenever he was alone in the woods he would find a protected place to lie out, and look up at the treetops bending and dancing in concert with each gust of wind.

William made sandwiches and packed them into a shoulder bag along with two bottles of soda. Hardy took Lilly to the garage and piled into the back seat of a new silver blue Chrysler station wagon his father had just bought the previous month. William opened the driver's side door, leaned down and set the seat back as far as it would go. At six-foot-six, his knees protruded out from each side of the steering wheel, leaving little room to maneuver. Hardy watched his father push in the clutch and shift the gears as they left the driveway and headed for Holt Hill. They parked at the base of the hill and began their hike, Hardy taking two steps for every one of his father's. William decided to take the steep path, which required much more effort on Hardy's part.

"Hardy, keep up."

"I'm trying Pop," Hardy called out.

Reaching the top of the hill, William tied Lilly to a metal gatepost at the bottom of the fire tower. The tower stairs were open to the top, and Hardy became anxious just thinking about the climb. He had a difficult time with heights, but never complained about it to his father.

"Ready to go Hardy?" his father asked.

"I guess so," Hardy replied.

The climb up was excruciating, made worse by the tower swaying in the wind. Hardy knew there were 171 steps to the top, each step memorized from the previous climbs he made with his father and brother. He counted each one, always looking up, never down. When they reached the top, his father pushed open the trap door leading to the observation box and climbed up the last six steps.

"Come on up Hardy," he called down.

Hardy's hands shook as he grabbed a braided rope and pulled himself up through the trap door. He sat down on a rough wooden bench, looking out across 50 miles of forest. It was the highest point in all of Essex County.

"Beautiful," William said. "We can almost see all the way to Boston."

Hardy sat quietly, thinking how his father always said the same thing when they reached the fire warden's lookout. William removed the sandwiches from his shoulder bag and handed one to Hardy along with a Coca-Cola.

"Have you ever noticed that natures first spring is gold Hardy?"

"What do you mean Pop?"

"The color of the forest Hardy, it's gold when the leaves begin to grow. Know who said that?"

"Nope," Hardy replied looking out at the forest.

"A man named Robert Frost."

They sat in silence, feeling the tower buffeted by the wind. When they finished their lunch, William opened the trap door and motioned to Hardy it was time for them to leave.

Hardy went first, gripping the rail tightly, his knuckles turning white. He kept his eyes straight ahead, counting the steps as he descended, pausing at each story. Going down always seemed much more difficult he thought. When they reached the bottom of the tower, he untied Lilly and they began their walk down the hill.

"Hardy, your mother and I will be leaving for Scotland next week to visit your grandfather. We've arranged for you to stay with your Aunt Mary. I want you to go to the house every day and take care of Lilly. Can you do that for us?"

"Yes Pop," Hardy replied thinking about the last time his mother and father left on a trip. His father referred to his mother and Aunt Mary as the two Mary's, and would always say that when they were together they stopped traffic. Whenever Aunt Mary heard him say this she would laugh a loud guffaw and invariably say, "Billy you're a wicked man!" Her house was on Apple Tree Lane, just off Salem Street and not far from his house, so taking care of Lilly would be easy enough.

Aunt Mary would always take care of him when his parents went away on trips. She lived alone and always said there were only two loves in her life, her son, and her husband who had died during the Second World War. She never considered another marriage even though there were quite a few men who asked. She had brown shoulder length hair, pale blue eyes the color of robin's eggs, and a sense of humor that was dry as a bone. Her highbred Boston Brahmin accent was similar to British, although not too British. Her words were clipped as if cut by a sharp pair of scissors, her laughter shrill, and she always referred to Hardy as "My Hardyboy." With her son away at college, she always looked forward to Hardy's visits.

As the week progressed and his mother started to prepare for the trip, Hardy thought about his Scottish grandfather, Gillies MacBean, who he had met when he was eight years old. He remembered he was quite a tall man, with ruddy face, white hair sprinkled with red and a large white beard. He had monstrous red eyebrows with thick hairs that made wild loops. Hardy had been mesmerized by two strands of hair that grew from the middle of his grandfather's massive forehead, coiled like springs and drooping. When his grandfather realized Hardy's fixation, he bellowed in his Scots dialect, "Dinna fash yerself, wee twa hairs thaur me brains." His father translated his fathers words for Hardy's benefit, "Don't worry yourself; these two small hairs are part of my brains." He remembered his grandfather lowering his head so he could have a closer look, flicking the coiled hairs with his index finger.

"Hardy, A'd like ye ta call me Gumpy," he bellowed.

"Yes, sir, Grumpy," Hardy replied to his grandfather's laughter. From that moment forward, everyone referred to Grandfather Gillies as Grumps. Hardy remembered the Gaelic and slang words his grandfather would use. During a hiking trip up Devils Point in the Cairngorm Mountains, his grandfather pronounced the Gaelic name for Devil's Point, "Bod An Deamhain," followed with the slang version "Penis of the Demon", of which he would repeat with the repetition he was known for.

On Monday morning, Hardy woke before six and did his chores. He gave Lilly her shot and boiled the syringe so it would be ready for that afternoon. At 7:30 he said goodbye to his parents and gave his mother a kiss before biking off. As he left Salem Street and headed to school, his thoughts of staying with his Aunt Mary began to sink in.

Chapter 9

"Over here Hardy, over here!" Aunt Mary called out. It was 3 p.m. and the Pike School bell sounded the end of classes for the day. Hardy looked out from the doorway when he heard his name called and saw Aunt Mary sitting in her son's bright red '54 Buick Roadmaster convertible with the top down.

"Hello, Aunt Mary," he called out as he retrieved his bicycle and walked toward the car.

"Put your bike in the trunk, Hardy, and I'll give you a lift back to my house. I've never driven my son's car and I thought I'd give it a little exercise." Hardy looked at the car and marveled at the polished red paint and shiny bumpers that reflected and magnified the size of his bike as he walked past.

"I feel a bit cold," Mary said as they left the school and headed up the road. She reached forward and pushed a button on the dash, activating the convertible top. Hardy looked with wide-eyed amazement as the white canvas top began to fill like a sail. He knew the trouble they were in as he watched the canvas begin to pull at the frame.

"Aunt Mary!" he yelled above the billowing noise of the canvas, "STOP!"

"Oh my god!" Mary exclaimed, "That isn't what I expected! Have I done something wrong?" She quickly pulled over to the side of the road and they both got out to inspect the damage.

"Oh my god!" Mary said again with alarm. "Let's see if we can get the top up Hardy."

Hardy struggled to pull the top forward as Aunt Mary reached into the car and pushed a second button. The metal frame jerked in an arc with the forward edge of the canvas top slowly closing onto the windshield frame.

"No harm done," Mary said, her voice rising to a nervous shrill as she inspected the top.

"Don't you say anything to Robby about this?"

"It's all right, Aunt Mary, it's our secret," Hardy replied and they both laughed. When they arrived back at Aunt Mary's house, Hardy removed his bike from the trunk.

"I'm going home to feed Lilly and give her a shot," he said as he climbed onto his bike.

"Okay, but don't forget to be home for supper. Six o'clock."

Hardy pushed away and pedaled his bike up Salem Street. When he arrived at his house, he found Lilly motionless on the kitchen floor, barely able to lift her head, her tail motionless.

"Dammit!" he exclaimed, quickly loading the syringe with insulin, his heart pumping, sticking her in the fatty section of her rear leg. He was overcome with sadness as he watched her regain her strength, stroking her white and black spotted head.

"It's okay Lilly, it's okay."

It was just Lilly and he. The house was silent except for the ticking of the grandfather clock. Within minutes, she was up, dancing on the kitchen floor, wagging her tail. Once more, all was right in Lilly's world. Hardy knew he had waited too long, and it seemed that it took longer for her to recover this time. He took the syringe to the sink, took it apart and placed it all in a pot filled with water onto the stove. He turned on the electric burner and headed up to the third floor.

There was a bedroom on the third floor, once used by an Irish girl who helped his mother cook and clean when his brother and sister were

41

living at home. After two years of visiting the dentist every week, she packed her bags and left in the middle of the night without a note or a goodbye. William MacBean would recollect how much her new teeth had cost him and her abrupt disappearance once they had been fixed.

"Gaud," he would always say in recounting the story, "her bloody teeth were falling out of her head when she came to us, and once we fixed em she ran off with her new boyfriend."

Hardy raced up the back stairway and stopped at the third floor landing out of breath. His brother's collection of Lionel trains was spread out between the bedroom and the bath. He entered the bedroom, the hair rising on the back of his neck. He approached the bed and with hesitation, lifted the dust ruffle in haste, flipping it up, leaning over and quickly checking for imagined ghouls. Next he inspected the closet, opening the door wide, expecting the worse. The coast clear, he briefly wondered why he didn't leave the closet door open, something about keeping the monsters contained he thought. He breathed a sigh of relief, opened a window and reached under the bureau to retrieve a pack of his father's Camel cigarettes. When his parents were away the previous fall, he had tried smoking for the first time. He remembered that after he inhaled, exhaled and coughed uncontrollably, he fell over dizzy onto the floor. He actually enjoyed the dizzy part of it for some reason. He wondered what it would feel like this time as he put the cigarette in his mouth, lit a match and pulled the first puff without inhaling, blowing the smoke out the window. Then he inhaled, exhaled and fell dizzily to his knees. The smoke stung his eyes. He wiped away tears with the back of his hand and put the cigarette out in an empty bottle of Pilsner beer. He reached under the bed for a full bottle, opened it and took a small sip. It tasted just as bitter as he remembered. He lit another cigarette, and after he inhaled and then swallowed another sip of beer, he cried out "Firewater" as he exhaled a cloud of smoke. He had learned this expression from his favorite TV show *Davy Crockett*, when the wild Indians would drink from jugs of whiskey. Hooting and hollering, they would all dance in a drunken stupor, igniting the whiskey as they splashed it on the fire shouting "Firewater". He sang the first verse of the *Davy Crockett* theme song as he put away the cigarettes and the newly opened bottle of beer.

"*Davy, Davy Crocket, King of the wild frontier.*"

"Shit," he exclaimed, suddenly remembering the syringe he had left on the stove. He raced down the stairs into the kitchen and found the water had long boiled away, the pot smoking with a blackened needle and the syringe and plunger cracked beyond recognition. Billows of steam rose from the sink as he ran cold water into the pot.

"Damn it," he said, glancing at the kitchen clock, realizing he had just enough time to feed Lilly and get back to Aunt Mary's for supper. He washed his hands and face, brushed his teeth and called Lilly from the back yard.

Chapter 10

On Thursday afternoon, as Hardy was leaving school, Emmylou Darling invited him to a party on Friday night. She had quite a figure for a 13-year-old girl, and Hardy had developed a crush on her the very first day of school. Her skin was olive color and her eyes almost black. Although he tried, he never gained the courage to ask her out. He didn't exactly know where he would take her if he did. He often imagined her without clothes when he paged through his father's *Playboy* magazine's his mother had hidden away.

43

All the boys knew Emmylou was a good French kisser, although Hardy never quite knew who had kissed her, or when, or, for that matter, what a French kiss really was. He kissed the girl next door on the lips when they played "doctor," but he didn't think that was a French kiss because he heard it had something to do with the tongue.

That afternoon Hardy gave Lilly a shot and let her out in the yard to do her business. He brought her back in, filled her bowl with food and left the house to return to Aunt Mary's. He was about to climb on his bike when he decided to detour to the garage, open the driver's side door of the car and try out the seat. He discovered he was too low to see out the windshield so he went back into the house and retrieved two pillows from the living room couch. The pillows made his height just right. He pulled the lever to adjust the seat forward as far as it would go. He was thrilled to be sitting in the driver's seat, pushing his feet against the pedals. He reached under the seat for the key and inserted it into the ignition. Turning the key, he was taken by surprise when the car lurched forward. He pushed the clutch pedal down, shifted into neutral and turned the key again with the engine bursting to life. Quite pleased by the even sound of the engine, he hardly noticed as the garage filled with exhaust. He began to feel sick as he turned off the engine and held his breath, stumbling from the car, opening the garage doors and letting the exhaust escape in a voluminous cloud.

On Friday morning, Hardy asked Aunt Mary if it would be all right for him to go to Emmylou's party that night.

"Where will the party be?" Mary asked.

"Over at the Darling house, close to my school off Pleasant Street."

"Well, alright," Mary said. "About what time will you be home?"

"I don't know, probably around 10 o'clock."

"What would your mother say?"

"She would say it's okay," he said, knowing full well that his mother wouldn't let him stay out past nine o'clock, and certainly wouldn't allow him to bike at that time of night.

"Well, all right, but no later than 10."

The afternoon school bell rang and Hardy was alone on the third floor of the old wooden frame building watching the students leave the front entrance. He opened the far right dormered window in the geography room and felt the heat from the building escape through the opening. The movement of air was just right he thought as he lit his cigarette, keeping his mouth at the level of the windowsill, exhaling. He felt a mixture of anxiety and thrill, knowing what would happen if he was caught. He put the cigarette out after two puffs, wrapped it in cellophane and put it away in his pocket. Descending the third story steps to the second level, he joined the last of the students leaving for the day, climbed on his bike and peddled for home.

Hardy went to his room to select clothes for Emmylou's party. He picked out a pair of brown corduroy pants along with a white button down shirt. "That should do," he thought, as he left his house and returned to Aunt Mary's for dinner. He thought Aunt Mary was a great cook and he relished eating whatever she would serve up. Tonight she was cooking his favorite; mashed potatoes, peas and hamburger. He thought about his mother, who would burn just about everything she cooked, even the TV dinners. Packaged in aluminum trays, with compartments separating the meat, vegetable and potato, Hardy found the food bland, tasteless and dreaded eating off the small collapsible tables in front of the television. It was the newest fad in frozen prepared foods. "No muss no fuss," his mother would say. The first time she heated one up she neglected to remove the cardboard seal from the top of the tray and the oven burst into flames leaving the kitchen filled with smoke.

"Thank you Aunt Mary. It was delicious," he said as he got up from the table and carried his plate to the sink.

"You're welcome Hardyboy, now don't be late."

"I won't be Aunt Mary."

He left the house and biked home to get ready for the party. After changing his clothes, he looked into the mirror. His hair was growing longer, accentuated by four cowlicks, two in the front and two in the back growing every which way. His mother always told him his cowlicks made a crown fit for a king. He used some of his father's 'Brillcream' to flatten them out and sang the Brillcream song advertised on TV.

"Brillcream, a little dab will do ya," he sang, hoping that Emmylou would like his slicked back hair.

Leaving the house, he patted Lilly on the head, picked up his guitar and closed the kitchen door on his way out to the garage. He had a sense of excitement as he opened the garage doors wide. He put his guitar onto the back seat, got in and adjusted the rear-view mirror once more. The pillows in place from the previous day, he pushed in the clutch and practiced moving the stick shift in the pattern displayed on the knob. Reverse was the most difficult, over to the left and up. He placed the knob in neutral and started the engine. Then he turned on the lights and dimmed them as he pushed the clutch in and shifted into reverse. The handle made a grinding noise and then a clunk, as he found reverse.

Letting the clutch out slowly, his foot slipped, and the car lurched from the garage. He pushed the clutch in as quickly as he could, intimidated by the jarring exit. His heart pounding, he turned the wheel to the left, shifted the car into first gear and slowly climbed up the driveway. Reaching the street, he turned off the headlights and the engine. He sat in the dark, his mind and emotions raced, and his hands beat a silent tune on the steering wheel. He waited for his best friend Abbot who lived two houses down. Hardy and Abbot were thick as thieves. Abbot also had his run-ins with Chief Harding, and the previous week he was caught shooting his BB gun at cars from his second story bedroom window. His father accompanied him to the station to speak with the chief, docked his allowance for a month and grounded him for a week. The week now completed, Abbot agreed to accompany Hardy on his maiden voyage. Earlier in the day, Hardy had studied the possible routes to Emmylou's house on his bike, avoiding the main road and eventually ending up out of sight behind the fence just beyond her porch. He never gave a thought about Chief Wesley Harding or what might happen if he was caught, he could only think of Emmylou.

Chapter 11

Abbot appeared at the driver's side window and Hardy motioned for him to get in.

"You still want to do this?" Abbot asked.

"Yep," Hardy replied. "Let's go, get in!"

Abbot opened the door and settled into the passenger seat. His slicked back hair was neatly combed and he wore a new dark blue navy pea coat. Abbot always wore the newest clothing compared to Hardy's, who mostly wore his brother's hand-me-downs or something his mother found at the local thrift shop. Much of the time Abbot and Hardy looked like the prince and the pauper. But tonight, Hardy wore his very best clothes.

Like an expert, Hardy turned the key and started the car. Looking out to the street, he turned on the radio and listened to the Everly Brothers newest hit 'All *I Have to Do Is Dream*'. It was 1962, and everything was possible for a boy of 13 sitting behind the wheel of a stick shift Chrysler Valiant on his way to experience his first French kiss.

They drove for about two miles when Hardy abruptly pulled off to the side of the road, turned off his lights and let a car pass that had been coming up fast behind them. He sat motionless, breathing short breaths, his forehead damp from the anxiety of not knowing, of suspicion. He breathed a sigh of relief when the car passed.

"I thought it might be a cop."

"What?" Abbott said.

They arrived at the Darling house driveway and Hardy turned off the engine and coasted past a long rambling white porch lit up with a string of Chinese lanterns hanging from the ceiling. They rolled down the driveway and came to a stop behind a hemlock hedge. Abbot opened the door and catapulted from the passenger seat, as if shot from a canon. He ran off into the darkness toward the house. Hardy sat looking at the open door wondering what Abbot was up to.

With her eyes open wide with surprise, Emmylou, along with three of her girlfriends, witnessed Hardy's arrival. She left the porch and ran to the car, hugging Hardy as he stood in the dim light, sticking her tongue deep into his mouth. He couldn't believe what he was feeling, not only to his tongue, which was being pressed and swallowed, but also the erection that was ballooning in his pants. As she pressed her body against his, he thought, "God, It was all worth it!" She loosened her embrace and grabbed his erection, squeezed twice, and with a shriek bounded back toward the porch, leaving him glary eyed, breathless and in a state of mental and physical intoxication. Not a word had been spoken between them. He leaned against the car watching her run up the porch steps, wondering what he should do.

His arousal fresh but fading and his throat dry, he reached into the car and removed his guitar from the back seat and walked to the porch. Once inside, he realized that he didn't know anyone and Abbot was nowhere to be seen. He took his Gibson Sunburst from its case and began playing a song by the Kingston Trio.

"Hang down your head Tom Dooley, hang down your head and cry," he sang as he watched Emmylou surrounded by three boys. She never once looked in his direction. He felt as if he were invisible. He finished singing, his face flushed; he put his guitar back in its case, closed the top and snapped the latches. He stood up without notice or a word from anyone and left the porch with the screen door slapping behind him. He opened the car door, put his guitar on the back seat, got behind the wheel and started the engine. No Abbot to ride with, no one to share the night's abandoned promise. He had never felt so alone.

Hardy turned into his driveway and drove into the garage. According to plan, he jacked up the left rear wheel, got back into the car, started it up and shifted into reverse gear, leaving the rear wheel spinning in space. He had studied the car's manual from front to back and had read that the odometer cable was connected to the rear axle on the driver's side. He thought that if he ran the car in reverse the odometer would turn backwards, erasing the mileage. And it did. He left the car running and went into the house to seek out his oldest and most enduring friend. He lay down next to Lilly on her bed against the cold kitchen stove, stroking her velvety black ears, repeating to her that everything would be okay as his eyes welled in tears.

Part 3

THE JOURNEY

Chapter 12

William and Mary's cab drove up to 57 Salem Street. A light rain fell as Hardy and Lilly appeared from behind the house, running quickly toward them. At that moment Hardy forgot how much alone he had felt. Mary hugged him and ran her hand across his hair, as she always did, paying special attention to his cowlicks. His father patted him on the shoulder.

"Mr. Hardy," William said, handing Hardy one of the bags with his right hand and reaching out and squeezing his neck with his left.

"Did you miss us?"

"Of course he did," Mary said as Hardy winced from his father's grip.

"We're going shopping for next week's groceries." William said as he walked toward the garage, "Come on, Hardy, and get a move on."

Hardy carried the bags into the house and left them in the front hall. He returned to the driveway with his mother as his father drove up from the garage. He climbed into the back seat and sat perched, looking over his father's shoulder. The odometer read two hundred fifty three and two tenths miles, slightly less mileage than when he drove off to Emmylou's. He breathed a sigh of relief when his father didn't seem to notice the difference. Mary climbed into the front seat and William began the drive out to Main Street.

"I had to readjust the seat. Anyone been fooling with the car?"

"No Pop, I haven't." Hardy's heartbeat quickened. How could he have forgotten the seat?

"Well that's odd, did you move the seat Mary?"

"I might have, I don't remember. Wait, I did use the car to take Hardy down town."

William pulled into the A&P and parked next to an eight-foot square cement clad box. Red, white and blue flags flapped in the breeze from two poles, each with loud speakers blaring away something about nuclear holocaust.

"What the hell is that? It looks like a trailer with a window." William exclaimed.

"The sign says it's one of those bomb shelters William. I'll do the shopping and I'll meet you back here in about a half an hour."

Hardy was relieved that the conversation about the car seat seemed to be over and forgotten. His mother climbed from the car and walked toward the market, and he followed his father to inspect the bomb shelter. They peered through a thick plate glass window and saw a steel bunk bed against the back wall with no mattress. A large sign faced Main Street.

'SURVIVE-ALL SHELTERS $735 NO MONEY DOWN FIVE YEARS TO PAY.'

The loudspeakers boomed sound effects of bombs exploding, with a man's voice shouting: "NUCLEAR HOLOCAUST IS POSSIBLE, A SHELTER WILL OFFER YOU PROTECTION." And then the sound of air-raid sirens pierced the air along with more sounds of exploding bombs and more shouting, repeating the dire warning over and over again. Hardy remembered the air raid sirens and drills when he was in first grade, huddled beneath his desk in front of his teacher's chair with a direct view up her skirt. She never wore any underwear, positioning herself just so, spreading her knees as far apart as her skirt would allow, giving him a sight he would never forget. After every drill, Miss Garrett would stand up and brush her hands down her skirt, giving Hardy a crooked smile, always saying, "Well then."

"This damn thing wouldn't protect a flea," his father said, bringing Hardy back to reality. "It's nothing but a way to part a man from his money. Let's join your mother Hardy," William said, as the loudspeaker repeated the warning to an empty audience.

"Your mother and I had a good visit with your grandfather and your Uncle Gillies. It was great to be home for a while. We visited a very nice boarding school when we were there, not far from your grandfather's house. We've arranged for you to have an interview with a friend of ours. Do you remember Mr. Minor? He's been over to our house a few times."

"I think so." Hardy said bewildered.

"He always wears a colorful bow tie and tweed coat, reddish hair? Remember him Hardy? He teaches over at Andover Academy. I'll take you over to see him next Saturday and he'll tell you all about the school we visited, okay?"

"Boarding school? B-B-Boarding school in *Scotland*?" Hardy stuttered, practically speechless. Memories about the time he visited Scotland, his grandfather and his Uncle Gillies swirled about in his head. He couldn't believe what his father was asking him. Why would he be sent so far away from home?

"Well, Hardy?" his father asked again.

"Yes, okay," Hardy, said halfheartedly.

"Okay."

Early Saturday morning, William drove Hardy to School Street.

"Here we are Hardy, I'm going to Hill's Hardware to pick up some paint, I'll be back to get you in about an hour."

"Okay, Pop" Hardy said as he got out of the car and climbed the steps to the house. He pushed the doorbell and heard a chime similar to the Andover bell tower that rang every hour on the half hour. He watched as a faint, distorted shadow appeared in the door's bull's-eye window. The shadow magnified, as it grew closer. He heard the floor creak as the door flung open with a pronounced swing with Mr. Minor standing high above. He was a stocky man with a large neck made more pronounced by a yellow bow tie with blue polka dots. He wore a blue button-down shirt with brown corduroy pants, a dark green tweed jacket and brown tasseled loafers. His copper colored hair was perfectly combed, not a hair out of place, and his thick eyebrows intensified his character.

"Well, hello there, Hardy, come on in!" he said in a welcoming, slightly graveled voice. He waved at William, then placed his hand squarely on Hardy's shoulder, ushering him into the house.

"Come with me, Hardy," he commanded.

Hardy followed him down a plush oriental rug covering the length of the hallway. Mr. Minor's gait was pronounced, having a defined forward pitch. Hardy would learn from his father that he was a captain during the war and had served in General Patton's Third Army. He also learned that Mr. Minor received the Bronze Star and the Croix de Guerre for his heroism during the German invasion. The house smelled of linseed oil and furniture polish, and the floors and furniture gleamed in the dull light.

"We'll go to the library," Mr. Minor said, opening the last door in the hall. "Come on in and make yourself comfortable."

Mr. Minor took his seat behind a large mahogany writing desk, inset with mother-of-pearl, ivory and ceramic. He took out his pipe and tobacco pouch, ground the pipe into the pouch, and tapped the tobacco with his index finger.

"I shipped this desk all the way back from Scotland, found it at an antique shop in Edinburgh. It was designed and made by Charles Rennie Mackintosh, a famous Scottish architect and designer. So you want to go to Gordonstoun, do you?"

He lit his pipe and blew a large burst of smoke into the air. Hardy became anxious as the question was asked, squeaking about his leather chair. This was the first time he had heard the name Gordonstoun.

"I don't know, sir. Pop told me that you were going to give me an interview and tell me all about the school."

Mr. Minor looked out through a cloud of blue smoke, pensive with his pipe stem pushed against his cheek.

"Well, if you don't know, then I don't know. Gordonstoun is one heck of a school. It caters to tough kids like you. Do you like sports?"

"Yes, sir, I like soccer and skiing." Mr. Minor's eyes narrowed.

"Hardy, they have soccer, but they call it football. They also have skiing with a mountain rescue team and they have a sailing program. Your father told me that you're a sailor."

"My grandfather lets me take his Beetle Cat out by myself."

"Where do you sail?"

"I sailed alone from Westport to Cutty Hunk and back last summer, about 14 miles."

Mr. Minor's eyes lit up at the thought of Hardy taking the risk and initiative at the age of 12.

"Gordonstoun isn't a very old school, Hardy; it opened with only two students in 1934. Today, there are about 250 students. If you decide to go, you'll be joining Prince Charles class."

Hardy heard about Prince Charles from his father but this was the first time he heard that he would be in the same class.

"The purpose of Gordonstoun is to make young men out of boys, Hardy. You wake up at five o'clock every morning and your day begins with a five mile run, no matter the weather, and much of the time in the dark. And when you finish your run, you take a cold shower! Then you have breakfast and hit the books until 3, with a half-hour off for lunch. After class you head to the sports field, the mountains or the sea, depending on which program you choose. During my time at Gordonstoun, I was an instructor in the sailing program, and in the winter I arranged expeditions in the Cairngorm Mountains. Gordonstoun has a great campus, with some buildings dating back to the early 16th century. There is quite a tale about Sir Gordon, who built the Gordonstoun House into its present shape. He also designed and built the Round Square House, which is a two-story circular stone structure with prominent garrets, a slate roof and shed dormers all around a circular court. Originally built as a stable, it's been converted into dormitories, classrooms and a library. Would you like to hear the tale, Hardy?"

Without waiting for Hardy's reply, he began his story.

"Around 1642, Sir Robert Gordon, Third Baronet of Gordonstoun, was known as 'The Wizard' by the residents of Moray. They regarded him with suspicion due to his study of alchemy and other mysterious activities rumored to take place in his laboratory.

56

According to legend, Sir Robert sold his soul to the Devil in return for knowledge. When the Devil arrived to collect his soul, he convinced the Devil to take his shadow in trade, but with an understanding. He promised the Devil that he would surrender his soul 25 years hence. And with a new lease on life, he designed and built a large round building, 180 feet in circumference, including dozens of rooms and a stable. He believed that when it came time to surrender his soul, he would escape from the Devil by running from one room to the next, always a step ahead, and never caught in a corner. When the time finally arrived for the Devil to collect his soul, Sir Robert enlisted the Parson of Duffus to sit with him in an attempt to ward the Devil away. With midnight approaching, along with howling winds, lashing rain and fierce crashing of thunder and lightning, Sir Robert lost his nerve and so did the parson. The parson urged him to find consecrated ground, where the Devils power would be useless. With desperate immediacy, Sir Robert mounted his horse and spurred him to full gallop, the hounds of hell and the thundering hooves of the Devil's black stallion close behind. When he neared the hallowed ground of Birnie Kirk, the Devil's hounds attacked his horse's flank as the clock struck midnight, throwing him off and causing him to break his neck upon the stone steps of the church. He died instantly; again leaving the Devil empty handed, and never to collect his soul."

Hardy conjured up a picture of a breathless, wizened old man, running from room to room, madly riding his horse into a ferocious storm. He didn't like the sound of Gordonstoun much, the five-mile run or the cold shower. And although he didn't much want to go, his father made it quite evident that he was scheduled to attend the fall semester.

August arrived and William made plans to travel with Hardy to Scotland. He wanted Hardy to be acclimated to the area before leaving him off at school, and he also wanted to spend time with his father and brother and take Hardy into Inverness to be measured and fitted up with his first kilt. He thought it important to introduce Hardy once again to his family heritage and Scottish history. Mary began to pack Hardy's suitcase from a clothing list that been provided by the school. The list included a reminder that the winter months were long.

Mary's eyes filled with tears at the thought of Hardy going off to school so far away. She had argued with William over his decision, but gave in when he promised that Hardy could return home during school breaks.

"If he is truly unhappy, he can leave Gordonstoun and return home." William said.

They agreed that they would travel to Scotland with Gillies and Eliza and spend Christmas with Hardy at Dalcross Castle.

"Mary," William said, "I believe that the structure of the Gordonstoun curriculum and the rigorous outdoor life is exactly what Hardy needs. Gordonstoun will give Hardy a much-needed regimen, a steady hand. We also have my father and brother close by if he is in need.

"I'm not so sure that your father or your brother are particularly well fitted in the parenting department."

"What do you mean?"

"I can only go on what you've told me. Your father seemed to be missing in action during most of your life and your brother isn't exactly known for his fidelity."

"About that I'm truly sorry about your friend, but Gillies has always been one for the ladies. She could have said no don't

58

you think? You did with me."

"This was our wedding William, and as far as I know your brother got her drunk the night before. It's too bad, I don't hear from her very often. It could have been different."

"What different?"

"Her moving away. It was only a year but our friendship was never the same."

William thought about his brother and their time together growing up at Dalcross. They attended the same boarding school before going off to university and Gillies always looked after him and helped him manage the rigors of life away from home. He knew he could depend upon his brother to watch after Hardy. Gillies had never married, nor did William think that he had any inclination to do so. There had been a Gillies MacBean present in every generation since the Battle of Culloden. His brother, Gillies MacBean VIII, appeared to be the last of his line and with his brothers blessing William named his first son Gillies. Although the line had not yet been broken, William was tempted to refer to his son as the ninth. His mother Margaret MacBean died soon after he was born, when Gillies was two years old. His father hired a village girl to help raise them and Gillies was kept at home until he was 10 and William eight when both were sent away to Merchiston Castle School in Edinburgh.

The brothers had formed a close bond with their nanny Sarah MacNiven, who stayed on the castle staff after they left and continued to greet them at the Dalcross railway station each holiday until they were both in university. Sarah fell in love with John Grant, who had been hired to fill the position of forester at Dalcross. They soon married and moved into the estate's farmhouse.

Over the next three years, Sarah gave birth to two daughters, Katherine and Winwood. Twenty years later, Katherine married and moved away to Edinburgh, and Winwood, who was somewhat of a free spirit, was hired on by Gillies to manage the staff and make sure the Castle guests were happy in their stay.

Chapter 13

On Friday, August 16, 1963, the MacBean family gathered for a cookout at Elephant Rock Beach to say goodbye to Hardy and wish him luck in his first year away from home. He was scheduled to enter Gordonstoun as a third former and bunk in with 13 other boys in one room. His mother tried to comfort him, saying they would all join him over Christmas, just four short months away.

"Hardy, did you give Lilly a shot this morning?" knowing full well that he had.

"Yes, Mum, I did. Promise to take care of her when I'm away?"

"I will Hardy, I'll take good care of our Lilly," knowing this would probably be the last time he would see his best friend. "Don't you worry, once in the morning and once in the afternoon?"

"Yes Mum."

Hardy ran his hand over Lilly's coat, beginning at her ears and running the full length of her body to her stubby tail. She lay against him with her eyes closed, as she always did. Her back leg jerked as she briefly relaxed, the air loudly escaping from her nostrils. A tear ran down Hardy's cheek as he kissed her face and silently said goodbye. Mary watched him, fighting back her tears as William walked up and announced the bags were packed away in the trunk and he was ready to go. Mary took Hardy's hand and walked him to the car as Lilly came round and became Hardy's shadow for the last time. His grandfather handed him an envelope.

"Hardy, I'm going to miss my first mate."

Sarah MacBean gave him a big hug.

"Hardy, now don't forget to write at least once a month."

"I won't forget" Hardy said, his voice trembling.

We'll see you this Christmas," Gillies and Eliza said in unison when Gillies reached out his hand and gripped Hardy's shoulder while Eliza hugged him around his waist.

William opened the driver's door and Mary reached over gripping Hardy's hand and kissed him goodbye once more.

"Promise me you'll write?" Eliza asked.

"Yes, yes, I will, I'll write to all of you," Hardy said, his voice trailing off.

"Okay, let's go, Hardy," William said, giving Mary a kiss and settling into the drivers seat. "I'll return the first week of September before Gillies and Eliza go off to school."

The family stood in the driveway on Atlantic Avenue and watched as William and Hardy drove out Acoaxset Road and disappeared from view.

Pan Am flight 115 landed in Heathrow on August 18 at 7 o'clock Saturday morning after a five-hour flight from Boston. William and Hardy flew first class aboard a new Douglas DC 8. They descended a portable ramp under sunny skies and walked toward Britannic Terminal Building 2.

"May I see your passport, please," a man in uniform said, holding out his empty hand.

"Why, yes," William said, handing three passports to the official.

"Is this your son here?" he asked.

"Yes, it is, William Hardy MacBean."

"And how long is your stay?" asked the official opening Hardy's U.S. passport.

"Hardy will be attending school in Scotland."

"Does he have a visa?"

"No, no he doesn't. He doesn't need one. He has dual citizenship. I also gave you his British Passport along with mine."

"Ah, so you did," and with a cursory glance the official opened and stamped the passports. "Do you have anything to declare?" he asked.

"No, nothing," William replied.

"Very good then, you are free to go." Hardy pushed the luggage cart with three suitcases and guitar through the exit door out to the main entrance. A man with a patch covering his left eye walked up to them.

"Why there you are, you old bloke!"

"David, you old dog you," William said smiling, turning to meet the voice.

"How are we so lucky?" knowing full well why David was there.

"The front office sent me a message with your arrival time and I thought I would meet you and your son and get you into one of our agency cars."

"God, and here I thought we were incognito! Hardy, meet my old friend David Stewart. Actually, he's really here to meet you, we've been friends since before you were born."

Hardy shook David's hand looking into his deep blue eye, the color reminding him of a cold winter sea.

"You have a fine handshake for such a young lad!"

"Thank you sir," Hardy said looking at David's black eye patch and the black band that disappeared into his snow-white hair.

"I can see your father has taught you well, a proper handshake, something we learned together in school way back when."

"Yes, those were the days," William piped up as they walked out to the parking lot toward a green 1962 four door Ford Cortina.

"Here you are," David said handing William the keys.

"Hardy and I will be driving out to Cambridge today. I'll be introducing him to Trinity and then we'll head up to the border. I have a couple of weeks to show him around before I drop him off at school. I'll catch up when I come back through," William said, handing David an envelope.

As William and Hardy drove off, David opened the envelope and read a note in William's handwriting. 'GPIDEAL, GPFLOOR, see what you can do with these, thanks.' "What the hell is this?" David thought. He knew the prefix GP was the type of digraph used by the CIA, but had never seen the same prefix used in two separate cryptonyms. Why would William come to him with this he wondered, why would he want to circumvent the company, and what clandestine operation might his old friend be mixed up in.

William drove to Cambridge and introduced Hardy to Trinity College and showed him where he had lived for five years. They drove past Bletchley Park, but William didn't stop to show Hardy where he had worked with his friend Alan Turing who invented the machine that broke German secret code during the summer of 1941.

Although in need of a fresh coat of paint, William knew the old building was still in use. He hoped that someday he could tell his children what he did during the war, but like all members of the intelligence service now and during the war, he was bound to secrecy.

They began the drive north toward the border, hoping to reach Scotland by dark. Hardy looked at the houses with thatched roofs and small paned windows as they travelled through Nottingham. William pointed out signs to Sherwood Forest, the Sherwood Forest Hardy's mother introduced him to when she read to him *Robin Hood and His Band of Merry Men*. Although he was quite young, and was confined to bed with a nasty bout of measles, he remembered his sadness when Robin lay on his deathbed asking Little John to string his bow, and then shooting his last arrow out the window, requesting his grave be dug "where this arrow lodges".

As daylight began to fade, they approached Scotland's border. William told Hardy about Hadrian's Wall and how it was built to keep the barbarian Picts from invading the northern region of the Roman Empire. They drove to the center of Carlisle and pulled up in front of the Crown and Mitre Hotel.

"We'll stay here for the night, Hardy. Tomorrow we'll rise early and drive straight away to Edinburgh. Take our bags to the main desk please and give the clerk our name. I'll meet you inside after I park the car."

"Okay, Pop" Hardy said, struggling with the suitcases. He climbed the steps to the hotel lobby and dragged the suitcases over to the front desk.

"May I help ya young lad?" the hotel clerk asked.

"No, thank you, I think I can get it," Hardy replied.

"Would you be in need of a room?

"Yes sir, thank you. Name is MacBean."

"Here you are, William MacBean for two."

"Here I am," William said stepping up to the desk and signing the register.

"The last time I stayed here was before the war, Hardy."

"Your key, sir, first floor, number 101, across from the loo."

William thanked the clerk, motioned to Hardy and said, "Let's go." The carpets were different than William remembered, but the hotel was a pleasant reminder of the past. They found their room and Hardy crawled into bed, immediately falling off to sleep. William tucked him in and went back down to the lobby and found a seat at the bar.

"Hey, *whattle* it be?"

"Scotch, neat," MacBean replied.

"You ever hear of the Beatles?"

"No, can't say as I have," William said.

"They used to be known as the Quarrymen, but now they're the Beatles. They was here in February, playing at the ABC Cinema down the street and they came in here after for a drink and a dance in the ballroom. And they was asked to leave — something about the way they was dressed, can you imagine that?"

"Well, I don't know," William said. "Who are they?"

"Well they're a right successful band ova heeya these days. Their first album was just released end a March and bin top of the charts eva since. You'll hear of 'em soon enough, the girls go fab over 'em, matta fact they call 'em the Fab Four," the bartender exclaimed.

"Time to get up, Hardy," William said shaking him.

"Do I have to?" Hardy asked?

"Yes, and by the time we get out of here it'll be 8 o'clock. I want to get up to Edinburgh by noon."

"Okay, Pop,"

Hardy swung his feet out onto the floor.

"I'll be down in a minute."

At precisely 8 a.m., William and Hardy loaded their luggage and began the journey to Edinburgh. Taking A7 North, they crossed the River Eden and left Hadrian's Wall behind. The road became a single lane with lay-bys, each placed within eyesight of each other marked by black and white horizontal striped posts. Hardy quickly learned that if his father passed the lay-by before the approaching traffic passed theirs they wouldn't need to give right of way and pull over. His father drove like a mad man, trying to avoid pulling off the road as much as possible, beating the oncoming cars to the striped post. More than once Hardy would exclaim, "Geese Pop," gripping the handle in front of his seat. Passing through the border town of Selkirk, William reduced his speed as they crossed over the River Tweed.

"Hardy! We're back home! Scotland!"

William rejoiced in his surroundings and Hardy loosened his grip when they left the bridge and entered the town of Galashiel. As noontime approached, they drove under the southeast end of the old Edinburgh-Carlisle railway viaduct in Newbattle Parish. Hardy found the viaduct impressive, with 24 arches of brick stretching 400 yards and rising 70 feet above the River Esk. He turned on the radio and listened with rapt attention to a song he had never heard before. The singers belted out words Hardy would never forget.

"Listen, do you want to know a secret, do you promise not to tell?"

"Arthur's Seat Hardy, It's the main peak in the hills," William said pointing. "The Queen's official residence is located at the entrance and it's called The Palace of Holyrood.'"

Hardy was oblivious to his father words, listening intently as the song ended. "The Beatles!" The announcer yelled.

William entered 'Old Town' Edinburgh, with Hardy asking him if he would scour London for Beatles sheet music and mail it to him. Leaving High Street and crossing over North Bridge into the 'New Town' of Edinburgh, William pointed out their hotel and a tower that looked like a castle made from sand.

"The Scott Monument," William said. "Named after Sir Walter Scott. It's the largest monument in the world built to commemorate a writer, stands 200 feet six inches high. Once we get settled, we'll have a visit."

They continued to the end of North Bridge, took a right onto Princess Street and then a quick U-turn arriving in front of the British Royal Hotel. A giant of a man stood at the hotel entrance. He wore a brilliant Cameron plaid kilt, military coat, Glengarry bonnet with white cockade, a long hair Royal Scots Guard Sporran and a sgian dubh tucked neatly into his plaid stocking.

"Walcome tae Dun Eideann," the kilted man said, as he opened Hardy's door.

William emerged from the car and handed the keys to the kilted giant and Hardy removed the suitcases from the trunk and placed them on the curb.

"Please, allow me," the man said, picking up both suitcases and carrying them through the main entrance door to the front desk.

"What does Dun Eideann mean, Pop?"

"Scottish Gaelic for Edinburgh. Did you notice the white ribbons? They signify allegiance to the Jacobite cause that supports a free and sovereign Scotland. Bonnie Prince Charlie of the Stuart Clan led the last bid for freedom. The British at the Battle of Culloden defeated him. Scotland lost its bid for freedom that April day in 1746, and has been part of the United Kingdom for more than 200 years. I'll be taking you to visit the battlefield when we stay with your grandfather."

Heavy rain began to sweep the city as they walked to the hotel. William approached the front desk with Hardy out of hearing range and asked if two tickets had been secured for the Royal Tattoo. He hoped to surprise Hardy later that evening with a trip to Edinburgh Castle and an introduction to a dozen marching bands, including the Royal Scots Regiment, the Royal Highland Fusiliers and the world renowned Black Watch Brigade. Made up of bagpipes, drums and highland dancers displaying a myriad of colorful tartans, William remembered watching the bands marching back and forth with precision when he was a young man, playing Scotland's battle-ready tunes and laments in front of hundreds of spectators at the castle entrance. He remembered the multiple canons that roared and the reek of the gunpowder rising from the castle floor along with thick clouds of smoke. He had often hoped that someday he would share the experience with his children and Hardy was the first.

Part 4

THE AWAKENING

Chapter 14

William MacBean drove slowly through the entrance to Dalcross Castle, past the ancient iron studded oak gates and headed up the long single lane drive. The stonewalls leading toward the castle reminded him of the walls in his adoptive home of Westport. Hardy looked through the rain crossing the windshield as the castle tower house and turrets came into view. The rain had not let up since it began the previous day. Hardy thought about his visit to the Scott monument and the claustrophobia he felt climbing up the damp stone steps, worn hollow by pilgrims who travelled from around the world to experience all things related to Sir Walter Scott. He left his father on the third level as William explained the last winding stairway was too narrow for him to navigate. His father urged him to continue up the stairs for a better view across the Princess Gardens to Old Town and Edinburgh Castle. He remembered running his hand across the stairway wall, touching the sandstone's beaded moisture, feeling his shoulders brush against the narrowing stairway walls. His breathing quickened, as he counted the last of 287 steps, then bursting from the stairway, gulping down the fresh air and stumbling to the rail to see Arthur's Seat rising above the city a mile to the east. Turning to the west, he saw Edinburg castle hovering above the mist, and then north to Leith where the city's seaport clung to the south shore of The Firth of Forth. The wind had been quite strong with rain horizontal, pelting his face. He had braced himself against the stone parapet, alone, without another soul in sight.

They came to a stop outside the castle entrance with Winwood Grant waving at them from the kitchen window. Moments later she swung open the main entrance weathered oaken door studded with large black iron bolts.

"William," she called out, "now who is that young man you have with you?"

"Why it's my son Hardy, don't you remember him?" William asked, knowing full well that she was expecting them both.

"Well, of course I do, William, but my, how Hardy has grown so," Winwood gushed in her soft Scots accent. Winwood had just celebrated her 30th birthday and her long, brilliant red hair, curvaceous figure and blue eyes captivated Hardy. He remembered her from his visit six years before when he first met his uncle and grandfather. She had just returned back from Edinburgh with a Doctor of Veterinary degree and his Uncle Gillies lost no time putting her to work looking after the estates growing sheep and highland cattle herd.

When her father and mother retired and moved in town to Inverness, her position was elevated to manager of the castle staff, which included a cook, a butler, two farm personnel and a forester.

"Where is everyone?" William asked as he embraced Winwood.

"I don't know about your brother, but your father is down at the river angling for tonight's supper. Let's hope he catches a few salmon so we can smoke what we don't eat," Winwood said as she reached out to give Hardy a hug, crushing him against her breast.

"My Hardy," Winwood said, "you've grown into such a handsome young man."

Hardy blushed as she released her hold, leaving a distinct scent of the rosemary she had picked from the kitchen garden.

"Come on men," Winwood ordered, "Get your bags and follow me. Hardy will have the third floor east turret looking out on the gardens and William will have his old room on the second floor."

They entered the Great Hall with beamed ceiling, tall windows with balconies, a grand fireplace and paneled walls with portraits of the MacBean ancestors hung along with landscape paintings depicting the River Nairn, the Moray Firth, and ships battling a stormy North Sea. They climbed the stone spiral stair to the second floor where William entered his room and Winwood continued climbing with Hardy up to the third.

"Here we are," Winwood said, opening the first door off the landing. "I hope you will be comfortable here Hardy, your grandfather should be home any minute now. So come on down as soon as you are situated."

Hardy looked out the turret window onto the garden and out to the hills beyond. Lost in thought, he was jarred back into the moment when he heard his grandfather's thunderous voice calling out.

"Winwood, I have eneuch salmon for denner and eneuch lave over for the smoke house! I see me boys have arrived?"

"Yes, they have," she exclaimed.

William descended the stairs and approached his father with his hands outstretched. His father held out his arms and embraced him, throwing the salmon over his back.

"Na glaikit havn frae me!"

"All right then," William said, "then no foolish hand from me either," and he stood back and looked at his father's smiling face. "Father, Please use the King's English. Hardy won't understand a word you're saying and I'd rather not be your interpreter."

"Alright, son, I'll do my best, I promise."

Hardy leaped down the stairs two at a time and ran into the hallway. His grandfather greeted him, forgetting for a moment what his son had asked him not to do.

"Ah Hardy, come gie yer auld-faither a hug, I mean come give your grandfather a hug," he said laughing. "I'll learn to speak guid one of these days Hardy!"

Gillies MacBean hosted his sons and grandson in the Dalcross Great Hall, where they sat at a long dining table made from oak harvested centuries before from the Dalcross forest.

"Hardy," his grandfather exclaimed, "at this very table, in 1746, sat the 'Butcher,' known as William Augustus, Duke of Cumberland, the son of King George II. His was the responsibility to rid our beautiful Scotland of its rightful king, Prince Charles Edward Stuart, and he did thus in a particularly gruesome manner, not more than two miles from where we sit. I'll tell you the whole story when we go for a shoot across the Culloden Moor."

William and his brother glanced at each other, feigning indifference to their fathers often repeated story of the "Butcher," a story intertwined with Dalcross Castle and the demise of the Stuart dynasty.

That afternoon, Winwood ordered the cook to prepare a feast of Cullen skink, poached salmon, colcannon, hairy tatties, potted game and minced collops. She wanted Hardy to experience true Scottish fare.

As the food was served on the table, Hardy's uncle called out to the kitchen.

"Winwood, Miss Grant, we need a woman's company, please come sit with us," he implored.

"All right," Winwood called back, "I'd love too! I'll be there in a minute, as soon as I tidy up."

Hardy noticed a smile come over his uncle's face when he heard Winwood's reply.

"Now Hardy," his grandfather said, "I hear that your father is taking you to Inverness tomorrow to fit up a kilt. I understand this is part of the required school dress at Gordonstoun."

"Yes sir," Hardy replied.

"Perhaps we can fish the Nairn tomorrow afternoon when you get back, I've picked out a very nice 'Hardy' J.J.H. Triumph fly fishing rod. Aptly named wouldn't you say?"

"I would like that very much Grumps" Hardy said.

Winwood appeared at the table dressed in a floor length skirt made from Grant tartan, a white ruffled high neck shirt with her hair tied up in a bun.

"Sorry to keep you all waiting, I was putting the finishing touches to the dessert."

"And what dessert might that be?" William asked.

"What might that be? Well, seeing how our raspberry patch has come into full harvest, I have taken the liberty to make raspberry cranachan for our very special guests!"

"I hope you used our private label Glenfiddich," Uncle Gillies said. "We need to educate young Hardy with an introduction to our local single malt whiskey."

"I most certainly did. Tis about time Hardy experienced the dew of the realm."

They laughed as Hardy sat in silence watching his grandfather.

His grandfather looked around the table with a thoughtful scowl. He then rested his eyes on Winwood, showing a noticeable calm around his eyes as he began to recite the daily prayer:

> *"Some have meat and canna eat,*
> *And some wad eat that want it.*
> *But we hae meat, and we can eat,*
> *And sae let the lord be thankit."*

"Amen" traveled across the table in unison.

Hardy watched his grandfather fill his plate, wondering how anyone could eat so much food. His father and uncle deferred to Winwood as she ladled a bowl of Cullen skink and Hardy helped himself to salmon and hairy taddies. He discovered the hairy taddies were made from smoked haddock mashed with potatoes and his first taste reminded him of the creamed fin and haddie his mother would often make him for breakfast.

"Tell us about your trip up from London," Hardy's grandfather asked.

"Pop showed me Trinity College, and then we drove up past Sherwood Forest. We stayed the night at the Crown and Mitre Hotel on the border and we saw Hadrian's Wall. Then we drove up to Edinburgh. We climbed up Sir Walter Scott's Monument too, but Pop couldn't climb the last stairway because he couldn't fit."

"Your father tells me you experienced the Royal Tattoo," Uncle Gillies chimed in.

"Yes, we did. It was pouring rain and the bagpipes were so loud they gave me goose bumps. I couldn't think of anything else until the cannons began to fire. I counted 21 blasts with each muzzle flashing one after another, and could smell the heavy gunpowder in the air with the thick smoke covering over the bagpipers and the crowd in the bleachers below. We were sitting high up at the end of the castle square and we could see it all happing as the smoke rose up to our seats. We watched the Jordanian army ride a dozen camels and the Edinburgh Fire Brigade put on a demonstration!"

"That's braw, Hardy, the skirl of the pipes," Grandfather Gillies joined in. "Camels at the Tattoo? I've never heard of such a thing! Someday we'll go and witness that pageantry together!"

"When does your father take you up to Gordonstoun?" Uncle Gillies questioned.

"We go up this next Sunday," William replied.

"You know, Hardy," Uncle Gillies offered, "you'll be less than an hour away and I can skip up anytime and bring you home for the weekend."

"Winwood," Hardy's grandfather exclaimed, "the meal is quite guid and the salmon is the best I've ever had."

"It ought to be, Mr. MacBean, you caught it!" Winwood exclaimed laughing.

"Here's to you, Hardy," his grandfather said, standing and raising his glass, "and to a very successful year at Gordonstoun, but make sure you stay away from the Prince and the House of Windsor, nothin good will come of it."

"What in the bloody hell are you talking about father?" William snapped.

"Just letting the boy knows what he's in for William. Everyone around here knows the story."

"And what might that be?

"You know as well as I do, the royals change their name when it suites em. They made up the name House of Windsor in 1917 and before the House of Windsor it was the House of Saxe-Coburg-Gotha. Nothing but a bunch of moochers I say. All they do is take from the people and live high off the hog."

"Father, you know that the name Saxe-Coburg-Gotha came with Prince Albert. Queen Victoria married the man for god's sake."

"I know that, William, although that's not the only German name in the mix. What I'm saying to you is the Windsor name was borrowed from Windsor Castle and they used it specifically to cover up the family ties to the German aristocracy. George V knew they were close to throwing him out and realized he better Anglicize the family name. Too many of our boys died in the Great War. Whatever the case, most of King George's cousins in Europe lost their power and many lost their lives, like his first cousin Nicolas II, the Emperor of Russia. And here we are a scant 45 years later and many believe the House of Windsor has been the House of Windsor since the dawn of time. I want my grandson to know that the Windsor name has very little to do with the history of the royal family name as it is, other than the castle they have lived in and used for the past 700 years."

"That's fair enough." William said. "However, Queen Elizabeth's direct lineage goes back more than 1,000 years. In fact, it reaches back at least 1,200 years to the Saxon King Alfred the Great, who ruled England from 871 to 899.

"Well, if you say so," his father replied. " But I say it's time for them to be removed. They are nothing but figureheads and they cost the taxpayers dearly! They've been around long enough! And now I will say goodnight!"

He pushed back his chair, stood up swaying for a moment and turned toward the stairs.

"I think it's time we went to bed, too," William said standing, "Come along Hardy. I dare say father, you're in no shape to climb the stairs unassisted."

"Done it many a time before William, but I'll let you assist me, just this once. Goodnight Winwood and goodnight Gillies, see you in the morn."

Hardy woke at first light, dressed and descended to the second floor landing. He followed the hallway to a secret stairway leading to the kitchen. As he passed by his uncles slightly ajar bedroom door he heard the muffled sounds of "Ah, ah, ah," and quietly stepped to the door. Holding his breath he peered through the opening, and to his amazement, he watched a beautiful and naked Winwood astride his Uncle Gillies. With his uncle's back against the headboard, Winwood faced away toward the foot of the bed with her knees bent and feet pushed up into the pillows, swinging her hips as if cantering a phantom horse. Gillies held her hips with his hands, her eyes were closed and her face tilted up as her pace quickened. She continued to make sounds that transfixed Hardy's gaze. By chance Gillies turned and glanced at the bedroom door and was caught by surprise when he saw Hardy looking back, mouth agape and eyes open wide. Winwood's cries of pleasure increased and Gillies smiled and winked once at Hardy, who jumped back behind the door, with his heart quickly beating, as he moved down the hall in haste. He was filled with anxiety and embarrassed for getting caught watching an event that would be forever seared in his memory.

Chapter 15

"We'll all be back for Christmas before you know it, Hardy, and your Uncle Gillies will be up to get you at midterm." They shook hands and his father turned and opened the car door.

"Study hard, play hard, and don't take any guff."

Hardy watched as his father's car disappeared from sight. His lip trembled slightly. He felt very much alone. His bag and guitar lay on the cobblestones outside the main building as he waited for a lift to Windmill Lodge.

The bus pulled up to a long, narrow thatch-covered structure and dropped Hardy off along with three other boys. He stood looking at the single-story boarding house, unsure of his next move when the eldest boy among them approached him.

"You there, collect my bags and follow me."

"Screw off, collect your own bag." Hardy replied.

Hardy watched as the boy moved swiftly in his direction.

"I'll be the one telling you to screw off!" the boy exclaimed.

The last thing Hardy remembered was a blow to his nose, then stars, then blackness. When he regained consciousness, he tasted blood flowing down the back of his throat. Blood saturated the front of his shirt.

"Jesus, you okay?" His assailant asked as he propped him up.

Hardy continued to bleed as the other boys gathered around.

"We better get him to the infirmary," one of them said.

The bus arrived with another load of students. The driver got out and saw Hardy lying on the gravel road.

"What is going on here?" the driver asked.

The older boy looked up from Hardy.

"I popped him one and he won't stop bleeding,"

"Awful lot of blood. Help me get him to the bus," the driver said. "You're in trouble now, Marcus. I dare say you'll lose your guardianship."

The infirmary was housed in a small brick building, sparkling clean in and out. The nurse opened the door and asked Hardy to sit down in the chair by her desk. He moved across the freshly washed gray tiled floor dropping bright spots of blood along his path.

"Bleeder," she said identifying the nostril in need of attention. "What's your name?"

"Hardy MacBean," he said, clearing his throat.

"Hardy, I want you to pinch your nose, like this," the nurse commanded.

"'I've been doing that, but I'm swallowing a lot of blood and it tastes terrible."

"Keep your head down," the nurse replied, "We'll need to cauterize. My name is Hood. You can call me Nurse Hood. This will only take a minute and it will burn a bit."

She reached into a white metal cabinet and withdrew a bottle of six-inch-long sticks that looked like wooden matches. She removed one stick and placed it on her desk.

"Let's clean you up Hardy MacBean, and see what's what," she said, taking a wet cloth and cleaning the blood from around his nose. "Alright then, head back, continue to pinch your nose."

She dipped the end of the stick into water to activate the silver nitrate tip.

"Now move your hand away Hardy," she commanded, "Hold onto the arms of the chair. You're gonna feel some burning."

She inserted the stick as far as she thought was necessary, rolling it in one direction.

"That will do," she said removing the stick from his nose, laying it down on a white paper napkin.

Hardy smelled burnt flesh and felt intense heat build in his right nostril. Incredible pain followed; almost equal to the blow he received from the boy he now knew was named Marcus. He gripped the arms of the chair, his knuckles turning white, thinking that his nose must be broken.

"FUCKING BASTARD ASSHOLE!" He cried out as the pain reached its zenith.

"There, there, that's a good boy, all done, I've heard worse Hardy," Nurse Hood exclaimed, pushing a wad of gauze up his nose. "You'll soon be good as new."

With the pain beginning to subside, Hardy realized with relief that the flow of blood had stopped.

"Now use the cludgie and clean up and I'll get you a fresh shirt."

"The what?" Hardy asked?

"The lavy, you know, the loo," Mrs. Hood replied.

She took hold of Hardy's arm and pointed him toward the bathroom.

"I will try and save your shirt, but no promises."

The phone rang as Hardy walked to the bathroom.

"Hello, Nurse Hood here. Aye, sir. Yes sir. Bye now."

Hardy returned and Nurse Hood handed him a clean shirt.

"I think this should fit."

"Thank you, Nurse Hood," Hardy whispered as he began to put on the shirt.

"I've just now been rung up and you're to be brought round to the Head Masters house as soon as you're able, and try not to swear over there Hardy. Here are some aspirin tablets," she said handing him the aspirin and a glass of water. "Take two now and two more before you go to bed."

The bus driver appeared at the door.

"Hello Nurse Hood. How's the patient?"

Nurse Hood thought about the young American and imagined she would be seeing more of him.

"I think he's seen better, Mr. Murray, but he'll do just fine and he's ready to go now. Hardy I'm afraid you have blood on your trousers, too. When you get back to your boarding house, make sure to soak them in cold water."

"No problem there," Mr. Murray said, "all's they have is cold water! Well alright, Hardy," Murray continued, "let's go see Headmaster Chew. We'll be heading back in the direction of your boarding house. My name is Robert Murray, but you can call me Bob."

"Mr. Murray, Bob," Hardy hesitated but repeated.

"Yes, it's Bob," Murray said, hoping he could make the third form student from America feel at ease. "Why not ride up front with me, Hardy? You've certainly had a tough day. How do you feel?"

"I've felt better Bob."

"Just a spot of blood, Hardy. You're on the mend," Murray said, starting the engine, looking down at the gauze packed with blood. He took a right turn off Gordonstoun Road and travelled down a long gravel drive that ended in front of the headmaster's house.

Murray signaled Hardy and they both got out and walked to the front door. The door opened and Hardy looked up to see a beautiful blue-eyed, blond haired woman who looked a lot like a model he remembered seeing on the front cover of his mother's July issue of *Vogue*. She wore a dark blue dress and her hair was swept up in a braided wrap.

"You must be Hardy," the woman said. "Please come in. Thank you Mr. Murray for bringing Hardy over. We'll return him to Windmill Lodge after tea."

"Alright, Mrs. Chew, I'll check in on Hardy later this afternoon." Murray turned and walked back to the bus.

Eva Chew put her hand lightly on Hardy's shoulder as her husband appeared in the entrance hall moving toward them in a mechanical fashion. He was a large man with close cropped brown hair, a pronounced receding hairline, rugged features and impeccably dressed in a Saville Row tailored suit.

"Hardy," Mrs. Chew began, "this is my husband, Mr. F.R.G. Chew, otherwise known as Robert, and I'm Eva. It's so nice to have you here at Gordonstoun. We understand you've had a bit of a dust up today and Mr. Chew thought it best if you came round for tea."

"Hello, Hardy MacBean, I see you've met Mrs. Chew. Let's go to my study and get acquainted, shall we? Mrs. Chew is fixing some tea and biscuits for us."

"Yes sir," Hardy said, following Mr. Chew.

Mr. Chew sat at a long low table completely clear of everything but blotter, paper and pen. Each book in his extensive library was in order of descending size, left to right. He pointed to a sofa along the wall and Hardy took a seat nearest the window.

He looked out at the sunlit sky and watched as flocks of starlings swooped in unison across the open fields catching the light, illuminating a mass of iridescent green and purple colors.

"Well, Hardy," Mr. Chew began, "Not a very fitting introduction to Gordonstoun, and It looks like you'll have two black eyes out of this."

Hardy sat in uncomfortable silence, both physically and mentally exhausted, wondering what was coming next.

"So I hear you had a bit of a boxing match. What was it about, Hardy?"

Hardy sat and contemplated his response.

"It wasn't a boxing match, sir. It was more like a sucker punch."

"What was it about?"

"Not much, it was a mistake, sir."

"Who might I ask did you have this mistake with?"

"I don't know his name," Hardy said.

Mrs. Chew knocked on the door, entered carrying a tray and placed on a tea caddy.

"Here you are. I have a couple of bottles of Irn-Bru, and a Tizer limeade if you would rather not take tea."

"Thank you, Mrs. Chew, I'll have the limeade, please."

"Alright then, I'll leave you men to your discussions," she said looking up at her husband.

Mr. Chew opened the limeade and handed it to Hardy along with a small plate with biscuit. He poured his tea and sat down looking out the window onto the stone terrace.

"You know, Hardy," he began, "life is hard enough without adding a sucker punch into the mix. I daresay whoever gave you that punch isn't exactly proud of it. The problem as I see it, is which one of you is going to start the discussion — you or him? I can't exactly tell you that you should speak with him, but in my life I've seen two wars Hardy, and perhaps if both sides had spoken with one another about the possible consequences they wouldn't have caused so much pain and tragedy. We all need to get along in this life and the year has just begun. What do you think you will do?"

Hardy placed his empty bottle on the tea caddy.

"I guess I'll try, sir. I'll try to speak with him."

"Good for you. You never know, you just might become friends in the end. I have a saying, Hardy; it never hurts to air your laundry, although it does matter how dirty the laundry is."

For the next hour, Mr. Chew spoke with Hardy about sailing off the Scottish coast and hiking in the Cairngorms and Grampian mountains. By the time he suggested that he drive Hardy back to his boarding house, Hardy had shared stories about his sailing off Westport and hiking he had done with his father and Uncle. Mr. Chew believed he had successfully brought Hardy back to a positive place from which to begin his new life at school.

"Remember, Hardy," Mr. Chew repeated when he dropped him off at Windmill Lodge, "you know where I live and you're always welcome to come round any time you wish."

Hardy thanked him and walked to the entrance of his new home. Once inside he recognized a boy from earlier that day.

"Hello," the boy said reaching out his hand, "My name is Colin Ferguson. I put your things by your bed. Come on, I'll show you the dormitory."

Ferguson was tall and lanky and about the same size as Hardy.

"Hardy MacBean," he said shaking Ferguson's hand.

They walked to the dormitory, where Hardy counted 14 beds, seven to a side. His bed was the sixth one against the wall to his left.

"Mine is to the right of yours. I guess that makes us bunk mates," Colin said.

The seven beds across the room were interspersed with four windows without curtain or shade. The walls were bare, covered with cement stucco and the floors were of dark oiled oak.

"Thanks for your help Collin," Hardy said, adding, "and thanks for watching over my stuff, especially my guitar."

"No problem, Hardy, I'm glad to help. Are you hungry?" he asked. "I have some crackers and smoked kippers to hold us over until the evening."

"I'd like that," Hardy replied.

Hardy and Colin sat on their beds, each eating crackers and kippers, watching as the room slowly filled with their dorm mates. Hardy figured that his altercation with Marcus Fielding was now a well-known fact. He counted 13 boys. Their glances in his direction were often and repetitive. The bed to his left remained empty.

"Who do you think is missing?" Hardy asked.

"I'm fairly sure that's the Prince," Colin replied.

Hardy thought about the information, Prince Charles sleeping next to him!" He imagined his grandfather would have a fit.

"I know he enrolled last summer and got himself in a whole heap of trouble out in Stornoway on the Isle of Lewis," Colin said.

"What did he do?"

"It was in all the papers. He ordered up a cherry brandy at the Crown Hotel. His bodyguard nipped him in the act and rushed him back to school hidden on the floor of his car. But it was all out by then.

Everyone in the pub saw it and the papers were agog over it." "They couldn't get enough of it. The Royals back in London denied it at first, and then changed their story when word got out. Chew didn't cane or demote him; there was nothing to demote him to. How do you demote a Prince? It all got swept under the rug. There was an investigation about serving under age, but there weren't any charges brought up and that too disappeared away. My father thought the whole mess was nothing but a bunch of rubbish. The papers had his age at 14, but he's 13 till November and my father thinks they used 14 so it wouldn't sound so bad. If it had been you or me we would have been caned, expelled or both! The buggers!"

"I'm surprised my grandfather didn't know about it," Hardy replied, "He doesn't think much of the Windsor family."

"Where does your grandfather live?"

"He lives in Dalcross, about an hour south from here, a few miles from Inverness."

"I'm from Inverness!" Colin exclaimed. "I've never been to Dalcross. He must not get the paper."

"I guess not, "Hardy replied as an older athletic looking man entered the dormitory. His hair was white, closely cropped and his cheeks were ruddy. He wore a checkered brown tweed, green plaid tie and flannel pants.

"Hello, men, I'm your house master, I'm Mr. Whitby. I'd like to welcome you all to Gordonstoun and Windmill Lodge, where I hope you'll enjoy yourselves for the duration. I'd like you all to know that Prince Charles will soon be joining us. I'm warning you now that any antagonistic behavior toward Charles will result in immediate expulsion. Also, smoking and drinking are against the rules and as such are punishable by caning, demotion and possible expulsion. Are there any questions?"

Colin raised his hand.

"Yes sir, I do, what punishment did Prince Charles receive when he was caught drinking this summer?" A murmur of voices circled the room.

"That matter has been dealt with and it's none of your business!" Whitby exclaimed, his face becoming a darker shade of red.

"Next? Well, I guess that sums it up then," he continued, "I want you to know that as Master in Charge of Cricket, I'm always looking for new cricketers. Anyone who is interested, please step up and let me know. Remember, we all rise at 5:00 each morning and have a run. We shower before breakfast, which is 7 o'clock sharp. I will see you later at the evening meal." He turned and abruptly left the room. Every last boy in the room except Hardy decided that Charles would get his due.

When Hardy returned from dinner, he found Charles siting on the bed next to his reading a magazine. He wore a blue button-down shirt, a pair of brown thick corduroys and a cashmere sweater. Hardy sat down, the shirt the nurse loaned him and his khaki pants were spattered with blood. Looking over at Charles he extended his hand.

"Hello, I'm Hardy MacBean."

Charles looked up from his magazine and noticed Hardy's swollen nose and eyes underlined with black and blue.

"What happened to you?" he asked, grasping Hardy's hand.

"I was on the wrong end of it," Hardy replied.

"The end of what?"

"The end of the Guardian's fist."

"Who is that?"

87

"The head boy," Hardy replied. "I told him to screw off when he asked me to carry his bags and he slugged me, almost broke my nose."

"God, you look positively awful," he said, turning back to his reading as Hardy removed his shoes and swung his legs up on to his bed.

"Hey, Hardy," Colin called out as he entered the dormitory, looking over at the Prince. "You hitting the sack now?

"Yes, I think so, I'm pretty tired."

A moment passed and Hardy breathed a sigh and was soon deep in sleep. Colin walked to his bed and spread a blanket over him.

"Goodnight, Hardy, see you in the morning my friend."

Later on that night, when lights were out, a shoe was thrown in the direction of the Prince and landed squarely on Hardy's nose.

"Owwwwwe! Fuuuuucking Bastard!" Hardy screamed, waking from a deep sleep. Complete silence fell over the room. Hardy held the shoe tightly in his right hand. "I'm going to beat the shit out of whoever owns this shoe, you can count on it!" He laid his head back on his pillow, waiting to taste the blood he was sure would follow.

"Foul," Charles whispered under his breath.

"What did you say?" Hardy asked. Once more the room fell into silence.

"You okay?" Colin whispered.

"I'll be okay when I find the bugger who threw this shoe."

Robert Whitby turned the dormitory lights on and rang the navy bell five times.

"Everyone rise and shine," Whitby announced, "time for the morning run." Hardy opened his swollen eyes. His watch read five o'clock exactly.

As the dormitory emptied onto the front drive, he could hear other dormitories in the distance up and about. This was the five-mile run that Mr. Miner had told him about. His nose had a dull ache. He knew that running would be difficult. He wondered what would be worse, a throbbing nose or a cold shower.

Chapter 16

William MacBean left Gordonstoun and headed south to London, stopping once to gas up. He arrived in Regents Park at 10 p.m. and parked the car directly across from David Stewart's home. The apartment was dark as William climbed the stairs to the front door and rang the buzzer. He peered through the sidelight, listening to a door open somewhere in the back hall and then watched as David emerged, turning on the light and slowly shuffling toward the front door.

"Come in, William," David announced, opening the door.

"Hello, David," William exclaimed. "How are you?"

"I'd be better if I'd been able to break the encryptions you left me. Bit of scotch, William?"

"Yes, that would be terrific," he said placing his bag on the floor.

"Good, let's go into the study, shall we?"

MacBean settled into a leather couch, tipping a glass of Glen Livet, enjoying the simple pleasure of sitting and relieved from driving the roads and highways of the United Kingdom.

"Where exactly did you happen upon these cryptonyms?"

"I was waiting for you to ask that. It was by accident. I was returning to Langley to button up newly installed listening devices when

I passed the Federal Reserve chief leaving by limousine. The window was down and no mistake about it, it was he. Normally I wouldn't think twice, but it was late afternoon on Saturday and the building is usually pretty much deserted over the weekend, just a few officers, staff and skeleton crew. But I asked myself, what was the chairman doing out at Langley? When I walked to the elevator, McCone drove past me, looking straight ahead, no acknowledgement."

"This was also odd as the director was not the type to show up on the weekends, at least not since he took over from Allen Dulles in '61. I didn't think much more about it until I got to my office and started to catalogue and clear the recordings from the past month. I started with McCone's office, normal informational meetings with Clara reading text. Then out of the blue McCone said, "We have GPFLOOR laying cover." And then I heard someone say, "Joe told us he'd play ball with us, but now we don't have much choice since his stroke, poor bastard. He can't speak a word for Christ sake. This is dangerous business. We could lose everything, and you could lose big, too. Bobby is beginning to think himself both Peter and Paul, saving his brother's presidency." McCone went on to say, "Don't worry, JPIDEAL will be taken care of." Chairs moved on the floor and then another other voice said, "We're counting on you," and then the door closed.

"Sorry to say we hadn't hooked up the cameras yet, but I'm going to dig up some old recordings and try and find out whom the mystery men sound like."

"Well, we know one of them is McCone, and we have two names, Joe and Bobby," David interjected. "I don't know, but couldn't they be Ambassador Kennedy and his son Robert?"

"Do you think JPIDEAL is Bobby?"

"Could be William, could be. But I don't understand what Joe Kennedy has to do with it. And I don't know what he means by 'playing ball,' we just don't know enough to make any assumptions."

"Alright, it's probably nothing, but I intend to pursue it. Thanks for your help, David, even though we're at square one, I appreciate it."

"You're quite welcome old boy, let's hit the hay, tomorrow's another day. Your room is at the top of the stairs, third door on your right, and have a good sleep." David swallowed the last of his scotch, collected Williams' glass and carried it to the butler's pantry.

Chapter 17

November 22, 1963, Hardy perched on his bike preparing to plunge down the hill to Hopeman Harbor at breakneck speed. The tide was coming on high and he took notice of the wind's velocity and direction coming off Moray Firth. He could see the spray rising from the jetty as the wind freshened and the waves gained in height. The sky was a remarkable pale blue color where it met a deep blue sea, with dancing white caps sparkling in the noonday sun.

His American grandfather would call a day like this "a blue northerly," while his grandmother referred to them as "blue, bell jar days." Hardy never understood what a blue bell jar was exactly, and although he never asked his grandmother for an explanation, his imagination conjured a ceramic jar with a top glazed the color of a robin's egg on the inside with a dark ocean blue exterior. Looking down at the boats lining the harbor wall, he picked out the masts of the schools twin 27-foot Montague Whalers.

"Race you to the bottom?" he asked glancing at his friend.

"You're on!" Colin replied, pushing away before Hardy could put foot to pedal.

They arrived together in a cloud of dust, skidding along the gravel, each proclaiming victory.

Commander Shaw stood in the doorway of the sail loft scratching his head with the stem of his pipe. Hardy and Colin were always first to arrive and the commander would put them to work immediately.

"Hello, boys, he said. "Today we're going to learn how to leather the oars before the rest of the crew shows up."

Entering the hut, Hardy smelled the newly coiled hemp rope and the hand tarred marline, the heavy canvas sails hanging from the loft and the newly varnished oars. He relished these smells that carried memories of his grandfather's Westport harbor boathouse.

"Hardy," the commander said, "find me a piece of leather in the blue chest, and make sure it's at least 18 inches long and as wide as possible."

Hardy returned with the leather and watched as Commander Shaw wrapped it around the middle of the oar, where it would cradle in the rowlock, and then he cut it to width, leaving about one quarter inch less than the circumference of the oar handle. He explained how it would allow for the laces to pull the leather together for a snug fit.

"Hardy, I want five more pieces exactly like this," he said holding up the leather.

As Colin and Hardy began to punch holes in the leather, the rest of the sailing class arrived and Commander Shaw ordered them all to change into their serge seaman trousers and course round-necked pullovers.

"Hardy," Shaw ordered, "you will captain the old whaler today. We're going to have a competition between the third and fourth forms. James Garrison will captain the new whaler. As captains it will be your job to set course from the harbor to Burghead Fort. I will be over there to view your progress. We have a 15- to 18-knot wind out of the north, with gusts to 22. You'll be on a fast beam reach, starboard tack. Use the white marker off the end of the harbor jetty as the starting point and I will blow the horn three times five minutes before the start and then again to begin the race. Now jump to it!"

Hardy's heart skipped a beat as the word "captain" sunk in.

"Let's go," Hardy called out.

Six boys climbed down the ladder with four settling into double-banked rowing seats. Hardy surveyed the fore and aft lugsails and asked Colin for a hand. He had given much thought about the stiff breeze they encountered the previous week, a lot like the weather they were about to experience; lee gunwales down, keeled over, taking occasional water as everyone perched on the windward side, often turning into the wind, sails flapping, the boat righting. He remembered what his grandfather used to say when they took the catboat out in similar conditions: "Hardy, a heeling vessel doesn't make speed; you've got to reef her. You want your mast as perpendicular to the sea as possible, a perpendicular sail means full speed." Hardy leaned down and pulled the foot of the lugsail, exposing the reef nettles.

"We'll use the first set of nettles, both on the main and mizzen," he called out to Colin, thinking that one set would be enough.

On Hardy's first day of sailing class, Commander Shaw had told them that the old whaler held a heavy ballast of pig iron, which was beneficial in a stiff breeze. The new whaler, he explained, had less ballast and was faster in light winds. Hardy didn't stop to think why Shaw had given him the old whaler that day and continued to show Colin how to roll the canvas up to the nettle and then tie it off with a square knot. Clenching his pipe with his teeth, Lieutenant Commander Shaw looked on from the jetty, a wide grin across his face.

"Rowlocks in," Hardy commanded, "Oars in, pull together!"

The old whaler slowly moved away from its harbor berth, well behind the new whaler that was nearing the harbor mouth with sails up, heeling, once away from the protection of the stone jetty. Hardy and Colin pulled on the main halyard and hoisted the lugsail up the mast. With the sail flapping in the wind, they moved in concert to hoist the mizzen. As the new whaler passed their bow, Hardy could see a look of confusion on James Garrison's face when he noticed the old cutters shortened, reefed sails. Whether or not Garrison knew how to reef a lugsail Hardy thought, he would need to lower his sails to do it.

Hardy cleated the sheet and tack downhaul lines and called out to his crew.

"Give way together, ship oars!"

Four oars pulled from the rowlocks in unison and were stowed at once under the seats with precision as three blasts from the horn sounded. Hardy glanced at his watch, counting, coming about, and counting. "Come on," he thought watching the sails fill, feeling the whaler come to speed.

"Coming about, hard-a-lee!" he shouted above the noise of the wind in the sails.

Then came the single horn blast and the race was on with the bow of the old whaler passing the marker within seconds and inches ahead of its competitor.

Sitting to windward, Hardy held the tiller tightly, more out of excitement than need as the old whaler pulled away from its rival and plied the waves with ease. His crew looked ahead to Burghead Point. A pair of cormorants skimmed across the bow and a raft of velvet scoters jumped from the whaler's path, arcing in concert toward the shore. Hardy looked back at the new whaler, heeling over and pointing into the wind with the crew lowering the mizzen. Nearing Burghead Fort, Hardy could make out Shaw waving from the sea wall. Pushing the tiller away and yelling "hard-a- lee!" once more, they came about as the top yard dipped around the mast and the sail drew away from them, putting the whaler on port tack. With no other boat in sight, they headed for home, slapping one another on their backs, each boy whooping with delight in their triumphant victory over the fourth form boys.

Chapter 18

William MacBean sat in his Langley office pondering the day's events. It was 8:15 p.m. on November 22, 1963. President John Fitzgerald Kennedy was dead and Vice President Lyndon Baines Johnson had just been sworn in aboard Air Force One as the 36th President of the United States. His phone rang twice.

"MacBean here."

"MacBean, this is McCone, please come to my office."

"Yes sir," William answered. "I'll be right there."

MacBean walked down the corridor to McCone's office. Knocking once on the door, he heard McCone's authoritative voice.

"Enter, MacBean."

Sitting alongside McCone at a long mahogany table was Clara Winston.

Hello, Miss Winston," MacBean said, acknowledging his old secretary from the OPC days.

"Why, hello, Mr. MacBean," Clara said in her southern drawl. "So nice to see you again." The director cleared his throat:

"Have a seat, MacBean. Let's get down to business. Clara is going to record the event."

MacBean thought this statement odd. He knew that McCone was fully aware of the listening devices that were installed during the construction of the new headquarters. He must want Clara as a witness, he thought.

"At 7:10 p.m., central daylight time," McCone began, "Lee Harvey Oswald was charged with the murder of Officer Tippet during what we believe was his attempt to flee Dallas after the assassination of President Kennedy. We also believe that he will soon be charged with the assassination of President Kennedy. We have received background on Oswald and due to your linguistic skills, as well as your familiarity with the various underground organizations in both Russia and Cuba, I want you to find out as much as you can and as quickly as you can about Oswald's history. During this investigation, we have assigned a cryptonym for both Oswald and President Kennedy. For Oswald, we'll use GPFLOOR, and for Kennedy we'll use GPIDEAL. You'll use these cryptonyms in all your correspondence."

MacBean felt as if the wind had been knocked out of him. His heart went cold, his mind raced. He used his years of training to hide a reaction. "You son of a bitch," he thought.

"Yes sir," William replied, pushing his chair back and standing up from the table, "If that is all?"

"Yes, it is," McCone, replied.

MacBean left McCone and Winston and walked back to his office. He had known of McCone since 1948 when Harry Truman appointed him as Special Deputy to Secretary of Defense James V. Forrestal, who resigned his position in 1949 and plunged to his death from the 16th floor of the National Naval Medical Center. All under suspicious circumstances, William never gave it a second thought. McCone was then appointed Undersecretary of the Air Force in 1950. It was well known that while in this post he gave out contracts to Standard Oil and Kaiser Aluminum, companies in which he had beneficial financial connections. Prior to his appointments within the U.S. government, he became extremely wealthy as the founder and part owner of Bechtel-McCone, which was provided lucrative government contracts during World War II. During the summer of 1940 it was said that Bechtel and McCone received inside information from Admiral Howard Vickery of the U.S. Maritime Commission and Admiral Emory Land, Maritime Commission Chairman, stating that America was headed to war and hundreds of vessels would be needed for the U.S. Merchant Navy. As a result, Bechtel and McCone built shipyards at Richmond and Sausalito, California, soon employing thousands of workmen who would build over 300 ships, including tankers, Liberty and Victory cargo ships and troop transports. The business became known as "Operation Calship." On January 7, 1942, a month after the Japanese attack on Pearl Harbor, the Maritime

Commission awarded Calship its first contract. Within a year, Calship would employ over 42,000 workers.

MacBean was also aware of a number of deals set up by McCone during the war. From fictitious and fraudulent charges that were paid by the U.S. government for aircraft that were never built, to building a refinery and pipeline that would run from the Canadian Northwest through the Yukon territory into Alaska and cost the American taxpayer $134 million. The refinery, known as the Canol project, was abandoned less than a year after it was finished. By the end of the war, John McCone would symbolize the deal making that would make him one of the most powerful and wealthiest men in America.

William turned off his office lights and sat in his chair looking out at a clear, star-filled sky. The November weather had been dry and warm with temperatures in the mid-'60s. He picked up the phone and called Mary, who was visiting for the week and waiting for him at their Georgetown apartment.

"Hello," Mary answered.

"Hi, sweetie."

"Oh, William, such a day."

"I know, I need to stay at the office. I'll catch a quick nap here and then work the rest of the night into the morning. I'm sorry I can't make it home tonight."

"I understand, I'll be waiting for you."

"I'll see you soon," William replied and pressed the button to end the call, holding the phone in his hand, wondering what his next move would be. "They killed the president," he thought, "why not me?" He set his alarm for 2 p.m. to call the U.S. embassy in Moscow.

William knew he had to go through the motions, find out as much as possible about Oswald, even though the end result in his mind was a forgone conclusion. "JPFLOOR laying cover," MacBean repeated over in his mind. McCone and his associates wouldn't leave any loose ends, he thought. "Do what your told," MacBean said to himself. "Don't be a hero."

When the call came in, he was speaking to the US consulate in Mexico. At 12:20 a.m. central time, November 24, exactly two days after the assassination of President Kennedy, Lee Harvey Oswald was gunned down and fatally wounded in the basement of the Dallas Police headquarters. MacBean hung up the phone. A chill rose up his spine. Ultimate power had tied up loose ends. "Dead men don't talk," MacBean thought, "keep your head down."

Part 5

COMING OF AGE

Chapter 19

Hardy sat on the wall outside Windmill Lodge waiting for his Uncle Gillies. It was half term break in his second year at Gordonstoun and he was looking forward to spending his time at Dalcross. Gillies arranged to pick him up when he visited Dalcross at the end of August. He remembered his father's surprise when Winwood met them at the front entrance, extremely pregnant and looking as if she would give birth at any moment. Gillies asked William to be his best man and the following week a group of friends congregated at the Castle to witness the marriage. Hardy, soon to be 16, had his first experience with dark highland beer. The following morning he descended the stairs to the kitchen, where his uncle was preparing a breakfast of hot scones, sausage, eggs and baked beans.

"Hardy, shall I clap my hands?" Gillies said smiling.

Hardy's grey face flushed when he sat down at the table.

"No sir, no thanks, please, no," Hardy said, his voice trailing off, his head throbbing.

"Well, that's alright, Hardy," Gillies said, "We'll just call this one of those rights of passage we all go through in life. What you need is a bit of the dog that bit ye. You need to drink a glass of my famous Dalcross Black Ale."

"Go ahead Hardy," his father said, "It's the only cure I know of, but don't tell your mother."

Gillies poured a glass of his homemade ale and placed it in front of Hardy. They applauded as Hardy sipped through the frothy foam.

Lost in thought when Gillies drove up and sounded his horn, Hardy turned and watched his uncle swing open the passenger door.

"Get in, Hardy, Time's a wasting."

Hardy threw his rucksack in the back and climbed in next to his uncle, excited to gain his freedom.

"Your grandfather has all kinds of plans, Hardy. He wants to shoot grouse with you on Culloden Moor."

"I'd like that," Hardy replied.

"And you'll get to meet my beautiful daughter Margret who is named after my mother, your grandmother. We call her Maggie for short. She'll be six weeks old tomorrow and she's finally sleeping through the night. Winwood can't wait to show her off. Your brother Gillies won't need to worry about a cousin with the same name, at least for now!"

Hardy thought about the morning he watched his uncle and Aunt Winwood in bed and how he froze as his uncle turned and gave him a wink. He was relieved that they had never discussed it. As the Land Rover passed through the castle gates, Hardy felt a keen sense of belonging. Scotland was his home now, and although he didn't quite understand, Dalcross Castle was as much imbedded in his soul, as it was his father's.

"I see Winwood and Maggie in the garden, Hardy. Let's say hello!"

Hardy followed Gillies into the garden and found Winwood weeding with Maggie strapped in a carry pack, wearing a white cap and sound asleep with her head leaning against her mother's back.

"Hello, sweeties," Gillies exclaimed. "How does your garden grow?"

"Ah...we missed you Gillies! Why Hardy! I didn't see you standing there! It's so nice to have you home! And Maggie, you've never met our Magpie. Isn't she just the sweetest thing? Are you hungry Hardy?" she asked not waiting for his reply.

"My bet he's always hungry," Gillies broke in, "Hardy's a growing boy."

"He's been out walking in the Cairngorms. He just climbed Ben Macdui, Hill of the Black Pig! Did ye know it's the home of 'Am Fear Liath Mor,' the 'Big Grey Man of Ben Macdui', Hardy?"

"We heard about the 'Big Grey Man' from Headmaster Chew, but we didn't see him. It was a day climb for us and we reached the summit by noon. We were all down and done by four."

"Remember climbing Devil's Point when you were a young lad? Bod an Deamhain? We could see Ben Macdui from the summit."

"I do, I especially remember Grandfather's name for it."

"How could ye forget that?" Gillies laughed. "Your grandfather certainly likes the old Gaelic names and his translation of them."

"I could never forget that old saying, Uncle Gillies. Where is Grandfather now?"

"He's speaking with our gamekeeper Malcolm Forbes about hiring beaters for the morning shoot," Winwood said. "He wants all to be ready at first light. Why don't you take your things up to your room and then go off and find him. I know he's quite looking forward to seeing you."

"Okay," Hardy replied, entering through the kitchen door, welcoming the smells of food he always identified with Dalcross. When he reached his bedroom, he retrieved a pack of Player's cigarettes and matches he had hidden away under the dresser during his stay in August.

102

He opened the window, looking down on the garden, lit up a Player and took a drag. The cigarette tasted stale, but he enjoyed it just the same. He took another drag and then extinguished it on the slate roof; fieldstripping what was left, watching the tobacco disperse into the wind.

"Grumps!" Hardy yelled when he spied his grandfather walking up the road from the barn. "How are you Grumps?" he called out as he watched his grandfather leaning on his cane in the midst of swirling red maple leaves spinning like tops along his path.

"I'm just fine, Hardy. I wish I didn't need this cane, "I have a touch of the gout."

"Sorry to hear that, Grumps. Winwood said that we'll be shooting grouse tomorrow morning."

"That we will, Hardy. We'll have the beaters drive 'em to us so I don't have to walk. We have the McEwen's joining us to make a party of six. Thirty brace we're after."

"How much is that Grumps?"

"Sixty birds altogether, Hardy. We'll get half."

"We supply the team of beaters and the McEwen's provide the loaders. You and your uncle will have four shotguns. You'll use the 20-gauge and your uncle the 12. I'll have my three single shot 12-gauge, that way the loader can keep up with me. The red grouse can fly 80 miles an hour with the wind behind 'em, Hardy. We'll be shooting where Captain Gillies MacBean fought to his death defending our Bonnie Prince Charlie."

Hardy and his grandfather walked to the castle, his grandfather asked him how his roommate Prince Charles was carrying on.

"He's alright Grumps, but the boys pick on him terribly. He needs to give one of them a good fight and then they'd lay off.

Hardy met his grandfather and Uncle Gillies as he walked into the kitchen at 7 a.m. The sky was beginning to lighten as Winwood prepared breakfast. Sunrise would come at 8 a.m. and Hardy's grandfather wanted to be settled along the south line of the stone butts ready for the first drive.

"Good morning, Mr. MacBean," Winwood, said as she stood by the stove stirring a pot of oatmeal. "How are you feeling today?"

"I took your advice, Winwood, and haven't had a drop of wine or beer for two days, not even a penny-weep. My toe feels much better, less pain thank you."

"You know the gout is caused by your consumption of spirits Mr. MacBean, wine and beer especially," Winwood replied. "I know you like your brew, but you best stay off it until you're all new."

"I will Winwood, I will." He replied with a sigh.

Gillies drove to Culloden Moor with his father sitting in the passenger seat with his black and white Springer beside him, shivering with anticipation.

"We'll soon be there, Lu-Lu," Hardy's grandfather said, stroking the Springer's head. Hardy and Malcolm Forbes sat in the back of the Land Rover with all the equipment. The smell of the oiled guns reminded Hardy of duck hunting with his American grandfather along the Westport River.

"Malcolm, how many beaters do you have for us today?"

"We have six beaters and six dogs' sir."

"That's what we had last year." Gillies said as he drove onto the moor and parked next to the Culloden Memorial Cairn.

"Lu-Lu is as good as all of the dogs put together," Grandfather MacBean exclaimed. "She's got a soft mouth and I've witnessed her retrieve three birds at once and return em without a mark. The Springer spaniel is the most ancient breed of bird dog known to man Hardy, and the only good thing the English ever gave to humanity. I've heard that the credit due might actually belong to the Spanish. I really don't know for sure. But Lu-Lu is a English Springer, aren't you girl!"

Hardy reached forward and rubbed Lu-Lu's ear. He thought about Lilly, who died shortly after he left for Scotland.

"Now Hardy," his grandfather continued, "what you see there is a memorial that marks the halfway point between the Jacobite and the English army front lines. It was erected in 1881, along with the stones marking the mounded graves of each clan. Dalcross Castle figures into the history of Culloden, but has never been spoken of much. The story told, Lady Anne Farquharson-Mackintosh rode the countryside dressed as a man, enlisting all clansmen sympathetic to the Jacobite cause and willing to fight for Prince Charles Stuart. She resided at Loch Moy Castle, the homeland and Clan seat of the Mackintosh, where she received Prince Charles before the battle. Her husband, Angus, the Mackintosh Chief, was a commander in the King's Black Watch at the time and fought alongside Lord Loudon's Highlanders against the Jacobite army. At the time of Culloden, Angus resided at Dalcross Castle, which had been part of the Mackintosh estate since 1702. Not much is said about Angus other than that he was commissioned before the rebellion began and was compelled to fight for the king. But before the Battle of Culloden, he was captured by Prince Charles' army at the Battle of Prestopans and later released in custody to his wife Ann. He then returned to his Black Watch commission. It is said that the Duke of Cumberland, son of King George II, was given accommodation at Dalcross Castle the night before the battle. Your great grandfather and his grandfather before him, who bought Dalcross in 1822 from Alexander Mackintosh, have always held Angus Mackintosh to account for the Jacobite loss. He was a traitor and a scoundrel they said, and a curse fell on all the Mackintosh chiefs the day Culloden was lost."

The beaters formed the shape of a horseshoe as they appeared from the mist-filled heather at the top northeast corner of Culloden Moor. The breeze freshened from the north as the hunters took their positions to the south end, spaced 200 feet apart, crouching out of sight along the stone butts. Hardy joined his Uncle Gillies, while the other shooters prepared to receive the first of the driven birds.

"Now Hardy," Gillies whispered, "when Malcolm blows his whistle, he'll shout out which direction the birds are coming from and we'll be on to them. Make sure to aim a little low, as the grouse will dip when we begin to fire. The wind is up pretty good, so they'll be coming in quick. Understand?"

"Yup," Hardy said, placing his 20-gauge across his knees.

The shrill of the whistle broke through the damp morning air and Forbes shouted, "Mark right!" Gillies and Hardy jumped, the thunder of grouse wings exploded above as the birds dipped and swerved head on. Hardy let off both barrels, handing his shotgun off as the loader pushed the replacement into his arms. Gillies unleashed his second round as Hardy took his mark and pulled two more times, with three birds crashing to the ground.

"Good God damned shot," Gillies called out to Hardy as he prepared for the next covey.

Within the hour, the hunting party had bagged 30 brace.

"When we consider we had the worst winter in memory last year it's a wonder the red grouse survived, Gillies said.

Grandfather Gillies sat against the stone butt drinking a hot cup of tea and asked how many grouse Hardy had shot.

"A total of six, my count," Gillies replied.

"Well, Hardyboy, I want to show you how to dress out these birds, just like I did with your uncle and your father. They need to be warm to clean em this way. Put the bird on his back and step on his wings. Get your feet right close to the body. That's right, now pull up on the legs slowly."

Hardy pulled the legs up, watching as the bird's feet and entrails separated away from the body, leaving the breast with the wings attached.

"Now smooth the skin off the breast and use your knife to remove the wings. It's that easy, Hardy, and the rest we leave for the animals."

Hardy removed the wings and held the bird's warm breast in his hand, processing what he had done before placing it into the cooler.

Chapter 20

Uncle Gillies loaded the Austin A40 van with two butchered lambs, six smoked salmon filets and 25 breasts of red grouse, along with a box each of kale, leeks and onions.

"Let's go, Hardy, we need to make the delivery by 3 p.m.,"

Hearing his uncle's voice, Hardy ran down the main hall stairs and into the kitchen.

"Don't you look nice, Mr. Hardy," Winwood exclaimed.

"Come on, Hardy, we'll be late," Gillies said. "Hardy and me are going to have dinner in town and nose around."

"Have fun, boys, and don't get into trouble," Winwood replied.

Gillies and Hardy left the Royal Highland Hotel and drove down Academy Street onto Queensgate, took a left on Church and parked on the corner of Bridge Street.

"We're a block away from River Ness," Gillies said. "We'll stop here and get a bite at Gellions Bar."

They walked down Bridge Street. Hardy could hear music playing.

"You ever had a girlfriend Hardy?"

"No," Hardy replied.

"Ever kissed one?"

"Just one."

"Is that all ye did?"

"Pretty much," Hardy replied.

"Well, now, let's get some fish and chips, the haddock is always good here."

Gillies looked around for an empty table and found one close to the bar. Hardy smelled beer and fried fish as he sat down. The music was so loud that Gillies had to point at the menu to order the fish and chips.

"Dark ale!" he shouted, holding up two fingers.

Hardy watched as the bar swelled with people of all ages, dancing in wild gyrations to three electric guitars, one saxophone and one bagpipe. "Wow," he thought, "wait until I tell the boys about this."

"Let's get you out on the dance floor," Gillies said finishing his fish and chips. I see a nice looking young girl over there against the wall in need of a partner." He motioned Hardy to get up from his seat and pushed him toward the girl. Hardy was embarrassed when Gillies leaned forward and asked her for a dance while pointing at him.

"Will you dance with a young lad?"

She smiled and held out her hand. Hardy took it and moved to the dance floor. Gillies looked on with a knowing smile.

"Come on now, Hardy, time to go," Gillies said after Hardy finished his third dance, "We've got more to do."

They left Gellions and walked back toward the van.

"Okay, Hardy, one more stop tonight. Follow me."

Hardy followed Gillies up Church Street and stopped outside a boarding house. They climbed the steps and Gillies knocked on the door twice. After a few moments a middle-aged woman with bleached blond hair opened the door.

"Why Gillies, I haven't seem ya in ova a yeaha. I hear youse been married."

"Hello, Stella, yes, I'm married and I have a beautiful daughter, too!"

"Sorray to lose yaw binness, Gillies, you was a right regula one you was."

"Why thank you, Stella, but I have my nephew here with me and I was wondering if you could provide him with a nice birthday present.

He's comin' on 16."

"He's kinda cute, Gillies," Stella remarked. "Maybe Darcy would. She's a new girl from Outa Hebrides, just 18, breaking her in we are. She'd be just right for your nephew. What's his name?"

"Hardy".

Hardy stood in the front hall, listening to their conversation, feeling like his knees were made from rubber.

"Darcy!" Stella yelled up the stairs, "I have a nice gentleman down heeya for yuh."

"Stella is going to fix you up fine Hardy, you just let the girl show you." Gillies said as Darcy appeared at the top of the stairs. "Now go on up. I'll be down here when you're through."

Hardy was shocked at what had just happened between his uncle and the woman he called Stella. Gillies had never discussed doing anything like this with him. He began to climb the stairs, grabbing the banister, pulling himself up. The closer he got to Darcy, the more anxious he became. She stood on the landing wearing a flowered robe with her thick red hair cascading about her shoulders in tiny ringlets. Her brilliant dark blue eyes were the color of the North Sea and her fair complexion bared a multitude of golden colored freckles. Hardy thought he had never seen such a beautiful girl.

"It's Hardy?"

"Yes," Hardy said as she took his hand and led him to her room.

The room had a double bed and nightstand with little available floor space. A shade-less table lamp cast shadows of them arcing against the wall and ceiling as Darcy closed the door and crawled onto the bed.

"My name is Darcy," she said with a distinct lilt in her voice. She opened her bathrobe, letting it slip down from her shoulders.

"I heard," he said, looking at her swollen pink nipples and her skin glowing in the faint light.

"Aren't you goanna get undressed?" she asked in her thick island brogue.

"Yes," Hardy replied unzipping his pants, lowering them to the floor and pulling his shirt over his head.

"How bout your shorts?"

"Yup, I'm going to," Hardy said hesitantly.

"Go on," Darcy said, sliding her hand over his shoulder and down across his chest. "Do ya need help?"

"No, I can do it," Hardy replied quietly, feeling anxious as he slipped off his boxers.

"Hardy," she said, moving her hand between his legs, "this your first time?"

"Yes."

"Doona worry, Hardy, there's always a first time ya know. Now lie down on the bed," her hand pushing against his chest.

Hardy lay back, looking up at the ceiling. She continued to fondle him until he grew hard.

"Now there, Hardy, you're ready," she said slipping on a condom, leaning back, and sitting on her ankles.

He watched as she mounted him, the nipples of her breasts moving close to his mouth. She guided him inside her, beginning to move, setting a rhythm with her thighs pitching forward and back. Looking down at him, she was consumed by a feeling that had once seemed unimaginable to her, she stopped midway in motion, clutched his shoulders and rolled with him, landing on her back.

"My turn Hardy."

She kept her hands on his hips and then released her grip as he gained pace.

"There you go, Hardy. You're all good now," she said, throwing her left hand back against the pillow. He opened his eyes and looked down at her face with her eyes closed, her mouth slightly agape. He took her right breast into his mouth sucking, feeling the hard nipple with his tongue. His pace quickened. Darcy began to shudder; her entire body seemed to lose control. He closed his eyes and quickened his speed. She opened her eyes and looked up, watching him, his face turning red.

"Breathe, Hardy," she gasped, "breathe for god's sake," jabbing his ribs with her hands.

He exhaled all at once, holding himself up with arms locked straight and his body rigid until his orgasm came to an end. Collapsing, he rolled away from her onto his back, breathing heavily in long bursts.

"Why that's a good job, Hardy," Darcy said, "good job."

"Thanks," Hardy gasped, between breaths, "First time, first time. I'll get better."

"I know you will, Hardy," she said. "You'll come back and we'll get better together. You best get dressed now; Stella doesn't like the customers hanging around much and she keeps a pretty good ear to the wall."

Hardy lay in the bed, thinking about what had just happened, wondering if he would see Darcy again. At that moment he hoped that he would.

"Darcy, I have a leave-out weekend in November, about a month away."

"What's a 'leave-out' weekend, Hardy?"

"A long weekend before the Christmas vacation."

"A leave-out from where?"

"From my school in Elgin."

"Where is Elgin?"

"It's about an hour away, east of here. Is it okay if I write to you?"

"Yes, it's okay."

"Can I have your last name and address then?"

Darcy leaned over the table and withdrew a piece of paper and pencil and wrote her name and address. Hardy looked at her body, her full pointed breasts, and began to get hard again. She noticed his erection and smiled, squeezing him as she lay back on the bed pulling him toward her. They kissed before he entered her. It was a long kiss and Darcy thought about what Stella had said to her the first day she arrived, "Show the customer to the door when he is finished." Two of Stella's cardinal rules were now broken, kissing and having sex more than once. Something about falling in love she had said to her.

"I guess she won't mind what she doesn't know," Darcy thought.

Hardy watched the headlights shine a hole through layers of mist as they drove back to Dalcross.

"How'd it go, Hardy?"

"It went okay," Hardy replied, thinking about Darcy's last name, Nicholson. He thought he loved her.

"You can consider it an early birthday present."

"Could you tell me how much it cost?"

"It was eight quid, and I hope worth every farthing."

Hardy thought about the money and calculated how much he had to last until Christmas.

"I have a leave out November 22."

"And you want to go back? It's fine with me, Hardy, but we'll need to keep tonight our secret."

"Okay," Hardy said as they drove through the castle entrance.

Chapter 21

"A Mr. Stewart is on the line," the operator announced.

"Right, pass him in. Hello David, how the hell are you?

"I'm in Washington. Can we have lunch?"

William was surprised by the call. They had not spoken to one another since he stayed at David's flat the previous August.

"Great to hear from you, David. I can't make lunch, but how about dinner?"

"Dinner will do. I'm here until Friday."

"You got a place to stay?"

"Is that an offer William?"

"Why, yes, yes it is," he laughed.

"I thought that you would never ask."

"That's great, David. I'll meet you at my house around six?"

"Perfect, it's 1504 Foxhall, right?"

"Same place, see you then," William said as he hung up the phone. He leaned back in his chair, thinking about the last time they were together. A lot had happened since then.

William drove into in his garage, closed the door, walked out to the street and knocked on the passenger side window of a black four-door Chevy sedan. David reached over and opened the door.

"Hey, William, right on time, 6 o'clock."

"Didn't want to keep you waiting. Let's go in town, five-minute ride, new restaurant I think you'll like. Its s called Clyde's."

"Sounds lovely," David said.

"We have to be careful, David, I don't trust anyone stateside these days. We can't discuss anything in my house, car, only public places," William warned.

"Fine by me," David replied.

William pointed to an open parking space near the restaurant. They entered Clyde's and walked to the back bar.

"They have terrific crab cakes, any beer you might want," William said as they sat down in a booth furthest from the door.

After dinner they parked along the waterfront, looking out over the Potomac River to Roosevelt Island.

"Let's take a walk," William said

"How much did you discover?" David asked.

"I don't know but I think the assassination was in-house," William replied, "God only knows how many are involved and how high up it goes. I do know that if I want to survive I have to go along and keep a distance. These guys are the most powerful people on earth and will stop at nothing. My wife, my children, all at risk."

"I have information," David began, "involving the Federal Reserve, Switzerland, the Vatican, Indonesia. It appears that you stumbled upon the initial directive to remove the president, and that was clearly the result of Kennedy's Executive Order No. 11110. He signed it last June. Effectively, it returned the power to issue currency to the U.S. government without going through the Federal Reserve. The order gave the Treasury power to issue currency backed by silver in the form of silver certificates and would essentially put the Federal Reserve out of business. Apparently, they weren't going to let Kennedy get away with it, and 50 years of printing money out of thin air and lending it to the government at usurious rates wasn't about to be dissolved by the president either. They thought they had a deal in place with his father before they got him elected. But when Joe had a stroke, all deals were off. The word on the street is Kennedy's brother Bobby had convinced him that constitutional law forbid private bankers from providing the nation's currency and charging interest."

"He also believed that creating an executive order eliminating the need for the Federal Reserve to print money would assure his brother's reelection."

"All water under the bridge," William interjected.

"Yes, it is, but according to the head of MI6 there is a larger conspiracy, and it seems the Vatican figures prominently."

"Nothing I can do about it, David, best let sleeping dogs lie."

"That seems the way of the spy business, always one step behind."

"Yeah, we have our Cambridge five and Kim Philby to contend with these days. Nothing stays secret forever."

"It will with me," William replied.

They returned to Foxhall Road, poured themselves each a large glass of scotch whiskey, spoke about old times at Trinity and then retired for the evening. This was the last time William would see his old friend.

116

David retired from MI6 at the end of the year and died suddenly one month to the day after he packed his brief case and walked out the office door. William never did find out the cause of David's death, but the old proverb "Dead men tell no tales," was never far from his mind.

Part 6

Rules of the Game

Chapter 22

"God, you really mean Church Street? You've got to be kidding?" Colin exclaimed.

"No, I'm not kidding."

"Can I go?"

"No," Hardy replied. "My uncle says you need to be at least 16."

"One of our mates just turned 16."

"What's that supposed to mean?"

"I'm just saying." Colin replied.

Hardy thought his discussion with Colin was finished until one week later when they were hiking together in the Cairngorm Mountains.

"Could you get some girls up to school last weekend before Christmas?" Colin asked.

"What?" why then?" Hardy replied.

"The school play, no one will be around Windmill after 6 o'clock. We will pay," Colin added, his voice rising. "How much do you think, Hardy?"

"I don't know, Colin, it's a long way to come," Hardy replied, hoping to end the conversation.

"But we'll pay extra!" Colin pleaded.

"Okay, I'll ask!" Hardy answered abruptly, hoping to end the conversation. He thought about the letter he received from Darcy expressing excitement about the upcoming weekend, and his call to Gillies asking if she could stay at Dalcross.

All was now arranged; Darcy would wait for him at 4 o'clock Friday afternoon on the corner of Church and Bridge.

Gillies arrived at Windmill Lodge along with Winwood and Maggie. Hardy greeted them as they drove up with window down.

"Hello, Winwood, hello Maggie, it's great to see you!"

"It's beautiful here, Hardy, a nice ride up, too. Maggie loves to ride!" Winwood replied.

"Get on in Hardy," Gillies said. "Where's your friend?"

"He's coming. Thanks for giving him a lift. His mother couldn't make it over, something about the car."

"Here he is. Meet my friend Colin Ferguson."

"Thanks so much for the lift," Colin said as he opened the rear passenger door.

"Not a problem, glad we can help out," Gillies and Winwood said in unison.

"Where'd you say we'd be taking Colin?" Gillies asked.

"If you could drop me off at my father's office on Church Street, please, that would be great," Colin replied.

"Okay," Gillies said. "We're off!"

An hour and a half later, Gillies turned the corner from Bridge onto Church Street.

"What number did ye say?"

"One hundred, just before the MacDougall Clansmen Hotel."

"Alright, here we are," Gillies said, coming to a complete stop.

Colin collected his bag, reached over and shook Gillies hand thanking him for the lift. He opened the door and stepped onto the curb.

"See you back at school Hardy."

"Okay," Hardy replied, with his eye on the dashboard clock.

"Don't worry, Hardy, we'll be there in time to pick up your girl," Gillies said as he put the Rover in gear and made a u-turn.

Hardy blushed at the mention of the words "his girl." His heart began to race when he spied a bright red dress in the distance.

"There she is," he exclaimed as they approached the corner of Church and Bridge.

Gillies pulled up to the curb as Hardy opened the door. Darcy stood clutching a small black bag, looking in the opposite direction.

"My God, Hardy," Winwood said, "is that really she?"
Darcy wore a short long-sleeve red wool dress with epaulettes and gold buttons along with high heels, all of which matched the color of her hair which was pulled back in a ponytail showing off small pearl earrings. She jumped when she heard Hardy's voice, turning toward him with a big smile.

"Hardy, you made it!"

"Yes, of course I have!" Hardy said climbing out from the back seat onto the cobblestones.

"Come on and get in," he said, taking her bag and stowing it in the boot. As he closed the door, he looked up the street and saw Colin with an older man walking toward them.

"Hey, Hardy." Colin called out walking up to the car, peering through the window.

"I'd like you to meet my father."

"Hello, Mr. Ferguson, sir," Hardy stammered, reaching out his hand. "Very nice to meet you. Sorry, but we're late and need to be off."

Gillies nodded and accelerated away from the curb making a right turn onto Bridge Street.

"Well, Hardy, a clean getaway of sorts," Gillies said, and they all laughed.

They left Inverness and headed south to Dalcross.

"I guess I'll need to teach Hardy his manners. I'm Winwood and this is our little Maggie. I believe you've already met Mr. MacBean."

"Not really," Darcy said blushing. "I mean, no one introduced me, ma'am," she said quietly.

"Please call me Winwood."

"Thank you very much, Winwood," Darcy replied.

"It's okay if you call me Gillies, too," Gillies exclaimed.

"Thank you, sir. "I haven't been out of Inverness since I arrived in September. It's so very nice of you to pick me up."

"We hope you like Dalcross," Winwood said. "Where are you from?"

"From Stornoway, Isle of Lewis, ma'am."

"Is your family from there?" .

"Yes, my father is a fisherman and my brother is his mate. Just the three of us, and then I came over to Inverness. The fishing hasn't been very good this year, my father's had a difficult time keeping up with the boat payments."

"Did you know Hardy is a sailor?" Gillies asked.

"Why no, he hasn't told me that, he hasn't told me much I guess."

"We hardly just met!" Hardy exclaimed.

Passing through the Dalcross gates, Gillies approached the castle slowly and parked by the front entrance. A small light shone above the front door and the windows were dark.

"I wonder what your grandfather is up to." Winwood questioned.

"I don't know," Gillies broke in. "He's been on the moor hunting all day, probably fallen off to sleep. Sunset was quarter to four today, getting dark earlier by the day."

"Hardy, please show Darcy her room, second floor, first on the right," Winwood said as they walked into the entrance hall. "Dinner is at 7."

"God, a huge place you have here, Hardy," Darcy whispered as they climbed the stairs to the second floor. "You never told me you lived in a castle."

"No, but I don't really live here. I visit my uncle and grandfather on holidays." He opened the bedroom door and turned on the light.

"I could get lost in here Hardy, the bed is bloody huge!"

"My room is a bit smaller, with a turret."

"Let's see your room then."

They climbed to the third floor and entered his room.

"This is nice," Darcy said sitting on the bed. "Come over here," patting the bed with her hand.

Hardy moved from the turret window to the bed and Darcy reached out and grabbed him by his belt, pulling him closer and then onto the bed, kissing him, lowering her hand.

"No problem here," she said laughing. "You have quite the walloper Hardy!"

Hardy embraced her, and they kissed. He moved his hands under her dress up to her breasts, pushing her bra up, reaching around her back, fumbling with the fastener. Darcy laughed and pulled her dress over her head, removing her bra as if by magic and then unbuckled Hardy's belt, pulling off his pants and boxers. She lay back on the bed as he moved

122

between her legs, kissing her and then sucking each breast until the nipples became hard. She guided him and sighed deeply as he began. She had dreamed of this moment since the last time they were together and it was everything she had dreamed of. Later when they lay next to each other, her head cradled in his arm, she thought she might be in love with him. She felt safe for the first time in a long while.

"Hardy, do you think I'm too old?"

"No, why would you think that?"

"Well I'm eighteen and you're not sixteen yet. But you make love better than anyone, Hardy," she whispered in his ear.

"I'll be 16 in March and I don't think we're that far apart in age."

"Okay, I just wondered."

"How many girls work at Stella's?"

"There are eight of us boarding there. Do you want someone else?"

"No, I want you, and only you."

"I just wondered if any of them would come up to my school, you know, for a visit."

"I don't know, Hardy But I'll ask Brenda, she has a car. Is that why you asked me to come?"

"Heck no. I made a mistake and told my friend about Stella's"

"Why did you do that?

"I dunno, I shouldn't have."

"I'll see what I can do."

"Okay, but I don't want you coming up. I'm in the school play and won't be around. The boys have asked me how much it will cost."

"I'll let you know if they want to go. Who are you in the play?"

"I'm the boatswain in Shakespeare's *Tempest*, a very small part with few lines."

"I wish I could come."

"No, you don't. I'm horrible at it. Let's get ready for dinner. You're going to meet Grumps."

"Who is that?"

"My grandfather."

The long dining table was set for five and Winwood had prepared Hardy's favorite meal of leg of lamb with roasted tatties. Hardy's grandfather appeared in the kitchen wearing his kilt and a tie made from the MacBean tartan, along with a regimental black highland jacket.

"Where have you been Grumps?"

"I've been taking a wee nap Hardy. What pretty lass is this?" he asked, gesturing toward Darcy.

"This is Darcy Nicholson."

"How do you do, Miss Nicholson? It's so very nice to meet you."

"Thank you, Mr. MacBean, your kilt is quite sharp."

"It's so nice to have another pretty girl in our midst."

"Certainly a beautiful tartan you're wearing, Darcy," Winwood exclaimed, "be careful with Mr. MacBean, he'll kill you with the compliments. Let's all move to the great hall, the food is on the table!"

The dinner lasted longer than usual as Hardy's grandfather gave a history of what he knew about the Nicholson Clan and its place in Scottish history.

"Nicholson's are descended from the Norsemen," he began.

"They're the oldest clan in the Hebrides, and they were quite a formidable family in their day. And what happened to you?" he asked Darcy. "You're quite a wee one."

"My mother was the same height as me, she was a MacLeod."

"Ahhh, MacLeod is an upright family, too!" They fought alongside the MacBeans at the Battle of Bannockburn, when our dear Scotland gained her independence from England in the year 1314!"

Grumps continued to expound upon centuries of hard fought independence, battles won and lost, and as always, ending with the last battle, Culloden. With dinner finished, Darcy joined Winwood in the kitchen, helping with the dishes, while Gillies discussed the day's ride up to Elgin.

"Darcy," Winwood asked, "would you be interested in moving to Dalcross and taking a job?"

Darcy froze, wondering why Winwood would ask her to take a job when she must know about Stella's. It took her completely off guard. She didn't answer immediately, with the silence broken only by the sound of pots knocking together in the sink.

"You needn't answer me right away. Since Maggie was born I've been a bit overwhelmed and Gillies and I thought we'd ask if you would be interested in moving out here. We'll pay 30 pounds a week plus room and board."

Darcy thought about what she was making with Stella, more than twice that amount every week, and most of it was going to her father.

"Thank you very much for the offer," she said blushing.

"I'll be honest with you, Darcy, you seem to be a nice girl and we felt you'd be better off here if you know what I mean. We don't think

Stella's is exactly the best situation for you. Now Hardy is a young lad and goes to boarding school, and whether or not you two continue to see each other is up to fate. But if Hardy is a passing fancy it doesn't much matter, he'll get over it. What we're offering you is a job and a safe place to work and live."

Darcy opened Hardy's tower room door and stepped lightly to his bed. She lay down next to him, listening to his even breathing. She reached out and touched him, and in moments Hardy was on to her, inside her. She put her arms around him, lost in passion.

Chapter 23

Darcy watched Hardy and Gillies drive off. She felt a sadness come over her as she climbed the steps to the boarding house. Her weekend with Hardy was like a dream, and now she was back to a reality. She knew she must continue to make the money her father so desperately needed and saw no other way to do it. For now she was resigned to live her life at Stella's.

"Welcome home, Darcy, the customers have missed you. Some mail for you here," Stella said, handing her a letter.

Darcy glanced at the letter and knew from the cursive handwriting that it was from her father.

"Thank you, Stella," she said, climbing the stairs to her room.

Placing her bag on the bed, she turned on the light and lay down, adjusting the pillow.

"Well now," she said out loud, "I wonder what Father has to say." She had just posted her weekly letter along with 40 pounds, for a total amount of 320 pounds over eight weeks. The letters must have crossed, she thought. This was the first letter he had written to her since she arrived. She thought about her life at Stella's and the different men she had slept with and the ones that returned and would only ask for her. Most of them were okay, but one of them scared her. She spoke to Stella about him. He had a wild look in his eyes, she said, and made her get into uncomfortable positions.

"Don't you worry, darlin'," Stella had said, "I'm right here and I'll protect ya."

"I don't know," Darcy remembered replying, "When he closes the door I have no idea what to expect. It's always something different. He's nothing like the others. The last time he was here, he hit me, slapped me, and it hurt."

"You never told me." Stella had said, "I'll have a talk with him the next time he comes. I promise I won't let anything bad happen to you."

Darcy ran her thumb and index finger along the envelope, turning it over and looking at the handwriting, and the ringed Isle of Lewis hand stamp. She lifted the edge of the back flap and slid her finger along, opening it in one motion. Before reading the letter, she held it in her hand, remembering how desperate they had been for money. She remembered meeting one of her friends at the end of August who introduced to a girl that told her about Stella's and how she had worked as a prostitute in Inverness.

"The money is good, you can make four times what you can on Lewis," Darcy remembered her say. She knew she was taking a risk. She knew she could never tell anyone on Lewis the truth.

She was so lonely away from home. She never imagined she would lose her virginity to a complete stranger. It was never supposed to be this way. She had graduated the top student of her secondary school. Her future seemed bright and university was within reach. She had always wanted to become a doctor and care for the people of Lewis. Nothing had prepared her for the desperate situation her father was in. Her mother would never have let it get to this point; she had always kept the family together. She unfolded the letter and began to read.

Dearest Darcy   November 21,1964

I am so sorry it has taken me this long to write to you. I have started to write many times but I had no good news and couldn't find the words. I very much appreciate the money you have sent to us. It has helped greatly in many ways, mostly with boat payments and putting food on the table. Last week we finished changing over the boats' rig to gill nets and have already had what I consider great success. It's a different kind of fishing, but much kinder on the boat than the constant dragging we used to do. We still need to learn the ins and outs of the fishery, but your brother seems to hold a good ability for it. This week I am proud to report we caught a couple of thousand pounds of mostly Salmon with a few Pollack, Sea Trout and Arctic Char. I can say a few more weeks like this one and we'll be well on our way to paying off our debts. There is no need for you to send us more of your hard earned money. I am so very proud of you and your job at the Royal Globe. We hope you will be able to take the time to make it home for Christmas.

Your loving father, Ian

Darcy read the letter twice, hands trembling as she folded it back into the envelope. She thought about the lies she had written to her father about her job. She thought about Winwood's offer. Overwhelmed with emotion, she quickly made her decision. She would tell Stella in the morning that she would be leaving, and ring up Winwood to accept her offer that same day.

Brenda steered her old Citroen up Duffus Road and took a right between the Gordonstoun gates. The drive took an hour and a half. Darcy's map had been accurate. In about a half mile she would loop by the schools main building and then proceed another half mile until she saw a sign on her left for Windmill Lodge. It was pitch black with few lights to mark the way.

"Want to wager a bet, girls?" Brenda asked her companions Nessie and Sally. "How long do you bet it will take us to do six young boys? I'd say we'd be done in 45 minutes. "How bout you, Nessie?"

"I don't know. If they've never been shagged I suspect it'll be over pretty fast. How much are they payin again?"

"Fifty quid each boy. Not a bad night's work. You girls owe me 10 quid each for the ride. You wanna bet or not?"

"No, I need the money."

"How bout you, Sally?"

"No, I'm good, but you never know about these young boys. Sometimes they'll surprise you."

Brenda drove to the front door of Windmill Lodge and shut off the engine. It was shortly after 6 o'clock.

"I'll go see where the boys are, you wait here," Brenda said. "If anyone asks you, tell em that we're visiting Colin Ferguson and he's family."

Brenda barely knocked on the door once before Colin opened it.

"Hi,' he said, looking Brenda up and down, "where are the girls?"

"You been waitin I see. Good ta meet you, Colin?" Brenda asked, waving at the car and motioning for the girls to come in. "I'm one of em."

Colin looked her over and watched as Nellie and Sally came to the door.

"Yeah, that's me. Where's the girl Hardy was with?

"Oh she don't work with us no more, she took another job."

"Oh?"

"Do ye have the money?"

"Yes, but there are only three of you."

"Then give it over. We'll each take two of you, one at a time of course, and I'll do the pickin first."

"I just thought," Collin said, his voice trailing off as he counted out 300 pounds in 10 pound notes.

"Follow me," he said leading them through the hall into the dormitory.

"Okay, boys, "Brenda said, "Who wants to go first?"

Colin and two boys stepped forward.

"Alright, I'll take you first," Brenda said pointing to Colin. Nessie and Sally each pointed at the boys nearest them. "Now the rest of you wait out in the hall till your turn," Brenda ordered in her raspy voice, "and turn off those damn lights!"

"God, less than 45 minutes for the lot," Brenda said starting the Citroen. "We'll be back to Inverness in time to get the Saturday night crowd. I guess I won the bet!"

"Yea, a bet with yourself Brenda. My two hardly got goin before they shot off," Nessie said. "It was sad, actually, neither of them knew what to do. Of course I patted them on the back and told them they'd get better at it, that they just needed practice."

"My second one was doin' it, didn't last more than three minutes. That Colin boy couldn't get hard. I whispered in his ear that I couldn't wait all night and that finished him off," Brenda said. "How bout you Sally?"

"The English chap and the foreigner, they both managed to get hard, but neither of 'em lasted long. They asked if I could come back. I told 'em to come visit me in Inverness and left 'em my number."

"God, you did what?" Brenda exclaimed, "We don't want em to know nothing about us."

"I could use the extra money. Got kids to feed."

"Jesus Sally, givin em your number for Christ sakes!"

"They'll probably lose it Brenda, don't worry yourself."

"I hope so Sally. Don't bring me into it," Brenda replied as they left the Gordonstoun gate behind and headed south.

Chapter 24

"Darcy," Stella yelled up the stairs, "one of your regulars called up and he's coming over."

"Stella, I'm all done. I'm being picked up in an hour."

"Come on Darcy, for old times' sake, he'll be angry if you're here and you won't take him."

"I'm all packed, Stella. I'm all done!"

"Please, please, Darcy, just this one last time."

Darcy looked into Stella's eyes and thought about leaving. She felt she owed Stella.

"All right, Stella, one last time," she said and climbed the stairs.

"You're the last one," Stella said as he entered the house, knowing that he was the one Darcy had the problems with.

"Last one what?"

"Darcy is leavin today, and you'll be a gentleman with her, do you understand?"

"Leaving for where?"

"I dunno, just leavin'."

"Well, I guess I'll be the last one then," he said in a cold voice and handed Stella a few pound notes as he climbed the stairs to Darcy's room.

"Now you mind what I said," Stella called after him, counting his money.

The yells for help began soon after he closed the door. Stella bounded up the stairs and heard a body slam against the wall.

"You'll do as I say, or I'll give your other eye a shiner too!"

"No, no, no!" Darcy cried out.

"Open this door; I'm goin to call the police!" Stella screamed.

The room became quiet as she leaned against the door out of breath, falling forward as it swung open.

"There, you can have her. I was the last one alright," he said as he descended the stairs.

"Oh Darcy, how could he?" Stella said looking at her with horror. Darcy's left eye was swollen and blood was running from the corner of her mouth. She sobbed in short bursts, imploring the invisible. "Why, why, why?"

"You wait here, Darcy; I'll get something to clean you up. You'll be okay," Stella said trying to calm her. "Jesus Christ!"

Winwood watched as a man burst from Darcy's building and walked quickly down the street. Sensing that something was wrong, she jumped from the car and ran up the steps through the open door. Hearing Darcy's cry coming from the second floor, she leapt two stairs at a time, almost knocking Stella over as she was leaving the room. She entered the room and looked over at Darcy lying on the bed with her eye battered and her lip bleeding,

"What in the God damned hell is going on here?" Winwood exclaimed in anger.

Chapter 25

"Central Intelligence Agency," the operator answered, "How may I direct your call?"

This is Mr. Chew, Headmaster of the Gordonstoun School. May I speak with William MacBean, please?"

"Just a moment, please."

"Mr. MacBean, a Mr. Chew is on the line, Headmaster of Gordonstoun School. Will you take the call sir?"

It was 9 a.m. and William MacBean leaned back in his chair, wondering what Mr. Chew could possibly want, if Hardy was ok.

"Yes, put him on."

"Hello, Mr. Chew, How are you, sir?"

"Not terribly good. I need to speak with you about your son."

"Yes, Mr. Chew?"

"We have a problem, a problem involving some high profile students."

"Yes, Mr. Chew? What does this have to do with Hardy?"

"In a nutshell Mr. MacBean, we have two students that have contracted gonorrhea and subsequently been removed by their families to finish out the year in other schools."

"The clap?" William muttered. "God, how unfortunate. But what does this have to do with Hardy?"

"We didn't catch him, but we have information from reliable sources that he was the conduit behind these women, or should I say prostitutes. Absolutely contrary to the school's code of ethics!"

"Exactly when did this happen Mr. Chew?"

"It happened on the last Saturday before the end of the autumn term, the night of the school play."

"The school play?" William repeated. "Wasn't my son involved in that?"

"Yes, he was. What does that have to do with it?"

"I'm just pointing out, Mr. Chew, that from what you're saying he was a busy boy."

"I find no humor in that!" Chew snapped.

"Do you know where these women came from?" William asked.

"Apparently, they came from Inverness, and the information we have puts your son visiting a brothel in Inverness over the November break."

William thought about his son and where he was during the November break. "Jesus Christ," he muttered.

"Where exactly did you get this information?"

"From one of the boys involved."

"He was involved with the women?"

"Yes, he was."

"Was he infected? Did he contract the disease?"

"No, he didn't."

"And where is this boy from?"

"Inverness."

"How do we know this wasn't his idea all along and he's not trying to put the blame on my son?"

"His father saw the girl."

"What girl? And how is his father involved?"

"Father *and* son both saw Hardy and a young girl, along with his uncle and aunt driving away together."

"God," William thought. "Gillies, God damn it!"

"Was this girl among the women at the school?"

"No sir, not to my knowledge Mr. MacBean."

"Then how on earth does that make my son responsible for these women at the school?"

"Whatever you may think, Mr. MacBean, Mr. Ferguson is a well-regarded lawyer. According to him, your son and the girl arranged for the prostitutes to visit Windmill Lodge during the school play and each of the boys paid 50 pounds for the pleasure of contracting gonorrhea, at least two of them did anyway."

"Accusations with not a shred of proof. What exactly do you want, Mr. Chew?"

"I think it best if your son leaves the school."

"Mr. Chew, I have paid tuition through the end of the year and I expect Hardy to complete the year unless you have proof. I suggest you concentrate on the boys who were involved with this mess and leave my son out of it. This is the end of the conversation, unless you have something to add."

He waited for a response and heard the phone click. He immediately dialed up his brother.

"Hello, Dalcross Castle Estates," his brother answered.

"Gillies!"

"William! What do I owe the pleasure?"

"No pleasure, Gillies, I just received a call from Hardy's headmaster."

"What did he want?"

"Something about Hardy being mixed up with a bunch of prostitutes from Inverness."

Gillies' heart skipped a beat: "Jesus Christ," he thought.

"Do you know anything about this?" William asked.

"No, can't say as I do."

"The headmaster is accusing Hardy of being the ringleader, providing prostitutes for his classmates. And two of them have caught the clap!"

"Jesus!" Gillies exclaimed containing his laughter.

"My sentiments exactly! Except some lawyer, along with his son, have implicated Hardy. They say they saw Hardy with a prostitute in Inverness." Gillies looked through the doorway into the kitchen and watched as Winwood and Darcy prepared dinner.

"They did? Who is this lawyer?"

"A man by the name of Robert Ferguson."

Gillies thought about the ride to Inverness. "Why that little shit," he thought.

"I gave a Colin Ferguson a ride from Elgin to Inverness. I saw him with his father for a brief moment when we picked up our kitchen help down the road from his father's office. I didn't catch his father's name, something Ferguson."

"As things stand now, Hardy can finish out the term."

"He could stay with us if need be and finish up at the Inverness Royal Academy."

"We'll discuss that later, Gillies. Have a talk with Ferguson, please."

"I'll stop by his office tomorrow," he replied, thankful that Winwood had managed to pack a beaten and bloodied Darcy into the Rover and driven off before the police arrived. He would confront Advocate Ferguson and suggest that he recant his story or he would make sure the press would identify his son as an admitted ringleader involved with prostitutes.

Part 7

The Hunt

Chapter 26

The steel grey November sky offered little comfort as a cold rain fell on Glasgow's waterfront. Hardy stood on the pier and watched as a crane lowered a bundle of Central American mahogany showing the stenciled letters R.A.M. He thought back to the day he received a letter from his Uncle Gillies offering him a job three months after he graduated from Gordonstoun.. The years he worked in the Dalcross forest, learning about trees, how to harvest them and how to make lumber on the portable sawmill were instrumental in securing the job with Mackenzie.

He counted 27 bundles stacked along the quayside in two rows with this, the last, making 28. He knew that the yachting and furniture companies would be quite pleased with the mahogany's length and width as well as the quality. He scanned the pier looking for 30 pallets of rosewood and lignum vitae logs also listed on the manifest. As he climbed the gangway to look in the tramper's hold, he heard his name called out from the Mackenzie warehouse. "Hardy," the man yelled, "we have the rosewood and lignum vitae over here." Relieved, Hardy thought about the orders he had for both. The rosewood was going to a local manufacturer of bagpipes. The lignum vitae, known for its natural oil and self-lubricating properties, would be cut into bearing stock and distributed to hydroelectric plants throughout the world. He was pleased with the recent bearing business he had developed. In late June, he received an inquiry from a Greek shipping company in need of bearing stock for a Liberty Ship built during WWII. As luck would have it, the triangular pie shaped blocks Mackenzie manufactured were interchangeable. Two weeks following the shipment of the bearings to Olympic Maritime S.A., Hardy received a call from a Mr. Aristotle Onassis, thanking him for his help and prompt delivery.

At first Hardy couldn't believe he was speaking with Mr. Onassis. He thought the call highly irregular, since he knew Onassis was the owner of Olympic Maritime as well as Olympic Airlines. He had researched Olympic Maritime prior to shipment and discovered the credit worthiness of his new customer was measured in the hundreds of millions of dollars and he was surprised that Onassis would acknowledge his company over such a relatively minor order. When Onassis insisted that he fly down to his main office in Monte Carlo, Hardy could barely contain his excitement. Two Olympic Airline tickets were hand delivered to the Glasgow office the following week along with a note that read: "Bring a friend, Ari."

Hardy and Darcy flew to Monte Carlo during the long summer holiday and Hardy soon discovered that Mr. Onassis frequently called his vendors no matter the size of the order.

My young lady, you are very beautiful," he said with a thick accent when they entered his office. "Mr. MacBean, you are a very lucky man. And I want you to know that each supplier to my company is relied upon and equally important to the success of my business. Besides, one never knows what opportunities may arise. Take Mackenzie for example, someday you may need Olympic Maritime to ship your lumber and logs, or maybe you go into business for yourself and you need financial backing. I am very pleased that you have come. We will fly to Scorpios for the weekend. Jackie is expecting us."

Hardy was astonished they would stay on Scorpios Island and also meet Jacqueline Kennedy Onassis. He remembered when he learned of President Kennedy's assassination the morning after his crew triumphed in the race against the fourth form boys, how he silently wept when the news was announced in study hall, and how at that moment he had felt so very far away from home.

They boarded the Onassis helicopter that had brought them to the Olympic Maritime office and returned to Cote d'Azur Airport where they boarded the Onassis private jet. Within two hours they landed in Greece and transferred by seaplane to Scorpios.

"Just in time for a swim," Onassis said as they landed in an open cove in front of the main house and taxied to a long floating dock. Jackie Onassis greeted them and personally showed them to their private cottage. She was every bit as attractive as the pictures Hardy had seen of her.

"We will see you on the beach," Jackie said in a soft, melodious voice, "follow the signs to East Beach and Mykonos house."

Hardy and Darcy met their hosts at the beach and within minutes they were asked to refer to them as Ari and Jackie. That evening they boarded a 40' launch, which ferried them to the Onassis luxury yacht *Christina*, moored in the Vlyho bay. When they arrived, Hardy and Darcy were each taken to private dressing rooms where they were asked to pick out formal attire for the evening. Hardy emerged wearing a tuxedo with black tie and Darcy appeared wearing an elegant, one shoulder pink chiffon evening gown. They met in the ships dining room where Ari complemented Darcy on her selection.

"I believe that you and my son Alexander are the same age," he said. "And I think you would enjoy each other's company."

"How old is Alexander?" Hardy asked.

"Twenty four last April. He just received his pilot's license."

"He is almost a year older than me. Have you flown with him?"

"Yes, on my jet, he is the co-pilot when we travel together."

The following morning, Hardy woke to a warm breeze coming off the Ionian Sea. He looked at Darcy asleep in the middle of the king size bed, thinking about how they had both had too much to drink the night before.

"Come on," he said, shaking her by the shoulder, "Get up, let's go for a swim."

They spent the day by themselves, swimming, beachcombing and walking about the Island. Ari had told them that when he bought the island there were no trees, no sand and little soil. Ten years later, the island displayed a burgeoning forest covering 74 acres, with more than 200 varieties of trees along with two beaches, all of which was brought over from the mainland. Food was delivered to the cottage during the day and in the evening a dinner of octopus, calamari and muscles arrived with spanakopita and revani, along with a note from Jackie wishing them well and "bon appetite."

The next morning they packed their bags and joined Ari and Jackie at the heliport above the main house and flew back to Aktion National Airport.

"Your skin is the color of your hair," Onassis said to Darcy as they settled into their seats.

"I'm afraid I don't get out in the sun much," she replied. "It will all be gone by tomorrow."

"I've found it is always wise to wear a hat," Jackie said.

"Actually, she burns and then peels, she doesn't tan," Hardy said. "Quite a sight actually." They all laughed as the jet landed and Hardy and Darcy thanked them both for a wonderful weekend.

Hardy began working for R.A. Mackenzie in the summer of 1970, successfully opening up new markets for exotic hardwoods, both in the U.K. and around the world. The price of raw material had become increasingly more expensive and the profit margin continued to dwindle. As he inspected rosewood and lignum vitae logs, he thought about the country of origin.

"Quite a nice lot of lignum vitae," Alan Mackenzie said, "not much sapwood."

"Yep," Hardy replied. "We should have a good overrun."

"Prices keep going up," Mackenzie added looking over the bills of lading. "They've asked for another 10 percent."

"I was expecting it," Hardy replied. "They obviously think we're a captive audience and it's time we did something about it."

"What's on your mind?" Mackenzie asked.

"I think we should buy directly, get rid of the middleman."

"Sounds good, but who will go?"

"I will!" Hardy said with conviction.

"You mean to tell me your girlfriend will let you go?"

"Darcy has too much work to miss me. She's working at the Glasgow Royal Infirmary at night and studying at medical school by day. It was all I could do to convince her to take a weekend off last July and fly to Monaco. We hardly see each other anymore."

"In that case, develop a plan and we'll consider it."

142

"Yes sir, I'll look into it," Hardy replied.

Darcy tiptoed into the bedroom. It was three in the morning.

"I hear you, don't tell me what time it is." He rolled over and watched Darcy's silhouette as she removed her clothes.

"How was your shift?"

"Same old, I've got to be up by 7, you?" she replied, lifting the covers and climbing into bed.

"Seven is good. I've got a lot of work to do."

"What kind of work?" she asked touching him.

"Do you want to?"

"Of course, you never need to ask," he replied.

"The alarm sounded waking Hardy from a deep sleep, dreaming of faraway places.

"What work did you say?" Darcy asked.

"I'm catching the 8 o'clock to London, I have an appointment at the Nicaraguan Consulate."

"What for?"

"We're thinking of buying directly, getting rid of the middleman."

"When will you go?"

"I don't know, just a preliminary fact finding mission. I'll be home late."

"Alright," Darcy said. "You know my schedule. I'll miss you."

"Yeah, always home late, but I'm not complaining, Dr. Nicholson."

"I'll be practicing next March if I graduate on time."

"That's terrific, we'll celebrate your graduation and my birthday at the same time."

"You're such a handsome young man."

"Yeah, and you're brainy *and* beautiful," he said, pulling her back onto the bed.

"I have to go, Hardy! Not now!"

"Okay, me, too. How about I join you in the shower?" he asked, following her into the bathroom.

"The soap, please?" she asked as she stood with her eyes closed under the shower spray.

Hardy placed the bar of soap in her hand, cupped her breast, lowered his mouth and sucked her nipple as the water cascaded over them.

"Hardy, stop it, that's all you think about!"

"No, not all, but a lot," he said pulling her close. "Darcy," he exclaimed as she reached out and put her arms around his neck and kissed him. The shower filled with steam as he lifted her, pressing her back against the tile wall.

"Go, Hardy, go" she whispered.

He found the Nicaraguan Consulate housed in a small office on Kensington Church Street. When he arrived, a young Nicaraguan woman greeted him. She was petite with delicate features; her bright red lipstick accentuated her coal black hair. Hardy couldn't help but notice her underwear with her black mini-dress rising above her thighs as she stood up.

"Good morning, Mr. MacBean," she said, smoothing her dress. "I'm afraid that your appointment will need to be rescheduled."

"Why Miss, Senorita?" keeping his gaze on her face.

"Vogel."

"Miss Vogel, I've come all the way from Glasgow and I was hoping to get some information about Nicaraguan hardwood and who I might contact."

"Well, that's easy, I'll give you my Uncle Herman's address."

"Is he in the industry?"

"What industry?"

"The lumber industry."

"What lumber industry?" She asked looking at him with a quizzical stare.

"Arboles, madera!" Hardy exclaimed.

"Ah, Madera, ahora entiendo, now I understand," she said.

"Uncle Herman knows about everything. He speaks perfect English. Please let me give you his address and phone number," handing Hardy a card.

"Gracias, senorita." Hardy said, taking the card.

The following day Hardy made contact with Herman Vogel. They telexed each other back and forth about availability and the possible shipment of Nicaraguan lumber to Scotland. He felt comfortable enough with Herman to discuss a trip to Central America with Alan Mackenzie.

"Yes, I've arranged to meet with him mid-month, That is, of course, if you think the project is worthwhile."

"What is Vogel's position over there?" Alan asked.

"He's an agent. He represents buyers and sellers."

"How much will he charge us?"

"Three percent of the invoice plus money for gas and food. If we don't buy he charges $50 per day for his services. He sets up meetings and will act as my interpreter and driver. He will take care of all the permitting when it comes time to ship logs and lumber.

"I'd like to know how many mills, the production, and the species we're talking about before we commit," Alan said.

Chapter 27

"Abrocharse los cinturones y apaquen sus cigarillos, por favor," the cabin speakers blared.

"Fasten your seatbelts and extinguish all cigarettes please." The stewardess repeated in English.

Hardy looked out his window at smoke rising from fires burning below.

"That's how they clear their land," a man said seated next to him.

Hardy heard a hissing noise from behind and the sound of heavy footsteps coming down the aisle as the jet began its decent. He listened to the landing gear snap into place as the engines reversed with a roar, slowing the jet and shaking the cabin. "A rookie pilot," Hardy thought.

"Hold your breath," the man said, "this DDT stuff is pretty nasty."

Hardy took a deep breath and watched the stewardess spray the cabin.

"Jesus," he said, his eyes stinging from the spray.

TACA International Airlines flight N1419 descended through a cloudless Saturday afternoon sky as Hardy exhaled the air he could no longer hold.

146

The smell of the DDT permeated the cabin as the plane landed at Managua International Airport.

"Enjoy your stay," the man said as the plane taxied to a halt. An audible sigh of relief rose from the passengers when the door opened and fresh air surged into the cabin.

The customs official took Hardy's passport, looked him in the face and stamped ENTRADA, handing it back with a snap of his wrist and motioning him toward the exit. Hardy emerged into a large open-air terminal and heard his name called out from a group of people standing behind a fence.

"Hello, a Mr. MacBean, please?" a man called out, holding a sign with MACBEAN in large block letters. Hardy looked over and saw a short stocky man with brown thinning hair, wearing an impeccably pressed short sleeve white cotton shirt and grey trousers.

"Herman?" he called out as Herman Vogel advanced through the crowd.

"Mr. MacBean?" Herman asked. "You fit your description completely; red beard, long hair, six foot one. Do you have luggage?" he asked as he folded his sign in half. Hardy could hear a Spanish accent with a hint of German.

"Just this one," he replied holding up his suitcase.

"Come," Herman said, taking hold of Hardy's suitcase, "I drive you to the Hotel."

Hardy felt the warm humid air press against his pants and shirt, a welcome relief from the cold and rainy Glasgow he had left behind.

His plans included one night in Managua, and then off to visit three sawmills, inspect lumber, return to Managua and catch a flight back to Glasgow on December 23.

"Are you hungry?" Herman asked.

"Si, Senor Vogel," he replied using what little Spanish he knew.

"We will stop at El Ray, a nice little restaurant on Lake Managua, You can pick your own fish from the tank, they swim around."

"Sounds terrific," Hardy said.

Leaving the airport at Las Mercedes, Herman joined a procession of cars on the way into Managua, each with honking horns, jockeying for position, winding in and out of carts and buses stopped to collect passengers, including chickens, goats and dogs. Herman's continuous beeping was either a nervous reaction or completely defensive, Hardy thought.

There appeared to be neither rules of the road nor police present during their drive to Managua. Hardy was entertained as drivers yelled out obscenities and made wild gestures. His senses were assaulted with the smells of a foreign land, different foods mingled with brief whiffs of sewage as they neared the city.

"We are in our dry season," Herman quipped as he pulled off the main road in front of a small wood and stucco building that looked out across Lake Managua. Triangular flags hanging from the open portico whipped in the afternoon breeze. "The beginning of our summer is the best time of year. Everything is green, a little rain maybe once a day now."

They entered the café and Hardy noticed two soldiers with semi-automatic M1 rifles standing at the end of the building.

"What is all that about?"

"You better not fart," Herman said in a whispered tone. "The Guardia Nacional will blow your ass off. Pick out a fish," he gestured towards an open tank as they entered the restaurant and walked to a table overlooking the lake.

"What kind of fish?"

"Guapote," It comes from the lake, delicious white meat, delicate. They grill it, sin espinas, or fry it in corn meal. If you don't want fish, you can have the carne."

"What kind of meat?"

"Some kind of meat, sometimes dog, sometimes goat."

"I'll have the fish," Hardy said quickly, thinking of his grandfather's dog Lu-Lu. Herman called out to a waitress.

"Senor Herman, como estas?" Todo elmundo sabre el senor Herman."

Si, everyone knows me," Herman repeated with a smile.

On the way into the city, Herman pointed to a pyramid shaped structure overlooking the lake. It appeared to Hardy to rise up above all the surrounding buildings.

"That is the Hotel Inter-Continental, the finest hotel in Nicaragua! I leave you off and tomorrow we go to Granada, 9 o'clock," Herman said tapping the steering wheel to a silent tune.

The shape of the hotel reminded Hardy of Mayan pyramids he had recently seen in *National Geographic*.

"El hotel mas bonito de toda Managua!" Herman exclaimed loudly as they entered the front lobby. He walked to the front desk, stopped and adjusted his stance. With his legs together, back straight, and shoulders at attention, he puffed his chest out, briefly lifting himself up on his toes and clicked his heels once lightly.

"Este es el Senor MacBean, hecho una reserve para el?" Herman inquired.

"Y que son?" the clerk asked.

"Senor Herman Vogel."

The clerk thumbed through the reservations. "Muy bueno el Senor Vogel, bienvenida."

"This way, Senor MacBean," Herman said, walking toward the elevator. "You are on the sixth floor."

"Gracias, Herman, I'll take it from here. See you in the morning then, 9 o'clock?

"Yes, 9 o'clock," Herman replied, reaching out and shaking Hardy's hand.

He entered his room and looked out across Lake Managua and saw a volcano releasing plumes of smoke. He had never seen a volcano much less an active one. He dropped his bag on the bed and decided to return to the lobby and find the bar. The bar was empty except for the bartender and a young blond woman sitting at a table looking out at the hotel pool.

"Que tipo de cerveza tiene usted?" Hardy asked.

"Cerveza Victoria," the bartender replied.

"Si, una cerveza Victoria, por favor."

"Si senor," the bartender said, opening the bottle and sliding it across the bar.

"Can you tell me the name of the volcano I see?"

"Momotombo is the large one. Momotombito is the smaller one. Nicaragua is the land of lakes and volcanoes," the blond woman said.

"Gracias, senorita, or is it senora? Are you from here?"

"Senorita! I am from Bogotá," She stood up and walked toward the bar. And what is your name?"

"Hardy MacBean."

"Nice to meet you, Senor Hardy MacBean, my name is Yolanda," she said, sitting down next to him. The bartender busied himself wiping the mahogany bar while casting glances at them, at Yolanda in particular.

"And where are you from, Senor Hardy?"

"Scotland."

"Where is this Scotland?"

"Northern U.K., north of England."

"London?"

"Yes, north from London."

"I have heard London is a great city, someday I go there."

"It is a great city," Hardy repeated.

"What do you do here?" he asked.

"I am visiting, and you?" she asked as the bartender glanced again in her direction.

"I'm here on business."

"Maybe we have dinner tonight?" she questioned.

"No, not tonight, thank you, it has been a long day and I need to get some sleep."

"Maybe I see you again?

"Maybe," he said as he rose from his seat and walked out of the bar.

Hardy woke early and watched the sun hit the slopes of Momotombo, gradually climbing to its peak. He showered, dressed and took the elevator down to the lobby to find food and coffee.

"Buenos dias, Senor MacBean," Herman said sitting down at Hardy's table in the InterContinental's brasserie.

"Would you like some coffee?" Hardy asked.

"No thank you, Senor MacBean, I've had mine today."

"Please call me Hardy."

"Yes sir, Senor Hardy."

"Beautiful temperature today," Hardy said. "Where are we going?

"It is cool now, but it will be hot this afternoon. Today we drive to Granada and tomorrow morning we visit Don Ramon. He has a grand sawmill. I told him that you want the genuine mahogany, like you said, also rosewood and lignum vitae logs. He has much to show you."

"Sounds great, Herman, I'm ready to go!"

"Vamanos," Herman replied, standing up from the table and leaving a tip.

There was little Sunday traffic on the road driving east from Managua. As they approached the airport, the road divided into four lanes. Herman slowed his Simca to a crawl and drove around an overturned wagon with a horse lying across the road, its lifeless tongue splayed on the pavement. Bananas scattered across both lanes. Parked to the side was a flatbed truck with a crushed front bumper. Steam spewed from the radiator. A young man with blood running down his face sat behind the steering wheel.

"These guys drive like maniacs," Herman said as he stepped on the gas pedal, sounding his horn with two quick beeps, squashing the bananas in his path. "The Guardia will come and take care of it, these accidents happen all the time."

Leaving the airport behind, Hardy looked at the one story buildings lining each side of the road.

"The buildings are constructed of taquezal," Herman said. "They have timber frame walls filled with stone and mud, finished with plaster. The roofs are made with unmortared clay tiles."

Many of the buildings displayed wooden doors and window frames painted in different shades of yellow, green, red and blue. A few buildings were painted entirely, some in bright turquoise with sparkling white doors and window trim and others in a light green with the window and door trim left unfinished. Hardy breathed in the sweet scent of the oleander trees, with their clusters of pink and white flowers and recognized the perfume smell from his stay on Scorpios. The traffic was punctuated by a few horse drawn wagons zigzagging in and out, trying to avoid potholes in the dirt road. Pedestrians covered their faces as cars and trucks whipped up the dust.

"I think we stop in Masaya and I will show you our famous markets," Herman said. "We have everything here, leather goods, wooden toys, pottery, art, food and clothing. Also very nice straw hats, the sun is strong."

Hardy listened to Herman as he looked at a volcano rising up from the east.

"How far are we from the mill?" Hardy asked.

"We are about an hour away. Celta de Nicaragua, they have very wide mahogany boards, over three feet. Don Ramon de Mercado has told me they sell two-inch thick mahogany boards to the casket companies. His family has these sawmills in Granada since the turn of the century. He attended Oxford when he was a young man and came back to run the family business. A very well respected family, the Mercado family. They came from Spain around 1825."

"Caskets," Hardy repeated. "A damn waste of wood, if you ask me. Put it in the ground to rot. Have you discussed prices with him?"

"The mahogany caskets do not get buried. They are placed in burial vaults above ground. I offered your prices out and Don Ramon accepted them. They have rows of lumber piles, all stacked and covered, waiting to be kiln dried."

Herman slowed his car as they approached Masaya, driving past a wall of single and two story buildings stretching the length of the street. He parked the car against the curb alongside the Masaya marketplace and signaled a young boy who approached the car holding out his hand.

"Cuidar el auto," Herman said handing him a one Cordoba note.

Hardy swung open the passenger door. His glance fell on a blind man kneeling in the entranceway to the market with begging bowl outstretched, his head covered with sores and his open eyes white and lifeless.

"Dinero para un pobre ciego." The blind man called out.

"Jesus, what is wrong with him?"

"I think he has syphilis, pobre enfermo," Herman replied.

Hardy bent down and placed a Córdoba in the beggar's bowl saying "buenos."

"Gracias, senor" the beggar said, tilting his head up toward Hardy's face with a smile.

"I'll follow you Herman," Hardy said standing.

154

They entered the market and walked past stalls separated by stacks of clothing and colored bales of cotton. They stopped at a booth brimming with handmade leather goods where Hardy noticed a prominent picture of a smiling President Kennedy hanging above a hand stitched leather saddle. The next booth had bright colored dresses. Hardy thought about Darcy and how beautiful she would look in one of them. He selected a white dress featuring an embroidered angelfish, with scalloped borders along the sleeves and the apron.

"It is for your wife?"

"My girlfriend."

"Angelfish for an angel," Herman said.

Hardy selected four additional dresses of equally vibrant color but with less embroidery.

"Summer dresses!" Hardy exclaimed. "I hope they fit."

On the way back to the car, Hardy stopped and looked at a wall of paintings created by local artists, each displaying a smoking volcano. A picture of Adolf Hitler hung from the wall, showing the tight-lipped mouth, cold autocratic stare, the ill-famed toothbrush mustache and the ever-present sun god symbol above the brim of his uniform hat.

"He is also revered here, the same as Kennedy," Herman said. "My family came here from Germany in 1934. My mother was a Jewess. My father knew well enough to get us the hell out of there. I was 10 years old, my brother 13. You will soon meet my brother Frederick."

Within the hour, they emerged from the market with Hardy wearing a wide brim straw hat.

Chapter 28

The road to Granada was hot and dusty with little traffic.

"We will stay with my brother tonight. His ranch is a few miles from the mill," Herman said as he turned off the main road and traveled down a single lane passing a herd of cattle. At the end of the road a spacious hacienda set up on a rise, framed by the lake and the islands beyond with Mombacho Volcano towering up to the northwest.

"Here we are," Herman said as they passed through the open gate into a courtyard. Hardy looked across the lake at two islands. He had never seen such a large lake and it looked like there was a vast sea beyond the islands where water and sky met on the horizon.

"Lago de Nicaragua is the ninth largest freshwater lake in the Americas and the largest in Central America. It covers 3,000 square miles. My brother raises cattle and sells his beef throughout Central America. The ranch has 1,435 hectares, about 3,500 acres."

A beautiful dark skinned woman appeared on the veranda and called out to Herman.

"Herman, hermano! Mucho gusto!"

"Mucho gusto, Avira!" Herman called back.

"Ah, my brother's wife, Avira, she speaks perfect English."

"Herman, pero Espanol es major?" Hardy asked.

"Okay then, we will try to speak Spanish only! Let me introduce you to Avira," putting his arm around her. "Avira Alvarenga de Santiago Vogel,"

Hardy reached out and shook her hand.

"Muy bonito conocerte."

"Y tambien se," Avira replied. "We don't have English here very often, especially English with an accent such as yours."

"Where is Frederick," Herman asked.

"Your brother is in town getting supplies. He will be back for dinner soon."

"Avira is mestizo, Hardy, 57 varieties, she is part Spanish, Portuguesa, Mayan, African, English and who knows what else. Exotico! My nieces are quite beautiful also, with their mother's color. Add in both German and Jew to the mixture and you have exquisite beauties. Frederick and his youngest, Maria, share the same birthday, which is today!"

"Girls!" Avira shouted out, "Your Uncle Herman is here."

Maria was first out the door.

"Uncle Herman, you remembered!" she called out.

"Of course, how could I forget your 16th birthday?" "I am your favorite uncle!"

"You are my only uncle," Maria laughed. Hardy looked up and watched as Maria skipped across the veranda toward Herman. She was as exquisite as Herman had described, her brown hair cascading over her shoulders displaying red highlights, her dark brown smiling eyes, sparkling and alive with passion. Her mid-calf skirt twirled as she jumped and turned with precision into Herman's arms, laughing all the way. Her sister Tanja, equally as beautiful, held back in the doorway watching, her eyes wide with anticipation.

"Me gustaria presentar Senor Hardy MacBean."

"Uncle Herman, please speak English," Maria implored, "I need to practice."

"Alright," Herman relented. "I'm very sorry, Hardy, but it is Maria's day, and if she wants to speak English then that is what we must

157

do. Maria and Tanja are fluent in Spanish, German and English. Tanja is named after my mother, Pauline Berthe Theodore Vogel, but we call her Tanja for short. She study's the law at Central American University. She will become president someday I think. We have many celebrations to look forward to."

"Come, everyone, let us show our guests to their rooms," Avira said. "Of course your Uncle Herman always gets the dormitorio supremo."

"I will show Senor MacBean to his room," Maria called out. "What kind of a name is MacBean?" she asked as she showed Hardy to his room. "It is funny to be called a bean, is it not?"

"Absolutely hilarious," Hardy replied laughing.

"The name Vogel means 'bird' in German. What does MacBean mean?"

"It means 'lively one' in Gaelic," Hardy replied.

"And if we get married I would be known as 'lively bird,'" Maria said laughing.

"That you are, I mean, would, Maria," he said, his face reddening.

Frederick and Avira Vogel sat at each end of the table and the girls sat along side both Herman and Hardy. Maria reserved the seat next to Hardy.

"How is Herman Junior?" Frederick asked.

"He is doing very well, teaching at the German school during the week, and every weekend he takes his scouts camping. He is a 'Ranger' now."

"Where does he take them?"

"To Ocotal and then into the Cordillera de Pilto Mountains, near

158

the Honduran border."

"I know of this area," Frederick said. "Coffee plantations and a few mines. Our ranch foreman comes from that region. He has told us of the growing MILPAS resistance."

"I don't know about this." Herman said.

"What is this MILPAS?" Hardy asked.

"It is a group of anti-Somoza fighters. MILPAS stands for 'Anti-Somoza Popular Militias.' But of course no one is to know. We have similar opposition groups south and east of here known as the FSLN, 'Frente Sandinista de Liberacion Nacional.' Some refer to them as Sandinistas. Their numbers are growing."

"And they were just here!" gushed Maria.

"Maria," Frederick said sternly, "we do not speak of this!"

"I am sorry Papa, I didn't mean to.

Chapter 29

Don Ramon stepped down from the porch and extended his hand. He was a tall elderly gentleman with elegant features, white hair, aquiline nose and lightly tanned skin.

"Bienvenido a Celta de Nicaragua," he said, greeting them.

"Gracias, Senor Don Ramon," Herman exclaimed introducing Hardy. "Esto es Senor Hardy MacBean."

"Buenos, come inside the office and we will discuss business," Don Ramon said in perfect English. "What can I do for you, Senor MacBean?" he asked as he sat down behind a large mahogany desk.

"I come to buy your lumber and logs."

"Yes, as Herman discussed, you require mahogany lumber, lignum vitae and rosewood logs. Do you have other requirements?"

"I need mahogany pattern stock, straight grained material."

"We develop straight grain material, maybe 30 percent of our production, but we don't saw for it, we pull out that which develops. Much of our lumber is sold ahead, but we will sell you two loads as a trial shipment. If you like we can take orders for next year. We are now beginning to accumulate logs from our concession across the lake. When the rainy season comes in May, the creeks fill up and the logs float down into the lake. We raft the logs together and pull them here to the mill."

"What do you use for equipment?" Hardy asked.

"We use oxen, this is the way we log and this is the way my father and grandfather logged. Last year, an American came here from California with a bulldozer and skidder. Somoza charged him a big import duty at the Port of Corinto, and then a tax through every town from Corinto to Granada. We were told that the American bought a timber concession next to ours from a gringo in the United States. I don't think General Somoza was very happy about the sale because he made no commission. By the time the equipment was finally barged across the lake, we were told it cost double the amount we would pay here. The American had only three weeks before the rains came and then his bulldozer and skidder got stuck in the mud. We bought what logs he brought to the lake. The last we heard the rebels had burned his equipment, incendiado, and he went home with nothing. We see many like him, soldiers of fortune who come here to enrich themselves and then leave penniless."

"The rebels try to overthrow Samoza," Herman exclaimed."

160

"Yes, that is what we hear," Don Ramon said. "But we never see them. I will show you the mahogany we have available and you are welcome to select out the straight grain. The lignum vitae and rosewood logs are waxed and bundled on separate pallets."

"Buenos," Hardy replied. "May I have two men to help me inspect the boards, Don Ramon?"

"Certainly, you may have more if you wish. Select the boards you want and Pedro will provide you with a piece tally and bundle count when you are finished."

"Gracias, Don Ramon," Hardy said.

Don Ramon stood up from his desk and motioned Hardy to follow him. "I want to show you another hardwood we have, our Central American black walnut. We call it nogal. We use it for parquet floors, furniture, and the veneer for musical instruments. Nogal grows along the riverbanks and it is impossible to dry a board that is more than one inch thick. Even then the board may spring and warp from tension after it is dried. The thin veneer is the most stable. Last year, we sawed a half million-board feet of two-inch-thick nogal for a lumber company from the United States located in Chicago. When they ordered, I informed them that two-inch was impossible to dry and they told me to go ahead, cut and ship, that they knew what they were doing. We told them they needed to pay us first, before we cut. Their money was good. The last we heard, they put the nogal into their kilns and used a drying schedule for North American black walnut, a completely different species. The lumber was ruined, the cell structure collapsed. We were told they lost over a million dollars and went bankrupt. We watch them come and go here, the gringos are always right, never wrong. They say they know more than us and we take their money."

Hardy thought about the U.S. passport he gave up when he was drafted for the Vietnam War. He remembered how his mother was relieved, and how his father was disappointed. His father said to him, "my country, right or wrong," when they shook hands and said goodbye that sunny day in September. He would never forget looking out from the porch, wondering if he would ever return to Westport. There wasn't a breath of wind; the ocean was like a big pond, flat as far as the eye could see. A good day for swordfishing he remembered thinking.

He graduated from Gordonstoun early that June and returned home to Westport. He found work on a swordfishing boat called the Wahoo, where he was hired on as a spotter and would spend the summer months in the "crows nest" searching the ocean for the telling crescent shaped dorsal fin. His fear of heights had never left him and climbing up and down the mast was terrifying. He remembered the first time he put the Wahoo close in to where Raymond could strike, sending the harpoon barb deep into flesh, the flash of the swordfish tail against the water, the giant unblinking eye disappearing into the deep, the wooden keg exploding off the deck following the noise of the rope spinning over the bow, all in an instant, blurred in his memory as the grand fish battled to a courageous death, using every ounce of his strength, then rising to the surface exhausted, vanquished.

It was late August when he received a letter from his Uncle Gillies asking him if he would like to work in the Dalcross forest. The next day, he received a notice from the United States Selective Service Department instructing him to report for a physical exam prior to his induction into the U.S Army. Without a second thought, he made arrangements to fly from Boston to Glasgow. He bought the ticket the next day and told his

162

mother and father he would be leaving.

On September 4, a day ahead of the physical, he remembered the relief he felt as the jetliner lifted off the Logan Airport runway. He did not know if he would ever return, but he knew that the Vietnam War was about as wrong as any war could be and he wouldn't go. On his return to Dalcross, Darcy met him at the door of the castle wearing an apron with remnants of flour on her cheeks and speckled throughout her long red hair. She jumped into his arms and hugged him with all her might, saying, "You're finally home, my Hardy." They kissed for a long while. He remembered leaning forward and whispering in her ear, "Yes, I'm home, and I won't be leaving soon." At the time, he never thought that his UK passport and the Scottish accent he had acquired would allow him cover from his American birth.

"Don Ramon," Herman said as the men stopped work for the day, "we will return tomorrow morning at 9 o'clock."

"Si," Don Ramon said, acknowledging the time.

As they drove back to Herman's brother's ranch, Hardy thought about the previous evening.

"They have these Sandinistas living around them?"

"My brother says they camp out on the southern slopes of Mombacho. They come down to buy or trade what they need. He thinks he is better off helping them and they have promised never to draw the Guardia Nacional to his ranch. He believes that someday they will be victorious. Somoza is a bad man. He controls everything. If you do business in Nicaragua, you deal with the Somoza family. I will have a meeting with his son to arrange shipment of your lumber and logs when they are shipped to Corinto. It is a required formality for everyone to pay and then we go about our business. Somoza always gets his money."

By noon on Tuesday Hardy finished up one trailer load of mahogany and a second load of lignum vitae and rosewood logs.

"My customers look forward to receiving your lumber and logs," Hardy said as he reached out his hand to Don Ramon.

"And we look forward to seeing you again," he said, shaking Hardy's hand. "Now that Pedro knows what you want, he will have the lumber prepared for you when you return."

"Gracias, Senor Don Ramon, Nos vemos el proximo ano."

"Yes, see you next year," Don Ramon replied, "Adios, Senor Hardy."

Hardy climbed into the Simca and Herman sounded his horn twice as they drove onto the main road.

"Where to now?" Hardy asked.

"Next we go to El Rama and take a boat to Bluefields. We will visit a mahogany and teak plantation. The mahogany and teak trees were planted by the United Fruit Company in 1920 after the banana blight came through. They have just begun to harvest the logs this year. An Englishman by the name of Baxter runs the business and he has arranged to pick us up at the dock Thursday morning. First we return to Managua. You can stay at my house tonight and we will leave early tomorrow morning. It will take us a full day to reach Rama."

"If I could borrow your telex, I'll find out what we can do with the teak before we go. We sell our mahogany to many of the boat yards in the United Kingdom, so it shouldn't be a problem."

"Yes, you can use my office," Herman replied.

As they approached the airport, Hardy saw vultures circling overhead and a few sitting on the fence that divided the highway, extending their wings as if stretching.

"Isn't that the horse we saw on our way to Granada?"

"Yes. It takes time to move such a big animal."

Herman slowed the car as they looked across the road and watched as two birds tore strips of flesh from the carcass and another plunged its' beak into an empty eye socket. Broken ribs extended through the hide of the horse's mangled body of rotting flesh.

"Those are black vultures," Herman said.

"Jesus," Hardy replied, looking at the oily tire tracks running north along the road. "It looks like she's been run over more than a few times."

"Jesus won't help her," Herman replied.

Hardy thought about what he had learned over the past few days. Nicaragua was a tropical paradise with desperate poverty, ruled by a ruthless dictator more interested in his personal wealth than the wellbeing of the Nicaraguan people. And then there was the dead horse, lying in front of the airport for last three days. He wondered if his time in Nicaragua would be a onetime occurrence. Was he just another foreigner who would leave empty handed? Or would he build a relationship with Herman and a few sawmills. As they entered the city, they left Carretera Norte and drove northwest toward the lake.

"We live in a walled compound called Colonia Dambach on the shore of Xolotlan, the Nicaraguan name for Lake Managua. My parents bought the house when we arrived from Germany. My father's friend Pablo Dambach built the neighborhood in 1928. He also constructed the Cathedral de Santiago, shipped here in pieces that were made in Belgium.

It is a beautiful cathedral about eight blocks west from here."

As they approached the compound, Hardy could see roofs of homes through tall flowering Ceibos trees lining the south wall. A tower with a high-pitched roof that made the compound resemble a fortress flanked the main entrance. Passing through the gate, he saw what appeared to be two story German Bauhaus type homes made from cement with angular dimensions. There were a few single story neo-colonial stucco timber and stone structures with arched windows and doors nearest the lake. Herman drove up to a large sand-washed colonial with a bright red front door.

"I have lived in this house since I was 10 years old, almost 40 years. Next year, we will have a celebration May 1 for my 50th birthday. Perhaps you will come?"

"Perhaps," Hardy replied, "Hopefully."

"Don't worry, Hardy, I take care of everything. All you have to do is sell."

"If that's all I have to do, it's a deal."

"Ah, my beautiful wife, Henrietta," Herman said as she appeared in the courtyard.

"Henrietta, this is our guest Hardy MacBean."

"Senor MacBean, it is my pleasure," Henrietta said with a slight accent.

A few inches taller than Herman, Henrietta had a thin athletic build, pale skin, light blue eyes and short brown hair peppered with gray. Hardy learned that her family escaped from Germany when she was barely six years old and settled into Colonial Dambach May 1, 1939, just in time to help celebrate Herman's 17th birthday. German's settled the entire compound and many of them were children of those who had been forced to flee Germany to avoid the death camps. Hardy could hear Herman's neighbors speak with one another as they walked by. "Guten tag," he heard them say as they greeted each other. "Good afternoon," he remembered from the little German he knew.

"Is Hermi at home?" Herman asked.

"No, but he will be here for dinner," Henrietta said

That evening four of them sat around the dining table and Hardy listened to young Herman rail against the Somoza government.

"Hermi," his father cautioned, "talk like that can get you into serious trouble and we will never see you again. Keep your head down, teach the boys how to speak German and take them camping in the mountains. Leave the fight to the rebels."

"I am and I do papa, but the Guardia is rounding up young men throughout the barrio as young as 12 years old and putting them in prison to keep them from joining the Sandinistas. Some are shot for no reason. Somoza is giving orders from his bunker on the hill and his guards do his bidding. The United States keeps him in power, and any of us who think we are safe from his Guardia Nacional is dreaming. We must overthrow Somoza before there is nothing left but our mothers and sisters to visit our graves!"

"Hermi," his father replied, "'you are all that your mother and I have. We need you to stay out of this conflict."

Chapter 30

The sun barely set when they drove into Rama. The drive from Managua had been a rough ride. Two hundred miles of dirt road shifting between single and double tracks over four bridges in various stages of construction. Along the way, they stopped in Tipitapa and then at Juilgalpa, where they walked along dusty streets and sat in small cafes drinking coffee, watching the locals go about their day. When they arrived in Rama, Herman parked in front of a thatched roofed hut overhanging the Escondido River. As the evening light faded into night, Hardy watched the river move along like a brown serpent, winding its way down to Bluefields Bay, spilling into the Caribbean Sea. He heard a whistle behind them and watched a man walk toward them holding a lamp casting long legged shadows.

"Herr Vogel?" a man's voice called out as the light from the lamp grew close.

"Si, Wolfe, you got my message."

"Guten Abend, wei geht es dir?"

"Good evening to you, too, Herr Bergmann. I am well, thank you."

"I hope you find zee accommodations acceptable?"

"It will do nicely," Herman said as Wolfgang Bergmann handed him a bottle of Flor de Cana.

"Please join us Wolfe? Acompanenos no le va?"

"Ich werde, danke."

"This is my friend Hardy MacBean, he doesn't speak much German."

"Oh, but of course, I will speak only the English," Bergmann said.

"I am Wolfgang, but you can call me Wolfe," he said offering Hardy a wooden cup.

"I have known Wolfe for almost 30 years," Herman interrupted, "His family arrived in Managua in 1944 and moved out here to Rama when there were no roads. They built these cabanas and rent them out to the migrant workers who come here to harvest the bananas."

"Do you know why we built these cabanas over the river Hardy?" Wolfgang asked.

"No, not really, perhaps it's cooler here over the water."

"You see that hole in the floor over there?" Wolfgang asked, and then answered before Hardy had a chance. "That is where you shit. Shit floats downstream, but don't fall through the hole, you'll be up to your alligators in it."

Hardy laughed in mid swallow, rum spewing from his nose.

"Getting another bottle," Wolfgang announced as he stood up abruptly and walked away into the darkness.

"Wolfe is married to Nora, the daughter of the Rama Chief MacCaig."

"That's a bloody Scot's name if I ever heard one," Hardy said feeling the rum cloud his senses.

"The name originates from Moravian missionaries who brought the Christian religion to Bluefields and the Mosquito Coast early in the 17th century." Herman explained. "MacCaig doubles as a Moravian pastor and married Nora and Wolfe. My family came down for Wolfe's wedding when the road was first opened. The Americans paid for it, and the Nicaraguans built it. And as we saw today it's still unfinished. I think Somoza stole most of the money. Back then it took us more than two days to get here and now only 10 hours with a couple of stops."

"Wolfgang's father Bruno was instrumental in helping us flee Germany. He was my father's childhood friend and our neighbor. After Hitler was appointed Chancellor of Germany, new laws proclaimed at Nuremberg made Jews second-class citizens. My father believed that our lives would be in danger if we stayed. He sold everything of value and transferred ownership of the house to Bruno, who later sold it and deposited the money in a Swiss bank."

"How did you get here?" Hardy asked.

"On a cold winter morning we boarded the train to Paris as if we were going away for the weekend."

"Did you know what was happening?"

"No, not then. When we arrived in Paris father told us we were going on a trip."

"I guess when I realized we were not going home I started to cry. I could only think of my little bear I left safely tucked in the covers of my bed. I remember looking up at my mother as tears streamed down her face. My father knelt down, reached out and held me close. He told me that I was a big boy and everything would be all right. From Paris we took the train to Le Havre and boarded a ship to Cuba. From Cuba we sailed to Honduras and took a bus over the mountains to Managua. It was quite a trip for us and quite an adventure for boy of 10. My father met Pablo Dambach in Belgium years before when he sold him steel for the Cathedral. They became friends and continued to correspond with each other after Pablo returned to Nicaragua. All was prepared for us when we finally arrived in Managua. Our house as it is today was fully furnished. Just before the end of the war, Bruno cabled my father and asked him for help with immigration and my father was able to return the favor. Bruno deserted from the German army and escaped with his wife and son through the port of Marseille when it was under German control and where he was stationed as port commander. He bribed his way onto a tramper bound for Panama and eventually they made their way to Puerto de Corinto. They arrived in September, six months before the German surrender. After staying with us for a few months, Bruno moved his family here to Rama. Back then the journey from Managua took more than a week by horse and wagon. He told my father then that he would live beyond the roads, but the roads eventually came to Rama and he died soon after. My father passed away in 1968 at the age 83."

Herman removed his shoes and climbed into a hammock and closed his eyes. "Tengo mucho sueno, buenas noches, Hardy."

"Good night Herman, sleep tight."

"I generally do Hardy, I generally do."

Wolfgang appeared at the door holding a bottle of rum in each hand. He sat down next to Hardy, reached into his pocket, pulled out a leather pouch and threw it on the table.

"Go ahead, open it," he said.

Hardy opened it and emptied a handful of coins onto the table.

"Pre-Columbian," Wolfe said, removing the cork from the bottle of rum and filling Hardy's glass.

"Go ahead, look at them. Beautiful, no?"

Hardy picked up a coin and held it up to the kerosene lantern. It had weight to it, although he couldn't tell what it was made of. He rubbed it on his shirt, then spit on it and rubbed it again. He could see a glimmer of silver shining on the raised letters circling the coin. He continued to rub it across his khaki pants. The coin was crude and misshapen with a visible circular stamp.

"HADRIANVS AVG COS IIIPP," Hardy read aloud, holding the

coin in the light, looking at a portrait of a man's head in relief. "HISPANIA" he read on the flip side as he studied a woman's figure in a long dress, holding a branch in her left hand and resting her elbow on a rock.

"Where'd you get these?" he asked.

Hardy knew from his studies of Hadrian's Wall that Hadrian was the fourteenth Emperor of Rome. In his drunken fog he couldn't remember what year Hadrian had ruled, but he remembered that the wall construction was started around 122AD.

"They came with my wife's dowry. I've been told the figure on the coin is a Roman emperor."

"Oh," Hardy said, his mind drifting, thinking he must secure the coins. "Is that right," he slurred, "where'd they come from?"

"They've been passed down from generation to generation, from one chief to the next. No one knows how long. What will you give me?"

"I have no idea, no idea. Herman," he called out, "what yah do?"

Herman lay in his hammock, snoring.

"Wake up, Herman," he called out again.

"I don't know Wolfe, how much you think?"

"Fifty U.S. and you can have the lot."

"Six coins? I'll give you 40."

"They're worth hundred at least," Wolfgang cried.

"Ah, bloody hell, I'll give ya 50," Hardy said, fearing he might lose the deal. He reached into his pocket and pulled out five 10-dollar bills and placed them on the table. Wolfgang looked at the money and then at Hardy. The lantern's shadows played across the room, leaving each man's expression shielded from view. Wolfe leaned forward in his seat, his eyes darting back and forth, showing hesitation.

"It's a deal! Drink up, Hardy!" he exclaimed as he swept the money from the table with one hand and filled Hardy's cup with the other.

"Next time I need to mix something with this," Hardy said.

"And ruin the flavor? Drink up, Hardy, you will have sweet dreams."

"I'm done, I'm going to sleep," Hardy said, climbing into his hammock. "See you in the morning. Nos vemos en la manana."

He fell off to sleep listening to the river running below, dreaming of the grand bargain he had made for the Roman coins.

Chapter 31

The trip to Bluefields was a success. With Herman's help Hardy was able to secure the mahogany at a lower price and the teak was half the cost of the Burmese teak that was selling in London. Although the plantation teak seemed to have less oil, Hardy knew he could sell it for a good profit to the yacht builders along the Thames.

The sawmill was built in the early 20th century. There were no date stampings on the cast iron gears and the carriage frame and head- block were made from wood. The production was small. Three men operated the mill, the sawyer, a man turning the log and another taking the boards away. They produced a little more than two cubic meters a day, where Celta de Nicaragua produced 20 cubic meters with six men. The product would need to be kiln dried at the Mackenzie kilns, whereas the lumber from Granada was kiln-dried at the mill and could be pre-sold before it arrived in Glasgow. But the price was right.

In less than a week, he had bought enough wood to pay for his expenses and make a 50 percent profit. That was if and when the lumber arrived in Glasgow. Time would tell, but it seemed that the decision to go direct to the source was well made.

The trip to and from Bluefields was uneventful, although the whine of the engines made Hardy's hangover all but unbearable. They arrived back in Rama at 5 p.m. and met Wolfe at the dock. He invited them to join him and his wife for dinner. Once there, Herman urged Hardy to drink another cup of rum.

"The best elixir, they call it the hair of the dog."

"I know, I know, the universal remedy, I've heard it all before. What I really need is an aspirin," Hardy replied.

Wolfgang put a bottle of rum on the table as his wife served a large bowl of gallo pinto along with whole fried fish smothered in tomato sauce. Hardy watched as Nora served them dinner in silence. She was exotic looking; tall with high cheekbones and straight black hair. Her eyes were an electric green, with specks of brown, and her complexion was lighter than the other Rama Indians he had encountered. They all sat down and Nora smiled as she poured coconut milk into Hardy's cup.

"Esto es bueno para usted," she said.

"Gracias," Hardy replied, sipping the milk.

"Have some rum with that," Wolfgang said.

"No thanks," Hardy replied. "This is just what the doctor ordered!"

They woke the following morning at six and began their drive back toward Managua.

"We go to Matagalpa," Herman said.

174

"Selva Negra, the Black Forest, some refer to it as the Cloud Forest. It is well known for the mahogany. Matagalpa is on the continental divide, between the Pacific Ocean and the Caribbean Sea. The high altitude is perfect for the coffee plantations."

"Apparently perfect for the rebels too," Hardy replied.

"Yes, that too."

As they drove west, the mountains loomed in the distance. Hardy thought of the hills and mountains of Scotland, about Christmas with his family just days away.

"We have a one o'clock appointment at the sawmill," Herman said as they retraced their drive to Managua. "We'll be back at the hotel in plenty of time for you to enjoy your last night in Managua. I am told it is the place to be on Friday night."

They reached the Pan American Highway and the town of San Benito just before noon, and drove north to Matagalpa. The dry season was more evident here as Hardy turned and looked at the dust billowing up behind them. Herman drove his Simca as fast as it would go, and within an hour they reached the main street of Sebaco.

"We're 10 minutes from the mill Hardy, how about some food?

"Great idea, Herman, I'm hungry, too."

"They have the sweetest corn tortillas in the entire country here," Herman said as he parked in front of a newly white washed adobe diner. 'Comedore de las Guirilas' was displayed in red block letters over the entrance. "Guirilas is the name for the sweet tortillas."

They entered the diner and sat at a wooden table in an open courtyard. Hardy looked out over the low walls and watched as a jeep with mounted machine gun moved slowly up the street.

A military transport holding a dozen or more Guardia Nacional troops followed close behind. Hardy motioned to Herman as a woman appeared from the kitchen and placed a bowl of gallo pinto on the table.

A loud explosion rocked the diner. Both Herman and Hardy dropped to the courtyard floor, knocking the wooden bowl of gallo pinto off the table with the contents raining down upon them. Machine gun fire erupted as the soldiers leapt from the truck and followed the jeep on foot. Hardy lifted his head and watched as another explosion stalled the jeep, with the driver falling out his door and the gunner clutching his face, falling backwards, momentarily holding on to the trigger, spewing one last burst of bullets into the air.

"What the fuck, Herman!"

"I don't know about what the fuck, but I think we get the hell out of here, fast!" Herman exclaimed, "Rapido!"

They crawled on the floor and peered out to the street. The car was close by the door but headed in the direction of the street battle. The gunfire was increasing but moving further away from them. The soldiers pulled the dead men from the jeep and one of them climbed up behind the machine gun, spewing bullets toward an unseen enemy as another drove the jeep up the street.

"I don't see them, Hardy, what do you think we should do?"

Hardy crawled his way over to Herman. It was just two of them. Everyone else in the diner had disappeared into the kitchen.

"I think we should get in the car and back up as fast as we can until we can turn around and head south."

"Okay!" Herman exclaimed as he crawled along the courtyard floor, out to the street and around the rear of the car to the driver's side. Crouching and close behind, Hardy opened the passenger door.

"Jesus Christ, Herman, get this god damned thing moving!"

Herman ducked into the driver's seat, peered above the dashboard while turning the ignition key, shifted into reverse, backing up as fast as he dared without losing control. He backed into an open lot, reversed direction, threw the car into first gear, sending clouds of dust into the air as he hit the road and headed south.

"I guess the mill will have to wait Hardy," Herman announced, short of breath.

"The hell with the mill, keep driving!" Hardy exclaimed.

They approached the airport in what Herman said was record time as they passed the carcass of what no longer resembled a horse.

"I never thought I'd like to see that again," Hardy said, as they drove past the airport and headed to the Inter-Continental. "Nothing but skin and bones."

Herman reached out his hand to Hardy as they drove up to the hotel entrance.

"I will pick you up tomorrow morning and give you a ride to the airport. We should be there by noon to clear customs. Adios, amigo, buenas tardes."

"See you tomorrow," Hardy replied, shaking Herman's hand.

He settled into his room and stood under the shower for a long time, washing off the dirt and fear acquired from the afternoon gun battle. He thought about Herman's son and the danger he faced.

Hardy sat at the bar lost in thought, surprised to find they had a bottle of Johnnie Walker. The bartender placed the scotch and a bottle of soda water with a glass of ice in front of him. He drank two glasses in succession and was on his third when he felt a tug on his arm.

"Senor Hardy, you've come back," Yolanda said with a big smile.

"Why, yes, I have. Yolanda, right? You're a lovely sight, can I offer you a drink?"

"Yes, you can," she replied. "Gracias por el complemento. I will have what you are having."

Hardy began to recount his trip to Granada, Rama and the aborted trip to Matagalpa. Yolanda listened in silence until he was finished.

"Matagalpa sounds crazy," she said, not showing much concern. "I think I prefer the beaches. I have been to the west coast, to a beautiful beach in Masachapa. Someday I would like to visit Bluefields."

The floor of the bar shook with a slight tremor. Hardy looked at his watch, 10:23 p.m.

"What the hell was that," he said, turning to the bartender.

"That was nothing, we have those shakings all the time."

"It's late, I need to go to bed Yolanda," Hardy announced. "I fly out tomorrow."

"Me, too, I ride up with you."

"You're flying out, too?"

"No, Hardy," Yolanda laughed, "I meant bed."

They walked to the elevator.

"What floor?"

"Your floor, Hardy."

They reached the sixth floor and Yolanda walked with him to his room.

"Okay, I will come in?" Yolanda said tentatively. "I need to use your bathroom."

Hardy sat at the edge of his bed as Yolanda appeared naked from the bathroom and walked toward him. "She was a real blonde," he thought.

"Let me help you," she said, unbuckling his belt and pulling off his pants.

"Now the shirt, Senor Hardy," she said, climbing onto the bed with a laugh.

He removed his shirt and moved up the bed toward her. She reached out and grabbed his erection, pulling him, laughing. Her blond hair fell about her shoulders; her breasts firm with nipples erect. She let out an audible sigh as he entered her. He listened to her quickened breath and cries of pleasure. His arms locked, holding himself above her, his pace quickened with each thrust.

"Faster Hardy, mas rapido!" She moaned, grasping him.

"El Beano Grande!" Yolanda cried out as the bed began to shake.

"What the hell was that?" Hardy said out of breath, rolling across the bed.

"That was beautiful," Yolanda cried.

"Not that!" Hardy exclaimed, "The shaking. It was a God damned earthquake."

They lay together, Hardy slowly gaining his breath. He reached out for the light, turning it on and off twice. "No God damned electricity. We're on the sixth floor with no fucking electricity. Jesus" he muttered. He swung his legs over the bed, stood up and walked to the window. "God damned fires down there. The floor started shaking again, violently, for about 10 seconds.

"Christ, I can hardly stand up," he said, falling back onto the bed. "We've got to get out!"

Pulling on his pants, he heard the approach of a helicopter. He walked to the window and watched as it climbed and hovered above the hotel roof. He looked down and saw the hotel entrance lights come alive along with the loud whine of generators.

"Good, we've got power. Get your things, Yolanda."

"I don't live here. I live out by the airport."

"Get dressed, we must get out, now!" Hardy exclaimed. "We'll take the stairs."

"Okay, I'll get dressed," Yolanda replied, "Un momento por favor."

Hardy felt the effects of the whiskey fade. He finished dressing and grabbed his suitcase. He remembered reading that a doorway was the safest place to be in a building during an earthquake. He moved to the bedroom door as Yolanda followed him with shoes on, buttoning her shirt. They reached the emergency exit, bounding down the stairs with hotel guests joining them at every level, running from the building with women screaming for help. The ground began to shake violently.

"Another earthquake," someone called out.

Hardy stood 100 yards away from the hotel and watched as the helicopter lifted off from a partially collapsed roof.

"What are they doing?" Hardy questioned a man he recognized from the front desk.

"They are rescuing Senor Howard Hughes," he replied, "our mystery guest. He has lived on the seventh and eighth floors since October. I don't think we will see him again, they will take him to the airport and he will leave Nicaragua as soon as it is possible, no longer a secret."

"A secret no more," Hardy said under his breath with a hopeless feeling as he watched the helicopter lights disappear toward the airport. He turned to speak with Yolanda and realized at that moment she was gone. He scanned the hotel grounds and saw a man pushing her into the back seat of an open top jeep. He had no time to react and was visibly shaken as he watched them drive off. "What in the hell?" he thought. He looked off to the north across Lake Managua and at the raging fires illuminating the night sky.

"Jesus," he said inaudibly, wondering what had just happened to Yolanda.

"Can I get a ride to the airport?" He called out to the man from the front desk.

"Fifty U.S. I take you," the man said.

"Vamanos," Hardy replied and followed the clerk to a Toyota pickup truck parked behind the hotel.

The road to the airport was empty of traffic. Buildings lay in ruin and more than a dozen fires burned out of control.

"That was once our fire station," the man said, pointing at a collapsed building, the nose of one truck poking out from the debris.

They arrived to a dark terminal building just past 2 o'clock.

"Gracias, senor," Hardy said handing the man a fifty dollar bill.

"De nada, senor," the man said. "Buena suerte."

Hardy raised his eyebrows and nodded his head in response as the man drove away. He sat on his bag in the dark. The terminal appeared empty and his flight wasn't scheduled to depart until 2 o'clock the following afternoon.

Hardy looked across the road and saw lights coming from a hotel that he had noticed the previous day on his way into Managua. He could hear the muffled hum of a generator as he picked up his bag and walked across the highway, careful to avoid the mound that was once a horse. Pretty soon there would be nothing to remove he thought, a fight between the buzzards and the daily traffic.

He walked into the hotel office and rang the handbell once. A dark haired man with a thick brush mustache opened the door behind the counter, rubbing his eyes.

"Si, senor?"

"Do you have a room available?"

"How many nights?"

"I don't know, it depends if my flight is cancelled," Hardy replied.

"Well, tonight then," the man said. "Maybe tomorrow. I know the airport was closed just after the earthquake. They have no electricity and the control tower lost windows. A captain in the Guardia informed me that the United States is sending troops and equipment from Panama tonight. When he left, as many as 20 trucks arrived at the airport and lit up the runway. I heard one jet take off."

"Si, Senor Howard Hughes escapa," Hardy said.

"Usted es un hombre con suerte," the man said, handing him a key. "The last room available. Welcome to Hotel Las Mercedes."

"Gracias, senor," Hardy replied, "Yes, lucky, lucky so far."

He took the key and followed the signs to room 33. The hotel was a series of single-story buildings covered with corrugated metal roofs. He saw no effects from the earthquake other than cracks in the cement walkway to his room. When he opened the door, he found a double bed, a night table, bureau, a small closet, and a bath with shower.

182

It was simple and clean. He barely lay out on the bed before he was sound asleep.

He awoke at first light to the sound of a plane landing. He dressed quickly and walked over to the terminal, looking for anyone who could provide information about his flight. Standing at the Taca Airline ticket counter, he watched as American and Nicaraguan military unloaded supplies from a C-130.

"Senor, there will be no flights in or out today." A young man in military fatigues said as he walked toward him. "All flights will continue tomorrow on schedule."

"Gracias," Hardy said, thinking he better get back to the hotel and reserve his room.

"Una cerveza, por favor," Hardy asked as he sat down at the hotel bar. He watched a young couple at the front desk, each with looks of disappointment, apparently having discovered there were no rooms available. They entered the bar and sat at a table next to him, depositing their bags in such a way to keep ownership.

"You just come from town?" Hardy asked.

" Yes," the woman said. "We were lucky to get out of our hotel alive."

"I left town last night about 1:30," Hardy said.

" All of the stores, restaurants, offices and houses within two miles of Avenida Central were either destroyed or severely damaged. Whole city blocks are roaring infernos with no water, no fire engines. Thousands are buried alive. As I said, we were lucky."

"I thought it was bad," Hardy said, "but didn't know how bad.

"Yes," the woman said, "we hope we can get the next plane out." Her companion was silent. He looked exhausted.

"I see you were over at the front desk," Hardy said.

"Yes, there are no rooms left," the woman's companion said.

"You are more than welcome to use my shower," Hardy said.

Before they could answer, he felt a tap on his right shoulder.

"El Beano, you are here!"

Hardy turned to see Yolanda smiling at him.

"What in hell, where did you come from? Where did you go? Who took you away last night?" he asked in quick succession.

"Oh, that. That was a friend. I'm so sorry I could not say goodbye, Hardy."

"I thought you had been kidnapped, or worse."

"What is this kidnapped?

" Carried away against your will..."

"Ahhh, secuestrar...No, just a mix-up, Hardy. I was hoping I would see you again."

"Well, here I am, waiting for my flight back to Miami. Why are you here?"

"I have a room here Hardy, would you like to see it?"

"Dos cervezas, por favor," he called out to the bartender "Here you go," he said handing her a beer, standing up from his seat. "Lead the way."

They walked to room 14, where Hardy found an exact replica of his room.

"This is the same setup as mine, closer to the bar."

He sat on the bed while Yolanda disappeared into the bathroom.

"Are you coming out naked?"

"Yes."

Hardy stripped off his clothes as the bathroom door opened. Yolanda walked toward him. They embraced, falling on the bed. Within minutes they were thrashing about, screwing each other as if there was no time left to waste. Yolanda gripped his shoulders and called out, "Fuck me, fuck me El Beano, fuck me," to his frantic rhythm with each thrust deeper and more forceful.

A loud banging on the door interrupted them in mid motion. Yolanda looked up at Hardy with alarm in her eyes, covering his mouth with her hand, holding her index finger to her lips.

"Who the hell is that?" Hardy whispered in her ear.

"Quickly, you must hide, my boyfriend's driver is here. I did not expect him this early!"

"Your what?" Hardy whispered in astonishment.

"Take your clothes, quickly," Yolanda whispered with panic in her voice. "Get in the closet."

"Just a minute, who is there?" Yolanda called out.

"Tomas."

"You are early Tomas, I am not ready."

Yolanda leaned her back against the closet door, buttoning her shirt, catching her breath, and exhaling in short spurts. Hardy stood naked in the closet, clutching his clothes to his chest, unable to move. He peered through the slanted louvers and watched the room briefly brighten as Yolanda opened the door.

"Buenas Tomas, por la manana."

"Si, Yolanda, buenos dias."

He listened to the door close and waited in silence. Slowly he opened the closet door, crept to the window and peered out the blinds. He watched Yolanda disappear behind the corner of the building, followed by a man wearing a pistol strapped to his waist.

"Jesus," he said in a whisper, exhaling. He dressed quickly, fumbling with the buttons on his shirt, peering out the room's window, casting glances up and down the walkway. He left the room walking in the opposite direction from Yolanda, the hair slightly rising on the back of his neck. He couldn't believe what had just happened. Men with guns, she was a crazy woman he thought. He returned to his room, stripped off his clothes and took a long hot shower.

It was early afternoon and he had nothing to do but wait until the following day. He wondered if he could get from Miami to New York and connect to a night flight out to Glasgow on Christmas Day. He sat at the bar filled with foreign refugees all waiting to get out on the next available flight. He felt unable to strike up a conversation with anyone as he sipped his beer. He thought about Dalcross and Darcy and about Yolanda. What had he been thinking? What had made him cheat on Darcy? He didn't know, near death experience, alcohol, earthquake, it didn't matter, Darcy would know. There was no excuse. He knew he wouldn't be able to keep it a secret. It would show in his eyes he thought, before a word could be spoken.

Part 8

Farewell

"Soraidh"

Chapter 32

"Darcy, is that you?

She heard his voice echo, "It's me Hardy, are you okay?

"I'm just fine," he said, relieved to hear her voice.

"I was so worried Hardy."

"I'm in Miami, I've booked a flight to Glasgow with a stopover in London. My flight arrives at 1 p.m. Tuesday. I'll tell you all about it when I get home. If you pick me up we can drive straight away to Dalcross."

"Of course I'll pick you up Hardy, I can't wait! What do you want me to pack?"

"My wool lined pants, a few warm shirts and sweaters and my kilt. Please call my parents, let them know I'm okay, I have to board now."

"Alright, I love you. I can't wait to see you!" she exclaimed.

He hung up the phone. I love you, too, he thought, realizing he forgot to say it. His guilt was heavy on his mind. He dreaded the future confession he knew would be forthcoming.

An icy mist covered the grounds of Dalcross Castle as the cold winter sun began to set across the Firth of Forth. Snow squalls marched across the fields as Hardy drove past the entrance gate and continued up the drive, stopping just past the front entrance. Snow clung to the castle roof and turrets and lay in furrows in the fields making a contrast with the gold winter grasses waving in the falling light. The long drive from Glasgow reminded Hardy of the unequalled beauty of Scotland.

From the tropical flowers and humid forests of Central America to the oft bleak, frozen tundra, gray skies and roaring winds of the Scottish winter, he reveled in the day's beauty with the gift of a cloudless blue sky and snowcapped mountains. Hardy was in his element. He was home and he couldn't wait to join his grandfather, his Uncle Gillies, Winwood, their two children, along with his mother and father, sister and brother, who had all traveled from different corners of the world to enjoy Christmas at Dalcross. Eliza greeted him at the door, jumping into his arms with a shriek.

"Well, look at you, Hardy MacBean!" she exclaimed standing back. "Long time no see, little brother."
His brother Gillies followed Eliza, giving him a bear hug.

"You've managed to bring him home safe and sound," Gillies said, extending his hand to Darcy. "It's wonderful to see you again."

"Yes," Eliza said. "What would we ever do without you?"

"Hardy will always return with or without me," Darcy replied. "Dalcross is forever in his blood, his compass."

They entered the great hall to see Grandfather Gillies sitting in front of a roaring fire, surrounded by Uncle Gillies, Aunt Winwood, Mary and William. Maggie played with her brother, helping him to construct a train from Lego's at the base of an immense Scots Pine covered with ornaments and burning wax tapers set in reflectors of polished tin.

"Well, it took you long enough!" Mary MacBean said when she saw Hardy appear at the door.

"What do you mean, Mum, I barely just landed.

"Not soon enough, Hardy, you've missed Christmas Day."

"Boxing Day must do! I'll fetch your presents, be right back."

"That can wait until after dinner, Hardy. Come say hello to Grumps immediately, you're all he can talk about."

"That is certainly true, Hardy," his father said, shaking Hardy's hand and giving Darcy an embrace.

"I hear you will soon be a practicing physician," he said, "We always did need a bright young doctor among us."

"Oh, William, leave her alone. First things first," Mary winked at Hardy.

Hardy registered his mother's statement with a pang of guilt, wondering how he would keep his indiscretion secret until he was back in Glasgow.

"It's time to eat," Winwood announced. "Everyone, please find your seat."

Three generations of MacBeans sat down in the great hall, ready to enjoy a Scottish highland meal with all the fixings, from roast leg of lamb to grilled salmon. Gillies IX sat between his grandfather and mother in an ancient high chair that had been used by most if not all of the MacBeans for more than 200 years. At two years old, he had a remarkable likeness to his grandfather, broad forehead, aquiline nose, large hands and feet, and a distinctly similar laugh.

"Four Gillies MacBeans at one table is quite a sight," Hardy exclaimed, raising his glass. "Who would have thought?"

"I, for one, never would," William said. "But it was the right thing to do, I mean the uninterrupted succession of it, and I know my son is fine with it. After all, there is a 26-year age difference."

"William, we all know I was a confirmed bachelor, never to have children," Gillies piped up. "At least ones I could acknowledge!"

"Gillies!" Winwood exclaimed.

"And it was with my blessing that my nephew received my name. But my darling wife convinced me that giving our son the name Gillies and the numeral nine after it was indeed a tradition that should be honored. Besides, I rather like having all these Gillies in the family. Now let us stand and toast our father, our patriarch, on this glorious Boxing Day. Let us give thanks for all that we have, and for our family gathered together this night. And let us give special thanks for keeping our Hardy from harm's way, as we will need him years hence.

May 1973 bring good health, joy and happiness to us all. Now let us raise a glass to our father, our grandfather, our patriarch, Gillies MacBean VII, and thank him for his continued strength and leadership of the MacBean family."

"Here, here," each voice said with glass raised in unison.

Hardy quickly left the hall to retrieve the presents, the dresses each wrapped in newspaper, a bottle of Nicaraguan rum and six coins in a leather pouch. Crème Brulee was served as Winwood set out a bottle of Grand Marnier and placed small dram glasses in front of each setting. Hardy circled the table, stopping at his mother's chair.

"Mum, this is for you. I love you. Merry Christmas," he said, putting the package down and kissing her on the cheek. He then placed a package in front of Winwood, Maggie and Eliza in succession, with a final stop at Darcy's chair.

"I hope you like this, sweetheart."

Darcy looked up and noticed something different in Hardy's expression, something she had never seen before, something odd she thought.

"This is for you, Grumps," placing the bottle on the table. I discovered this rum on the east coast of Nicaragua, in a town called Rama on my way to Bluefields."

"Should I take a dram Hardy?"

"Of course, Grumps, "but first let me recite your favorite Bobby Burns poem, *Bottle and a Friend*."

> *Here's a bottle and honest friend*
> *What wad ye wish for mair, man?*
> *What kens, before his life may end,*
> *What his share may be o' care, man?*
> *Then catch the moments as they fly,*
> *And use them as ye ought, man;*
> *Believe me, happiness is shy,*
> *And comes no ay when sought, man!*

The table erupted in cheers and Hardy took an exaggerated bow.

"That was quite tosh, Hardy, now pour me some of that rum, lad, and pour every dram that's a calling," his grandfather commanded. He then stood and looked around the table, raising his prolific bushy eyebrows, and with the words "drinkin drams" he began to recite:

> *He ance was holy*
> *An' melancholy,*
> *Till he found the folly*
> *O singin' psalms*
> *He's now red's a rose*
> *And there's pimples on his nose*
> *And in size it daily grows*
> *By drinkin drams.*

Once more the table erupted in cheers while Grandfather Gillies raised his hand motioning for silence. In his deep bass voice he began to sing *Scotland the Brave* with Gillies, William, Hardy and his brother all standing and joining in harmony.

"Hark when the night is falling,"
"Hear! Hear the pipes are calling,"
Loudly and proudly calling,
Down thro' the glen.
There where the hills are sleeping,
Now feel the blood a-leaping,
High as the spirits of the old Highland men.

Towering in gallant fame,
Scotland my mountain hame,
High may your proud standards gloriously wave,
Land of my high endeavor,
Land of the shining river,
Land of my heart for ever,
Scotland the brave.

High in the misty Highlands,
Out by the purple islands,
Brave are the hearts that beat
Beneath Scottish skies.
Wild are the winds to meet you,
Staunch are the friends that greet you,
Kind as the love that shines
from fair maidens' eyes."

"Far off in sunlit places,
Sad are the Scottish faces,
Yearning to feel the kiss
Of sweet Scottish rain.
Where tropic skies are beaming,
Love sets the heart a-dreaming,
Longing and dreaming for the homeland again."

The last words sung reverberated throughout the hall and the table fell silent.

Grandfather Gillies raised his dram glass and boomed, "Kinchyle", with the family standing, each raising their glass and repeating twice again, "Kinchyle! Kinchyle!"

"Alright ladies," William said, "It's time you opened your presents."

"Marvelous, Hardy, beautiful!" Mary exclaimed opening her present, "We should put on a fashion show!"

"We can turn up the heat and have a showing tomorrow!" Winwood exclaimed. "Don't you love your dress, Maggie?" Maggie smiled broadly holding her dress by the shoulders with its high neck tucked under her chin.

"Fantastic!" Eliza chimed in.

Darcy looked at all the dresses and knew Hardy had made a special effort. She gave him a kiss and again saw an odd expression come over his face.

"There's more!" Hardy exclaimed. "I have gifts for the men and young Gillies IX! When I visited the east coast of Nicaragua, I met a man who was married to a Rama Indian princess. The princess had a dowry of pre-Columbian coins of which I managed to buy a few. You will see that each is embossed with the Roman Emperor Hadrian's name. Although I haven't had time to do research, I thought you might enjoy them notwithstanding. They were minted in the second century, when Hadrian's Wall was built to separate the Romans from the barbarian tribes in the Scottish Lowlands. And as we all know, Scots didn't emigrate from Ireland for at least another two centuries. But I think we were definitely there in spirit, if not perhaps in some distant lineage. This one is for Grumps," placing the coin in his grandfather's open hand. "And this one for little Gillies IX, and this one for Uncle Gillies," handing them both to his uncle. "This one is for you, Pop, and this the last, is for you, my big brother," holding it up and handing it to Gillies. "We now each have a coin, we MacBean men do, to be handed down to the sons of MacBeans in perpetuity, along with a story of how the coins came to be, and soon to become part of the MacBean historical lore. With that I give you leave to your imagination. But if by chance there are no male stirpes, then I would regard the girls most worthy!"

The women shrieked with laughter, with Mary the loudest.

"Hardy, you are a wicked boy!" Mary said, "It's time for us to clear the table and clean up. Do you think the MacBean male stirpes are worthy enough to join in?"

"I think we can handle that," Hardy laughed.

He opened the door to his old room. Moonlight poured through the turret window marking a pattern of squares on the floor.

"It's so nice to be back in our room, Hardy, I've missed you so much."

"Yes, it has been a long time. Quick, into bed with you and warm
194

it up, I'm not used to this cold."

"At your service," Darcy laughed. "Orders, always orders!"

She moved into his arms, shivering.

"I love you, Hardy."

"I love you, too, sweetie. I'm so bloody tired."

"Is that what's wrong?"

"What do you mean, wrong with me?"

"You seem a bit off."

"I'm okay. A long trip that was full of hazard. I'm just tired, goodnight sweetie, sweet dreams."

He turned off the light and faced away, gathering the covers over his shoulder, closing his eyes. Sleep seemed evasive as his mind raced, thinking about Central America.

A loud knock on the bedroom door woke Hardy from a deep sleep.

"Yes?"

"Hardy," William said standing outside the door, "you best get your clothes on and come down. I'll wait for you in the kitchen."

"Okay, Pop, I'll be right down," Hardy replied, yawning.

"What's going on?" Darcy asked, pulling her knees into the warm spot Hardy left when he climbed from the bed.

"I don't know. Pop sounded serious. I hope Mum is okay."

"I'll be down in a minute," Darcy said.

"No, you stay in bed, it's early. I'll bring you some tea. Thanks for bringing my lined pants. Frost's on the window this morning."

"All that heavy breathing, Hardy."

He descended the stairs and walked out to the kitchen.

Winwood sat with Uncle Gillies, her eyes were red and she burst into tears when Hardy appeared in the kitchen door.

"Oh, Hardy, Grumps is gone."

Hardy looked over at his father who was pacing the kitchen floor in a box-like pattern. His uncle wiped away a tear.

"You couldn't ask for a better way," Gillies said. "Eighty-eight, with his whole family here. You'd think he'd planned it."

Hardy felt a wave of emotion flow over him. Tears fell in streams down his face.

"He was just fine last night," he said, choking back his tears. He looked at his father.

"You want to go up?" William asked.

Hardy wiped away his tears, and slowly came to the realization that Grumps was gone from this life and never coming back. The past 10 years of memories seemed a blur.

"I guess so, pop."

"Do you want me to come?"

"No, I would like to sit with him alone, if I might."

"Okay then." His father answered.

Hardy shuffled to the kitchen table. His uncle stood up and embraced him.

"It's okay, Hardy, it's never a good time, he was ready," Winwood said hugging him, grasping his face in her hands. "He waited for you. You were his breagha mic-mac. He loved you best of all," she said. "The days you sat with him along the stone butts, waiting for the first of the grouse to come in, and the hours you stood by him fishing the Nairn for the next record salmon that he would throw on the kitchen counter with glee. Go on up. Take as long as you need to say goodbye."

He turned and left the kitchen. Reaching the stairs, his feet felt like cement. He climbed slowly to the second floor landing, stopping at the first door. He looked at the door, hesitated and then opened it.

Lu-Lu laid alongside him; lifting her head up when Hardy entered the room, and then resting it back on her masters lifeless leg with a profound exhale passing through her nose like a whistle. His grandfather lay as if he were sleeping. Hardy bent down and kissed his forehead. It felt cold and damp to his lips with a faint taste of salt. His grandfather gave off a mixture of smells; smells Hardy remembered from their last embrace, from every past embrace, a sweet smell he could never identify. It was just Grumps, it was the smell of Grumps. He slowly sat down on the bed, looking out the window at the gray morning sky, and then back to his grandfather's face. The tears flowed uncontrolably. He wondered if he had had pain in death, if he was dreaming of his brave Scotland of which he sang with such wonderful fervor the night before, the last night of his remarkable life. Was the cry "Kinchyle" his last will to stand with his namesake, his kinsmen, in the murderous Culloden defeat? Was it his last testament in life to hear the battle cry before rushing into the madness of war? Or was it his last connection to this life before he joined his fathers before him and his long departed wife Margaret? He knew that he loved this man that lay before him like no other. He reached out and squeezed his grandfather's hand twice, and held it for a moment. "Goodbye, my wonderful grandfather," he whispered, "May I see you again." With that he stood up, and quietly left the room, closing the door slowly until he heard the lever click. He descended the stairs into the great hall and walked directly out the front entrance, breathing the cold winters' air deep into his lungs, looking ahead, blinded by his tears.

The sky had turned blue and the morning sun glistened off the frost collected on the bushes and trees. "Heavy dew," he could hear his grandfather say as the mist settled on the fields. He headed toward the barn, remembering him, cane in hand, telling him to slow down and wait for his poor old grandfather. He walked the forest for hours, heading home when the sun climbed high above.

"There you are," Darcy exclaimed as she met him halfway up from the barn. "Are you okay, Hardy?"

"I'm okay. We'll need to stick around and give Grumps a grand sendoff."

"I know. I'm so sorry, Hardy. Of course we'll stay. I'll call the hospital and let them know. I'm sure they won't mind. I've never missed a day."

"Thanks, sweetie," he said clasping his hand in hers. "I would like you to be here. He was as much your grandfather as he was mine."

"I know he was very special to you," she replied, "He was to me. It will be a different Dalcross without him. But we have Gillies and Winwood to come back to. I love Maggie, and little Gillies has grown so."

"He certainly has. He looks a lot like him."

"Who else could he look like?" she said, laughing, hoping to cheer him. "He's a little Grumps of course! Of course!"

"I've made the arrangements," William said, as Hardy walked into the kitchen. "Your uncle is undone over your grandfather, as am I, "But they have lived their whole lives together.

"I know, Pop."

198

"I've contacted every chief in the Chattan Confederation, except Macpherson. He's arriving back from Edinburgh tomorrow. Winwood says a possible count with all 12 chiefs, limited family and septs could exceed 300. We will all need to pitch in and give your grandfather a sendoff befitting the MacBean of MacBean. Winwood has begun to order food and spirits, Uncle Gillies is preparing pigs and lambs for roasting, and I hired a tent large enough to accommodate the guests."

"Tell me about your trip Hardy, we were very worried about you. The American Consulate is in ruins. We called your Glasgow office to find out where you were and they told us what we already knew, and they had no idea where you were. We were at our wits end when Darcy called us with the news you were on your way home."

"Yes, it was good to hear Darcy's voice. The earthquake caused tremendous, unbelievable destruction. I don't know if the lumber and logs I bought will ever be delivered. I visited two sawmills, one in Granada and one in Bluefields. I was on my way to another mill in the mountains when we ran into armed confrontation between Somoza's troops and the rebels. I saw at least two soldiers shot down. I never saw the rebels. We got the hell out of there as quickly as possible and returned to Managua. And then the earthquake came the following morning about 12:30. I haven't spoken with the man I hired and I couldn't get in touch with him before I flew out. I don't know if he is alive or not. I think his house was in the epicenter of the earthquake along the lake. Hopefully, he'll telex the office soon."

"From what I understand the quake damage was localized to Managua," William said. "If you want me to find out about your man, I will call Washington and have them relay the information to our people and find out what happened to him."

"I would appreciate that. His name is Herman Vogel. I'll give you his address."

"Consider it as good as done," William said.

"Thanks, Pop, I appreciate it."

"Tell me more about this armed conflict."

"Wrong place, wrong time. Somoza's Guardia Nacional shooting up the place. Somoza is a tyrant."

"Yes, he is, but the State Department says he's *our* tyrant."

"Most Nicaraguans believe America is the power behind Somoza."

"I'm sure they do, Hardy, but it isn't as simple as that. The Somoza family has done the bidding of the U.S. government for more than 35 years. The powers that be have no wish to abandon Somoza as long as he's helpful and does what he's told. He's a West Point graduate and I've been told he speaks English better than he does Spanish. His son went to Harvard."

"I don't think you understand," Hardy said, his anger noticeable. "Where he went to school, where his son went to school has very little to do with what is happening in Nicaragua. Innocent men and boys are being imprisoned and murdered by Somoza's Guardia Nacional. He's killing the poor before they can join the rebels. But the rebels are a growing force and the talk of revolution and freedom is widespread throughout the country between wealthy and poor alike."

"Maybe so, but he has might on his side."

"Might?" Hardy said with disgust. "That doesn't make it right. Just look at Vietnam, for God's sake, 12 years of war for nothing, thousands of American men shipped back in wooden boxes. Don't you think the United States would have been better off building schools and feeding the poor? The United States will no more win the war in Vietnam than it will keep Somoza in power. The democratic principles espoused by the United States government are simply what those in power want the American public to believe. In the history of Nicaragua, Honduras, Guatemala and El Salvador, the United States government is complicit in the killing of thousands of defenseless citizens."

William listened to his son and noticed his reasoning had become more spirited and hardened since the last time they had spoken about war and the United States.

"I know you don't agree with what I do, Hardy, and I know that might isn't always right, but I'd like to think that my work makes the world a better place. The good that we do isn't necessarily recognized by the general public, but trust me, there are good reasons for what we do to protect our way of life."

"Protect our way of life," Hardy said angrily. "How can you say that when the Ohio National Guard shoots 14 unarmed students at Kent State? They killed four students for Christ sakes, four *innocent* students, and they got away with it. Jesus, Pop, a better place? A country that claims it's the greatest democracy in the world? I made the right decision when I gave up my passport." Hardy turned and abruptly left the kitchen.

The morning's first light was pink. Hardy lay in bed watching the sky change to gray. He remembered that it would be mid February before the morning sun would strike his turret window, flooding his room with blinding light on its journey north. Grumps funeral was today, and less than a week since he had died. Winwood was now expecting 350 to 400 clansmen and women, including the whole of Dalcross village of 27.

Uncle Gillies butchered a half dozen lambs and brought two 25-gallon casks of his aged Dalcross dark ale from the cellar. Hardy would travel to Inverness to collect four cases of Glen Livet Malt Whiskey and five cases of Drappier Pinot Noir rose champagne, his grandfather's favorites.

"Darcy, time to get up. Do you want to ride to Inverness with me?"

"No thanks, I need to stay and help Winwood."

"Okay, I'll see you when I get back."

Hardy drove the 11 miles to Inverness, remembering the trips he made to the Royal Highland Hotel delivering lamb and the occasional catch of salmon. He retraced his old route onto Church Street and was startled when he passed by an empty lot that had once held Stella's boarding house. He thought about the first time he laid his eyes on Darcy. She was the love of his life he thought. He would need to tell her today. He had been unable to find the courage, but now he was ready. He couldn't live a lie with the woman that he loved.

His kilt and military jacket lay out on the bed. He wondered where Darcy was. He began to remove his clothes, hearing the pipers in the courtyard warming their instruments to a stable pitch, adjusting their drones and chanter notes. Chills ran the length of his body as one piper played seven bars of *Scotland the Brave*. He looked down on the courtyard and watched a flurry of tartans gathering together three abreast with his brother in the lead.

"God damn," he thought, "Grumps would've enjoyed this."

"There you are," Darcy exclaimed, opening the door.

"Where have you been?" he asked.

"Last minute touches. Your grandfather's casket was brought into the tent and we decorated it with flowers. The pipe and drums are here, too, but I guess you heard them."

"Yes, I did. I need to talk with you about my trip,"

"What about,"

"There is no easy way to say this Darcy, I cheated on you. I'm so sorry, I didn't think."

"What do you mean you cheated on me? You mean you slept with another woman?"

"Yes."

Darcy's face screwed up with anguish, her eyes closed, her mouth silently repeating, "Damn, damn."

"For god's sakes Hardy, you don't want me anymore?"

"I want you more than ever. I know you may leave me, but I couldn't live with you any longer without telling you."

"Is that why we haven't made love since you came home?"

"Yes. I feel so guilty Darcy."

Darcy wiped away a single tear running down her face.

"God damn you, Hardy MacBean! You think you're going to get rid of me that easy? Cause you won't. I still love you, Hardy. Sometimes I think you forget how we started out. I wasn't exactly the kind of girl you would bring home to the family, was I? You loved me, and you accepted me, and I've loved you ever since. You overlooked my past then and I'm going to overlook yours now. Do you understand me, Hardy? Do you?"

"I guess so, I just didn't think you would forgive me."

"Oh, you didn't, did you? You came home to me Hardy, I'm yours and I'm god damned horny. I'd like to know what you're going to do about that?"

He watched Darcy as she unbuttoned her shirt, her breasts spilling out as she unclipped her bra. He dropped his boxers, moving to her side, caressing her face, kissing her deeply with his tongue. She pulled him to the bed and pushed him down, and then mounted him, her legs astride, guiding him, slowly gaining a rhythmic pace, placing her hands on his chest with her eyes closed and hips swaying.

"You're mine, Hardy, you're god damn mine," she gasped; bringing herself to the climax she desperately needed.

Hardy and Darcy descended the stairs into the great hall. Winwood was supervising the placement of food and drink, and Gillies was giving last minute instructions to the bartenders.

"I want you to pay special attention, lads," he said. "I don't want a disaster on my hands. If you think anyone has had too much to drink, they probably have. Cut em off and send em to me if they cause trouble. I'll have no collie shangles here today. This is my father's day in heaven and I want it to be full of good remembrance. No guttered Highlander is going to ruin it." He turned to see Hardy and Darcy and called out to them, "Hello kids, the tent's filling fast. We're all sitting in the first row. Mary, William and Eliza waited for you but they've taken their seats. We'll be along with the kids as soon as your brother and his pipers begin to play."

They sat in the first row looking beyond the casket, watching his brother lead a cowerson of pipers and half dozen drummers, all representing the 12 clans of the Chattan Confederation. He could hear the music's declared cadence from the sound of the gravel beneath their feet as the band marched up the drive toward them. Gillies blew through his bagpipe's mouthpiece, inflating the bag, quickly striking it with his right hand and then squeezed it with his left arm. His fingers engaged the chanter; his pipes resonated with a piercing wail, signaling to the others who then joined with the skirl of 18 additional bagpipes. Kilts swinging, backs straight, his grandfather's beloved *Scotland the Brave* came alive along with a sharp rata tat-tat from the drums. The band marched three abreast in eight rows to a measured and abrupt halt adjacent to the casket, leaving silence in the air reigning absolute. Uncle Gillies stood up and moved to the front of the casket.

"As you may know, our father was a good Presbyterian, who as moderator of the General Assembly of the Church of Scotland was instrumental in the ordination of the first woman elder in 1966. It was his hope that the assembly would embrace women to be fully ordained ministers of word and sacraments. It is my sincere privilege to welcome Reverend Catherine McEwen, one of the first women to be ordained and a longtime friend of our family. The Reverend is the wife of my father's oldest and dearest friend, Alexander McEwen. Together they hunted the moors and all the guid pubs from here to Aberdeen, but don't tell that to the reverend, please!"

The crowd roared with laughter and applause as Catherine McEwen stood and waved to the crowd, making her way to the casket.

"Good afternoon," she began. "I would like you all to know that there were many times that I joined Gillies and Alex in their quest for the perfect single-malt, and I must confess we found quite a few!"

Again the crowd roared, with a few men standing, swinging their fists in the air in cheerful agreement.

"Gillies hasn't been to church much in the past few years," she continued, "but his spirit was always present with us. We did discuss his wishes for this day's eventuality and he asked me to read two poems that he felt would best describe his parting thoughts. He wanted no scripture, no prayer, and above all, no sadness. He wanted you all to enjoy yourselves in the celebration of a life well lived and enjoy the wonderful food and spirits he hoped his sons would provide. And with that, let us begin.

I'd like the memory of me to be a happy one.
I'd like to leave an afterglow of smiles when my life is done.
I'd like to leave an echo whispering softly across the waves,
Of happy times and laughing times and bright and sunny days.
I'd like the tears of those who grieve, to dry before the sun;
Of happy memories that I leave when my life is done."

The reverend waited a moment, tapped her foot once and then cleared her throat.

"One more poem for which Gillies chose to share with you all, and he forbid me to dally, because he wanted you to enjoy yourselves altogether and toast in his memory.

Don't grieve for me, for now I'm free
I'm following paths God made for me
I took his hand, I heard him call
Then turned, and bid farewell to all
I could na stay another day
To laugh, to love, to sing, to play
Tasks left undone must stay that way

206

I found my peace…at the close of play
And if my parting leaves a void
Then fill it with remembered joy
A friendship shared, a laugh, a kiss
Ah yes, these things I too will miss.
Perhaps my time seemed all too brief
Please don't lengthen it now with grief
Lift up your hearts and share with me,
God wants me now…. He set me free.

The tent was silent as Catherine looked over the crowd.

"Your presence here today speaks volumes about the love you had for Gillies MacBean. It is rare for such a multitude of friends to gather together to pay their last respects. Gillies had a saying to anyone who believed him or herself lacking in friendship, and it was simply that if you could count your friends on one hand, you were indeed a fortunate man. And by this I think he meant that each friend was precious and to fill one's hand was quite extraordinary. As I look out and see a host of hands, I realize more than ever that Gillies MacBean treated each man, each woman, and each child with equal respect, bringing hope and often joy to those who needed it most. He was a man who stood up for the downtrodden and cared deeply for his clansmen and his country. Today we say farewell and goodbye to Gillies MacBean, the MacBean of MacBean, who in his 88 years has been a good steward of Dalcross, a good father and grandfather to his children and grandchildren, a good friend to many, and always true to his word. I raise my voice and call out to him in his mother's Gaidhlig tongue, Mar sin Leibh!"

Four hundred and thirty-two men, woman and children, each

wearing their clan tartan, stood in a mass of color and repeated in unison, "Mar sin Leibh!"

Gillies walked to the casket as the reverend returned to her seat.

"I would like you all to remain standing and join together in song. My nephew Gillies is going to play a tune he adapted to the bagpipes, which became my father's favorite. You will find the words on the back of the memorial program. As you know, my father was a true Jacobite who yearned for the day our country would be free and it was his hope this song would become our national anthem. He never wavered in his want for Scotland's independence, and as many of you know, he was keen in the history of our bonnie land. This melody commemorates the Battle of Bannockburn, one of the most decisive battles fought for Scottish independence. Let us all now sing "Flower of Scotland".

OH Flower of Scotland
When will we see
Your like again
That fought and died for
Your wee bit Hill and Glen
And stood against him
Proud Edward's Army
And sent him homeward
Tae think again.

The hills are bare now
And autumn leaves lie thick and still
O'er land that is lost now
Which those so dearly held
And stood against him
Proud Edward's army
And sent him homeward
Tae think again

Those days are passed now
And in the past they must remain
But we can still rise now
And be the nation again
And stood against him
Proud Edward's army
And sent him homeward
Tae think again

Eleven Clan Chattan Chiefs walked forward and stood in front of the casket. Each in succession came to attention and saluted Gillies MacBean VIII, recognizing him as the MacBean clan chief, the MacBean of MacBean.

Part 9

Revolution

Chapter 33

Hardy looked up from his desk when the clacking sound of the teletypewriter came alive with its banging keystrokes and ringing bell. He walked over to the telex and watched as the message unfolded, still marveling at the technology that had been around for so many years but new to the Mackenzie office.

0594 EST

VIA WUI

MAC W

TO: MACKENZIE LUMBER   ATTENTION: HARDY MACBEAN

FROM: H.VOGEL   SUBJECT: SHIPMENT LOGS/LUMBER

DATE: JANUARY 25, 1973   PAGES: (INCLUDING THIS ONE) 4

GREETINGS FROM NICARAGUA.

His heart skipped a beat. Herman! God, it was Herman! He held his breath.

The clatter of the telex keys filled the room. He tore the bottom of the first page away as it folded over the top of the machine and began to read answers to many of the questions he had since leaving the ruins and desperate madness of Managua a month before.

FAMILY ALL OK. TELEX UP AND RUNNING. PHONE SERVICE REPAIRED. HOUSE DEMOLISHED.   LUMBR/ LOGS SHIPPED RAMA/BLUEFIELDS.

MOVED FAMILY TO BROTHER FREDERICK/GRANADA. WILL REBUILD.

BEST REGARDS HERMAN.

Hardy scanned the next three pages consisting of packing lists, Bills of Lading and shipping schedules.

ETD: 15.02.1973 MAMENIC LINE BARGE SERVICE/ BLUEFIELDS-HOUSTON

ETA: 22.02.1973 HOUSTON

ETD: 01.03.1973 HOUSTON-GLASGOW VESSEL MV MONTEREY RA0102

ETA: 17.03.1973 GLASGOW

IRREVOCABLE LETTER OF CREDIT/BANCO DE NICARAGUA

The lumber would arrive in two months, he thought, just in time for his birthday and Darcy's graduation. He set a new tape and began typing.

HERMAN, GREAT YOUR MESSAGE.

RELEASE LC AGAINST ON BOARD DOCUMENTS.

LET US KNOW WHAT WE CAN DO. RELIEVED YOU AND LOVED ONES SAFE. LOOK FORWARD TO ARRIVAL/FUTURE BUSINESS.

BEST REGARDS TO YOU AND FAMILY.

HARDY.

He leaned back in his chair, activated the tape and watched the machine burst into action, relieved that the lumber and logs were on the way. He reached for the phone and called Darcy.

"Hello, Darcy Nicholson speaking."

"When do you get off? It's time to celebrate."

"I'm glad you called, I get off early today, at six."

"Great, I'll pick you up and we'll go out."

"What's the occasion?"

"I've just heard from Nicaragua, Herman and his family are safe and the lumber is on the way!"

"That's wonderful, Hardy. I'll be out front, ten minutes."

"Okay, we're going to Sloans. They have a band tonight."

Hardy drove up to the hospital entrance. It was cold and snowing. Darcy's face lit up with a smile when she saw the car approach.

"Jesus, Hardy, it's so cold," she said opening the passenger door.

"We'll have some hot food and we'll dance. That should warm you up."

"Sounds terrific!"

They settled into a booth and ordered the sea bass and a bottle of Drappier Pinot Noir rose champagne.

"Darcy, if the lumber is good I will need to fly to Nicaragua again."

"I know that Hardy."

"Maybe I could take you with me next time.

"Maybe, I'd like that."

"Good, I'll speak with Mackenzie about it."

They danced until midnight, drove home and crawled into bed.

"Hardy?" Darcy asked, "Will you marry me?"

He looked at her, the streetlight outside the bedroom window illuminating her face. Moments of silence seemed like minutes. He pulled away and watched as her lower lip began to tremble. He always thought it was his job to ask, but never felt the time was right.

"Is that the champagne talking Darcy? He said breaking the silence. "No one has ever asked me that question before."

There was more silence. Darcy's eye's widened.

"Okay, okay sweetie, I will marry you!" he exclaimed.

"You bugger! You sure waited long enough Hardy MacBean!"

She leaned back and poked him in the solar plexus, briefly knocking the wind out of him.

"But I'm your bugger, yours forever! He said catching his breath. "When do you want to get married anyway?"

"I don't know, Hardy, how about this summer, when it's warm?"

"That will give us enough time to make plans, I'll call up Uncle Gillies and see if we can have Dalcross. We could pretty much fill it up. You'll need to invite your father, your brother and his family."

"I know, but I'm not sure my father will come."

"That's too bad, his loss. We'll have your brother walk you down the aisle. How about early September, we could travel to Nicaragua for our honeymoon."

"You mean travel for business, Hardy, I know you."

"Well, mostly honeymoon, what do you say?"

"I love you, Hardy. Anywhere, anytime you want."

They lay in each other's arms and Hardy listened to her fall off to sleep.

Chapter 34

"First time to Nicaragua?" the woman asked with a heavy accent. Darcy turned away from the window as the jet began to descend, waiting for the smell of pesticide spray.

"This is my second trip. My first was a couple years back during my honeymoon. It rained every day.

"What month was that?" the woman asked.

"The end of September, early October," she replied.

"You will like it better in February. Hot days and cool nights. A lot has happened in two years," the woman said. "Do you know?"

" Know what?" Darcy asked.

"There has been much trouble since the kidnapping and the Sandinista declaration," the woman said. "Somoza is furious. They held his family and the ambassador from Chile, among others. He had to pay them two million American dollars in ransom, let them make their manifesto declaration on the radio and release 14 of their comrades from jail. He gave them free passage through the streets of Managua, then flew them to Cuba and to freedom."

"The nica's cheered them on their way to the airport. Somoza's government was humiliated."

"Why are you coming to Nicaragua," Darcy asked.

"I am coming to see my mother, she is very ill. I immigrated to the United States five years ago with my American boyfriend. I opened a beauty shop last year and tried to get my mother to come live with us. But she will not come to Miami, so I must come here."

"I'm sorry about your mother. I'm meeting my husband for a vacation."

"I hope you have a safe visit. I do not know where safe is in Nicaragua today, so be careful."

"I'm sure my husband has it all planned out."

"I hope he does," she said as the jet touched down.

Hardy stood behind a rope separating the waiting area from the customs desk. Darcy looked up and could see him smile as her passport was stamped.

"Welcome to Nicaragua," the customs clerk said. "Enjoy your stay."

"Gracias," she said, trying out what little Spanish she knew. She walked through the open door into Hardy's arms.

"God, I've missed you sweetie, let's get your bag."

Hardy guided her to the luggage area. They claimed her bag and then walked to a small red two-door Toyota Corolla.

"We've got air conditioning," Hardy said, getting into the driver's seat. "It's rather hot here, but a nice change from the gray skies and cold weather of Glasgow."

"Where are we headed sweetie?"

"We're off to Granada. Herman's brother has found us a little 25-foot sloop. From his description it has a cabin with two births, a galley, a toilet and enough room in the cockpit for us to lie under an awning. It was brought down from Miami about five years ago by barge and then motored up the San Juan River to San Carlos. We're going to sail the Solentinames, an archipelago of more than 30 Islands. We'll also visit San Carlos."

"That sounds wonderful Hardy, I can't wait!"

"We're off then!" Hardy exclaimed as he drove the car away from

215

the airport and headed toward Granada.

"Buenas tardes! Senor Hardy y Senora Darcy," Avira exclaimed as she met them in the courtyard..

"Your lake is so beautiful, magical!" Darcy exclaimed looking out from the porch across to the islands. "I can't believe Hardy is taking me sailing, a big surprise!"

"La bienvenida a nuestro pequeno rancho, Senora MacBean," Frederick said as he appeared from the house and walked onto the porch.

"Pequeno rancho? I think that means small," Darcy replied.

"Not very," Hardy joined in. "But thank you so much, Frederick, great to be back here."

"Come in, come in," Frederick motioned with outstretched hands. Tell me, how is my brother and my daughters doing in Managua?"

"They are all well, Frederick, but you know that, you speak with them every day. Your brother's new house is beautiful, built up high with a view the lake."

"Yes, steel from America and reinforced concrete, Somoza concrete, and the seismic specifications exceed those that were used to build the Hotel Inter-Continental, certainly a big change from our father's old house. My brother tells me it will withstand a magnitude seven. Have you decided where you are going to sail?"

"The Solentiname Islands, and I thought we would also visit San Carlos.

"Certainly a great adventure, But who will sail?"

"Hardy never told you about sailing the North Sea and the New England coast?"

"First I've heard of it Senora Darcy. Hardy hasn't told me about his sailing days, but I assumed he knew how, or at least would learn quickly," Frederick laughed.

"He learned to sail with his American grandfather off the New England coast. He also attended school in Scotland and sailed the North Sea," Darcy explained.

"I didn't know about your American grandfather Hardy. Is he near Boston?"

"Not far away, my brother runs an offshore lobster vessel out of New Bedford.

"Where is this New Bedford?" Frederick asked.

"About 50 miles south of Boston."

"What size is your brother's boat?"

"100 feet. One hundred sixty gross tons."

"And how far out does he go?"

"They sail out anywhere from 25 to 100 miles, depending on the weather."

"Let's go down and see your little sloop," Avira said motioning to her husband.

"Okay, let's go," Frederick agreed getting up from his chair.

"They brought her today! It is a beautiful sight under sail. Ramon stocked your cooler with ice and drinks and supplied fresh baked bread for your voyage. He also filled the fuel and water tanks."

"I guess now is as good a time as any to take inventory," Hardy said, "What's her name?"

"*Mar Dulce*," Avira said. "It means Sweet Sea."

"A fitting name," Hardy said. "A freshwater sea!"

They followed Frederick and Avira down a long dirt road to the lake where they reached a small open roofed structure built on peers over the water. A 200-foot dock extended into the lake with a bright red sloop at the end, bow heading out.

"My God, Darcy, it's a bloody Nordic Folkboat, a blue water cruiser. Isn't she beautiful? Two of them sailed in the first Singlehanded Transatlantic Race a few years back. We're going to have a blast Darcy!"

"I hope so," she said as they walked down the dock to the boat.

"Let's get our gear stowed away."

Hardy dropped their bags in the boat's cockpit.

"Frederick! You didn't just get us any boat, you got us the famous Folkboat! I've always wanted to sail one. They're quite a popular racer in the UK."

"My friend says it is the fastest sailing boat on all of Lago de Granada," Frederick said walking toward the boat.

"She is quite beautiful," Darcy exclaimed, climbing aboard.

"Everything seems to be ship shape here, we'll just hoist sail and cast off if you don't mind."

"No, we don't mind, don't forget to give Father Ernesto my letter of introduction when you reach Mancarron Island. He will feed you and give you a place to sleep," Frederick said. "The charts are down below. You can't miss Mancarron, it's the largest one of them all."

"I will, Frederick. See you and Avira next week and thanks again for everything," Hardy said, shaking Frederick's hand.

They watched as Hardy raised the mainsail and then untied the stern line from the dock.

"Adios amigos," Hardy said with a big grin as the western breeze filled the mainsail.

"Adios, and have a great sail," Frederick and Avira called out.

The boathouse and hacienda beyond faded in the distance as Hardy set the jib and barked orders at Darcy to watch the mainsail and hold the tiller steady.

"Yes sir, captain, all under control."

Darcy's face beamed, ecstatic to be of help to her husband while keeping the sloop dead east by compass. Hardy pulled in the main sheet, letting the jib cup the wind as he placed his hand on the tiller, pushing away and bringing the boat onto port tack.

"Why don't you take over," Darcy said laughing.

"Thanks, sweetie, I just did."

Darcy moved to the companionway, sitting against the cabin trunk out of the wind. The breeze freshened, increasing the boat's speed, sending spray up from the bow.

"First time I ever tasted fresh water sailing a boat," Hardy said, wiping the spray from his eyes. The sun was hot in a cloudless blue sky as Darcy lay out on cushions.

"I guess no one can see us now," she said looking back at the shore and then out to the islands.

She began to remove her clothes and glanced back at Hardy, as he looked on, the red color of her hair becoming all the more pronounced against her porcelain white skin.

"Naked as a jaybird you are Darcy. Your skin is going to turn beet red if you're not careful. What are you trying to do, steer me off course?"

"It's been a while, Hardy."

"What do you want me to do about it?"

"What do you think?"

219

He looked up at the mainsail and let it out just enough to level the boat, then tied the tiller off, setting course for the islands.

"Here?" he asked.

"Yes, here, with the wind and the sun."

He moved forward and stood looking down at her, holding the grab rail running along the cabin roof. She unbuckled his belt and pulled his pants to the deck. He looked off the stern as her lips and tongue enveloped his senses.

"I'd say you're ready, Mr. Hardy MacBean!"

"Come on, Darcy, let's go."

"What, and leave the cockpit?" She asked with a laugh.

"Come on, Darcy, let's go," he repeated, clutching her hand, pulling her after him, disappearing below the deck as the *Mar Dulce* sped along toward the islands with its invisible crew.

Chapter 35

"Can we tie up here?" Hardy called out to a young man fishing off the dock, "Podemos amarrar nuestro barco?"

"Tirar una cuerda," the man said holding his hands up.

"Darcy, throw him the bow rope please," Hardy said, as he put the engine in reverse, increasing the throttle, slowing the boats speed.

They glided alongside the wooden dock and Hardy stepped off, tying a rope to a wooden post, bringing the sloop to an abrupt halt.

"Gracias," Hardy said, handing the young man two Córdoba notes.

"Me puede decir donde esta el Padre Ernesto Cardenal?"

"He is on the hill," the young man said smiling."

"You know English?" Hardy asked.

"Si, senor, un poco," he replied.

"What is your name?"

"I am Elvis Chavarria," he said with a smile.

"My name is Hardy and this is Darcy MacBean. How old are you, Elvis?

"I am 17."

"Lead the way," Hardy said with a sweep of his hand.

They followed Elvis up a steep path to a cleared plateau, where they found a small adobe church and four out buildings. Three were made from stone and pointed with cement and one was a long open structure with tables and benches. Two women cooking over an open fire watched intently as Elvis ushered them toward a man with a shock of long white hair. Sitting around him were men, women and children of all ages, each with canvas and brush, painting beautiful imaginary scenes of the island and volcanoes rising up with birds and jaguars placed about in each painting. The paintings were primitive in style with bold, captivating colors.

"I'd love to have a few of these paintings for our home." Darcy said

"We'll see what we can do," Hardy replied as Elvis introduced them to Father Ernesto.

"Padre, este hombre ha pedido conocerte."

"Si, Elvis," he said, looking up at Hardy.

"You American?"

"Scotland," Hardy replied. "Como se hace Padre Cardenal, esta es mi esposa Darcy y yo soy Hardy MacBean."

"Welcome to our island, Senor y Senora MacBean. No need to speak in Spanish. I lived in Culvertown, Kentucky, and studied at the Trappist monastery years ago. I learned to speak English there. I think we have something in common, Senor MacBean."

"What's that?"

"Both our countries are not free." he replied.

"My grandfather would have agreed with you on that."

"He is no more?"

"No, he passed away two years ago."

"I am sorry to hear that he passed away before his country became free. I hope I will live long enough to see Nicaragua free." And you, do you feel as your grandfather did?"

"I think Scotland should be free, I just don't know how it could happen. We have many British in Scotland, and they are good people. Over the past 300 years we've managed to live together and I can't see us Scots going to war over it. Maybe we will vote to leave the United Kingdom someday, but peaceably."

Hardy handed Frederick's letter to Father Ernesto.

"It is from Frederick Vogel," Hardy said.

"Ah, Frederick, my good friend, he is well?"

"Yes, Frederick, Avira and the girls are all well."

"Good," Father Ernesto said. "Now we eat! Ahora comemos! Jose, come sit with us at my table, we have guests from Scotland!"

A middle-aged man looked up from the table where he was showing two boys how to carve a wooden parakeet from a block of cedar. Smiling, he stood up brushing the wood shavings off his shirt. He was tall and lanky, with a dark complexion. His short curly black hair and carefully cropped goatee accentuated his riveting cobalt blue eyes,

222

magnified behind the thick lenses of a heavy pair of black-framed glasses.

"Gracias, Padre," he said, as he approached them and introduced himself to Hardy and Darcy. "Buenos, I am Carlos Fonseca. The padre calls me by my Christian name, Jose. But I am Carlos to everyone else."

"Very good to meet you, Carlos." This is my wife, Darcy MacBean and I'm Hardy."

"Did you take the panga from San Carlos?" he asked.

"No, we sailed here from Granada. We're visiting the islands, also San Carlos I think."

"He is Frederick's guest in Granada," Father Ernesto broke in.

Carlos carefully looked Hardy up and down.

"Frederick, I know him well. He is a good man," Carlos said.

"Maybe Jose can sail with you back to Granada," Father Ernesto suggested.

"Why not?" Hardy said, looking at Darcy. "We can stop on our way back in a few days. Friday morning okay?"

"That would be great," Carlos said, looking over at the women standing by the fire pit.

A fillet of largetooth Sawfish hissed over a bed of coals. Spattering oil from the frying pans filled with breaded and deboned Guapote ignited, sending the smoke curling up and away through a darkened hole in the metal roof. The younger of the two women removed tortillas from the adobe stove, wrapped them in a cloth and placed them over a large wooden bowl filled with guayo pinto. She carried it, as if an offering, and placed it in front of Father Ernesto.

"Comer padre."

"Que hermoso plato, Juanita," Father Ernesto exclaimed, reaching out and pinching her bottom.

She playfully shrieked and returned to the stove.

"These woman are not only good cooks, but beautiful, too," Ernesto said as he filled a small wooden bowl and handed it to Darcy. "Pass it down, please, I see many hungry faces. This is the best guayo pinto in all of Nicaragua. We also have fish to eat. Elvis brought us Sawfish and Guapote today. The fried Guapote is my favorite; the skin is crisp, delicious. Elvis is fantastico fisherman, is he not?" Ernesto continued as Elvis broke out with a pronounced smile but appeared embarrassed by the complement.

"I think I will set a hook when we sail back from San Carlos," Hardy said, "maybe I'll get lucky.

"And I will give you some bait to use," Elvis chimed in. "You will catch a big fish!"

"Good idea, "Father Ernesto added as he filled his bowl and began to eat.

"How long have you been staying in Granada?" Carlos asked.

"We just arrived today. Frederick arranged for our sloop and we left from his dock. I've been in Nicaragua for the past week working with Frederick's brother Herman. Darcy flew in from Miami this morning."

"What have you been doing here?"

"I've been buying hardwood lumber and logs for my company. This is my fourth year traveling to Nicaragua."

"And how do you find it, Nicaragua?"

"I don't know, exactly, but from what I hear, Somoza has become more and more oppressive. My friend has told me it's getting dangerous in Managua and the countryside is under constant assault from the Guardia Nacional."

"Where in the countryside?"

"In the mountains, Matagalpa north to Jinotega and along the Honduras border. A few years ago, I was on my way to visit a mill up there and the Guardia was shooting up the place. I've never gone back. The mill in Granada is able to provide all the lumber we need."

"Oh," Carlos said, lifting his eyes briefly from his food.

"Yes, the Guardia is making trouble in San Carlos. So far they stay away from the islands, but I fear we will see them soon enough. We will fight them when they come, or we will fight them in San Carlos. No es cierto Elvis?" Elvis looked up from his bowl and nodded briefly. "You see, Hardy," Ernesto continued. "It is right that we cut the head from the snake. Until we do, Somoza will continue to oppress the people. It is time we rise up."

The wind blew out of the northwest, giving Hardy a dead beat to Granada and the ranch. After five days of sailing the islands and one night in San Carlos, both he and Darcy were ready to return to Scotland. Carlos Fonseca sat in the bow leaning against the cabin. He didn't say much when he boarded except "Buenos Dias," and then he retreated to the bow when Hardy began to raise the mainsail. Darcy wore a wide brim straw hat, a long sleeve shirt and huddled in the companionway away from the sun. Hardy had warned her about the suns strength on their first day out but she still managed to burn her shoulders. "That's what you get for being a red head," he said when he applied aloe to her burns. Nearing the shore, Hardy could see the sun's reflection off a car windshield as it descended from the Vogel hacienda, leaving clouds of thick dust in its' wake.

He watched as two figures emerged from Frederick's jeep and walk toward the dock with one of them breaking into a run.

"Hello, hello, Hardy MacBean!" Maria shouted out, as Hardy jumped from the sloop and fastened the stern line to an iron ring. He smiled with affection and shouted back.

"Hola, Maria. Buenos Dias, Frederick!"

He finished tying the bow and spring line as Carlos climbed onto the dock and embraced Frederick, holding him at arm's length, looking at him with the affection only longtime friends could show one another.

"Muy bueno verte, mi amigo."

"Igualmente," Frederick replied.

"Bienvenido!" Maria called out leaving her father side, "Bienvenido! We are going to meet Uncle Herman and my sister for lunch in Masaya. We thought you would like to join us on your way back to the airport."

"Absolutely," Hardy said. "I'm sure Darcy would like to get in some last minute shopping."

"I would love to go, but we don't need another thing," Darcy said.

"Don't forget the paintings, Darcy," Hardy said throwing their bags onto the dock.

"I won't forget, Hardy, they are *my* paintings, you know."

Carlos and Frederick walked along the dock toward the jeep in animated conversation. Hardy overheard the words "la ley marcial," which he knew meant martial law. He turned to Maria.

"Why don't you ride up with us?"

"Papa," Maria called out, "I'll ride with Hardy and Darcy." Her father waved back and started the jeep, speeding off to the hacienda.

Hardy emerged from the shower and looked out the window to the north. He saw Carlos standing near the barn speaking with a man dressed in camouflage fatigues, wearing a green bush hat with the brim tied up along one side and a rifle slung over his right shoulder.

"Are you ready to go Hardy?" Darcy asked knocking on the bathroom door.

Hardy opened the door and walked into the room throwing his towel on the bed.

"I'll be ready in a minute," he replied, thinking about Carlos and the man with the rifle.

"Maria said they are ready to go now."

"Ask Maria where we can meet them, tell her we'll be along shortly."

"Okay," Darcy said leaving the bedroom.

Hardy looked out the window again and Carlos and the man had vanished.

"She says meet them at the old market restaurant."

"Tell them to go ahead," Hardy said, combing his hair.

He heard Frederick call out to Avira and Maria, and listened to their Mercedes-Benz roar to life and speed up the drive. "I'm glad we have our own car. Frederick drives like a maniac."

Hardy found a parking place along Avenida El Progresso. He locked the car and they began to walk toward the old market. The hot midday sun bore down on them as they ducked into the shade of the old Spanish fort. They heard a commotion and then a dozen young men ran past them. Hardy could see fear in their faces as they looked back.

227

He followed their gaze up the street and saw two Guardia Nacional troop carriers lumbering into view, coming to an abrupt stop in the middle of San Miguel with soldiers jumping to the street.

"Jesus!" Hardy said, grabbing Darcy's hand. "Come with me, quickly!"

"What's wrong, Hardy?"

An explosive burst of gunfire followed them into the fort. He pulled Darcy in the opposite direction of bullets whizzing overhead ricocheting off stone, smacking into the plaster walls. They ran past sacks of beans and rice stacked in rows along the hallway, diving between them as more gunfire erupted. People ran in from the street. A woman shrieked.

"God damn," Hardy said as they huddled behind the sacks.

"We have to find Herman and Frederick."

The shooting stopped almost as quickly as it began. They listened to the soldiers yelling orders back and forth as the trucks began to move further down the street, slowly fading away with sounds of sporadic gunfire. They crept along a central corridor toward an open arch doorway. Hardy peered down the empty street before they emerged and saw a pool of blood trailing along the sidewalk. They walked one door up where the blood stopped and a young man lay dead. They entered the old market restaurant to find tables overturned with chairs scattered about. Herman leaned over Frederick, applying pressure to his abdomen with a white linen napkin covered with blood. Avira sat weeping uncontrollably, her daughter Tanja holding her shoulders while she cradled Maria in her arms. Darcy rushed over to them and searched for Maria's pulse. She looked up at Hardy and shook her head. Frederick looked to Avira, moving his mouth without words. Avira wailed again and again. No one could find comfort.

Hardy sent a message to Glasgow that afternoon explaining his need to stay in Nicaragua for a few more days. And Darcy sent off a telegram that signaled she wouldn't be back in Scotland until the end of the week. The next day Frederick discharged himself from the hospital over the protestations of his brother. The bullet had gone clean through and did not damage any of his organs. He was in pain, but not enough to prevent him from being with his family and attend the "vela" and the following celebration of "nueva dias."

Herman drove Frederick to the ranch, where Hardy and Darcy, along with Father Ernesto and many close family friends sat in silence around Maria's open casket. Hardy watched as Frederick crossed himself and leaned over Maria, kissing her lips. He gasped his daughters name and cried out in anguish. Tears flowed from every eye as Herman steadied his brother and led him to his seat next to Avira, who cried out in the agony only a mother who had lost her child so young could achieve.

The funeral took place the following day in Granada at La Merced church, where Maria had been baptized when she was just 10 weeks old. The priest, who had performed Maria's baptism less than 20 years before, sprinkled holy water along the open white casket surrounded by burning candles. Exchanging the holy water vessel for a silver box filled with burning incense, the priest swung the box once up and down each side of the casket and then across, and then pronounced the prayer of absolution. Dressed in a white wedding dress, Maria lay lifelike, as beautiful as Hardy could ever remember. The priest then called upon the family to give Maria one last kiss before closing the casket lid. Hardy watched as Frederick's tears dropped onto Maria's face for the last time.

The sky was a dark blue, cloudless and cool for the time of year. It seemed as if the entire community of Granada was in attendance, spilling out from the entrance of the gleaming white stucco church. The casket was placed in a polished timeworn white Cadillac LaSalle, with its chrome gleaming in the sunlight, ready to lead a long funeral procession back to the ranch where the congregation would stand on a bluff overlooking the lake.

A few hundred people encircled the casket, while the priest said a single prayer consecrating the newly built burial vault.

"This was Maria's favorite place," Frederick said standing next to the casket, choking back his tears. "She would always stop here on her way home and sit and look into the distance across the lake. It is fitting that this will be her final resting place." He glanced at the priest, who again asked that Maria's soul rest in peace. The priest turned to Frederick, offering the holy water sprinkler and stood back as each relative starting with Avira cast holy water on the casket. The burial ended as the priest swung his silver box of burning incense back and forth along the casket and said another prayer for mercy. Hardy listened as the casket slid across the cement and brick enclosure, making a grading noise as it was interred into the brick vault. He could only think of darkness as the door closed with the mason waiting along side, ready to seal off the last vestige of light. At that moment, Hardy felt a loneliness of spirit that would haunt him in the months to come.

"Flor de Cana," announced the priest, as the crowd queued up and walked two abreast toward the hacienda with drum, trumpet, clarinet and marimba, all playing together in celebration of Maria's life.

Frederick held Avira's hand as they walked to the jeep. "Come join us," he called out to Hardy. Hardy waved them off as he and Darcy joined the end of the long procession of mourners.

"My uncle told me that your brother has a hundred foot fishing boat in New England," Herman Jr. said.

"Yes, that's true."

"We need your help, Hardy."

"How could I possibly help you?"

"We need guns, Hardy."

"We can get the guns, we just don't have the way to get them here."

"We need a boat to pick them up and a boat to ferry them to us. We have the money, Somoza's ransom money, blood money. The bastard's money will buy the guns. We will avenge Maria and all the others."

Hardy thought about Herman's request. He wasn't pleading; he was being honest and forthright in his position.

"How would we communicate?" Hardy asked not knowing what he would do.

"We can communicate through my father's telex, but only at six in the morning, and only after I signal that I am there, waiting. You can also reach me through our comrades in Costa Rica," he said handing Hardy a slip of paper with a phone number. "They will send word to us."

"I'm still not sure how I can help you," Hardy said.

"Clan Na Gael is an organization that provides weapons to the Provisional Irish Republican Army," Herman replied. "They will also provide weapons to us."

"Where are they located?

"Boston." The name Boston echoed in Hardy's head.

"I guess you want me to get my brother involved," he said, staring off at the lake.

"We need more than your brother to make this work."

"I understand," Hardy replied. "I'll think about it."

Hardy looked out his window as the jet gained altitude. The Nicaraguan countryside fell away below puffy white clouds shaped like balls of cotton. Darcy could see a pronounced worried look across Hardy's creased brow.

"Jesus Christ," he muttered.

"What?" she asked.

"I said Jesus Christ," he replied above the roar of the jet engines. "God's will, I hope I never hear that again."

"What are you talking about, Hardy?"

"God, and God's will. People who are getting murdered for no reason, much less bringing God into it."

'Hardy, the funeral is necessary for the grieving family and friends. No one can make sense out of death, any death. Look at your grandfather's funeral."

"My grandfather died in his sleep for Christ sakes. His funeral was sad but joyous. He had a long and wonderful life. Maria was shot to death by Somoza's thugs, no Goddamn joy there, just sadness, emptiness, darkness. Maria was barely twenty, just a kid."

"I know Hardy, but every family has their own way to grieve."

"I know, I know, children, their families. What choice do I have Darcy. I need to help them."

232

"What do you mean, help?" Darcy asked.

"Herman has asked me to help the cause. He is a Sandinista, they need supplies...guns." Darcy looked at him with disbelief.

"Hardy, don't be ridiculous, you know nothing about these guns! I didn't study ten years to become a doctor to find out my husband is a gunrunner. Guns take life Hardy. I save them."

"You don't understand Darcy. They need my help."

"But if you don't help them someone else will!" Darcy exclaimed.

Chapter 36

In the early morning hours, two weeks after returning to Glasgow, Hardy boarded a British Airways flight to Paris.

"You are here on business?" the customs official asked as he stamped the passport.

"Yes, just the day."

He picked up his briefcase, walked out the terminal door and hailed a taxi.

"Number 88 Avenue Foch, s'il vous plait," He said, placing his briefcase in the front seat and climbing in next to the driver. "I hope you don't mind, I like the view."

"Pas de probleme," the driver said. "Of course."

It had been years since Hardy traveled to Paris. The late February sky was gray with a light rain falling, more like a thick mist smearing the taxi window with each pass of the wipers. The city smog was pronounced with the smell of coal and diesel fumes. It had been a different Paris, with blooming flowers and bright blue skies the summer his grandfather brought him for a vineyard tour all those years ago. He remembered how Grumps would sigh and comment on the French women, saying in his thick Scottish brogue, "My, Hardyboy, I'd love to take one of these beauties back to Dalcross with me."

"Penthouse, s'il vous plait." Hardy asked a young man dressed in a high stand-collared blue tunic, with four gold colored buttons and a round blue cap embroidered with two gold stripes. He glanced at the elevator's iron gate and the intricate embellishment from the upper crest to the medallion centering a large Fleur De Lys.

He stepped from the elevator into an alcove and turned a mechanical twist doorbell once. A woman with blond hair appeared at the door, dressed in a brown woolen suit, wearing brown leather high heels.

"Oui?" she asked opening the door.

"Hardy MacBean to see Mr. Onassis."

"Please come in, Mr. MacBean, Mr. Onassis is expecting you. This way, please."

He followed her into a large open living room with floor length windows looking out at the Arc de Triomphe and the Eiffel Tower.

"There you are, Hardy, punctual as always," Onassis said, looking up from his desk.

"It has been a long time since we have seen each other, over two years."

"Wonderful of you to see me on such short notice sir."

"You sounded anxious, Hardy. What can I do for you? Have you finally sprouted your wings? Are you leaving Mackenzie to go out on your own?"

"No, not yet, I've been in Central America buying hardwood."

"Where about?"

"Nicaragua."

"Not necessarily a nice place to be these days," Ari said.

"No, it isn't. That's the reason I'm here. The Nicaraguans have asked me for my help."

"Which Nicaraguans are these?"

"The Sandinistas."

"And you want to help them?"

"Yes, I do. Somoza is killing an entire generation. The young have no chance in Nicaragua. They are killed because Somoza fears that they too will become Sandinistas."

"I know about Somoza," Ari said. "He kills with the full faith and backing of the United States government. Their actions are calculated. The people don't matter. It's about power, and world domination. Enough of that, how can I help you?"

"I need a small freighter that can get in close to Nicaragua," Hardy began, "And I need a crew that can be trusted. We will transfer cargo off the New England coast."

"I can see that you are passionate about wanting to help the Nicaraguan people. I had hoped that my son would find that kind of passion during his short life."

"Your son has died?

"Yes, it has been a little more than two years. He was instructing a new pilot when his plane went down in a flight lasting no more than 15 seconds; a tragedy and I think the CIA had a hand in it. But that was then and this is now. I have a boat in mind Hardy but I will pay."

"But I have the money," Hardy protested.

"Yes, but it is better this way. The captain will be paid before he leaves the dock. I will arrange for medical supplies and other equipment. After a certain point in life Hardy, money is meaningless. My goal is to make a positive difference wherever and whenever I can until I breathe my last. Don't worry; I have the captain and crew you need. Provide me with Loran coordinates and the boat will be off the New England coast by mid-March. By my estimate that gives you three weeks to get your side ready."

"I was hoping you would say that, but don't you want to know what I will take to Nicaragua?" Hardy asked, handing Ari the Loran coordinates, call number and radio channel for his brother's boat.

"No, that is unnecessary. All I need to know is that you are trying to help the Nicaraguan people.

"How fast is she?"

"As I remember, up to 15 knots, cruises around 12. She will hold enough fuel for the trip. How much weight do you think you will have?"

"I don't know, somewhere around four tons."

"Good," Ari said.

"March 15 then," Hardy replied, "Saturday, we'll plan on it. Tell the captain the transfer will take place at first light."

"I will. Take good care of yourself, and have a happy birthday."

"They shook hands and Hardy turned and walked toward the

door. Onassis looked out at the Eifel Tower and whispered under his breath, "Good luck young man, god speed."

Hardy boarded his flight back to Glasgow. "My birthday," he thought, "I'll be damned, he remembered."

Chapter 37

A U-Haul truck with Florida tags drove slowly onto the New Bedford Maritime Terminal dock and pulled alongside a large steel vessel with a red hull and a white forward pilothouse. KINCHYLE was painted along the bow in large white block letters. It was midnight and the wharf was shrouded in darkness except for one lone flickering mercury vapor lamp at the end of the pier.

"They're here, Gillies," Hardy said, looking down at the truck.

"Jesus Christ, Hardy, here we go," Gillies replied, "Let's not keep them waiting. We'll stow em on deck below the crane in the pen. Wake up Arthur on your way down and I'll turn on the deck light."

"Okay," Hardy replied as he left the wheelhouse and descended onto the deck.

A man stepped down from the trucks passenger side door. He was dressed in a navy pea coat with a stocking cap pulled down across his forehead, covering his eyebrows.

"You be Hardy?" the man asked with a slight Irish accent.

"Yes," Hardy said.

He heard the latch on the truck's roll-up door release.

"Where do you want them," the man asked.

"We'll put them on deck in the pen below the stacking crane."

237

"Okay, there are three of us. How many of you?"

"Three of us, too."

"Lucky we have high tide."

"No matter, we'll use the crane." Hardy said.

"How many boxes in all?"

"Five hundred, each weigh about 15 pounds. You get two AR-18 assault rifles in a box, each with a 20-round clip, 750 rounds a minute. 200 scopes go with them. Another truck is behind us with 40,000 rounds of ammunition."

"Jesus!" Hardy said. "Let's get going!"

The men worked feverishly unloading the truck and loading the boxes onto pallets. Hardy took the last box up to the wheelhouse, while Gillies and Arthur used the crane to transfer the pallets onto the deck. As the last pallet landed on deck a black pickup truck rolled onto the dock and parked parallel with the boat. Gillies climbed up onto the dock and surveyed the wooden crate in the trucks open bed with chains draped along the top.

"Arthur, you run the crane," he called out.

The U-Haul started up and slowly disappeared into the darkness. An older man with graying hair wearing a thick pair of black-rimmed glasses stepped from the darkness and climbed onto the truck bed. He grasped the chain in his right hand and waited.

"I was hoping you had a crane," the man said, clipping the hook under the chain, "Otherwise, we'd be here all night."

Gillies looked up, his gaze fell on the man's left eye, staring ahead without motion, his right eye darting back and forth from the crane's hook back to the boat. The crane lifted the crate from the pickup and swung it on to the deck.

"Are you Hardy?" the man called over in a thick Irish accent.

"No, he's on the bridge. You?"

"George," he said. "I'd like to give Hardy some instruction on the AR-18."

"Hardy, come down here," Gillies called out, "And bring a box."

"George," the man said to Hardy, reaching for the rifle. "We call this the widdah-makah in Ireland. Won't take me but a minute. You got to explain to them that a clean weapon is important, and it can be the difference between life and death, theirs. This is a gas operated, magazine fed, air-cooled selective fire assault rifle. The gas action features a short piston stroke, rotating bolt-locking mechanism. The piston has a cupped head and its own return spring. The bolt carrier is mounted inside the receiver on two guide rods, with each rod carrying its own return spring. Watch carefully, these special end plates, bolt link rods, bolt carrier, return springs, and guide rods can be removed from the rifle as a single unit. You field strip the AR-18 by pressing the guide rods forward like this, by this special lever at the rear of the receiver, then by folding the lower receiver down and forward. Now we can clean and oil your weapon. Now you put it back together."

Hardy took the rifle and repeated the steps backwards, giving the rifle back to George in less than a minute.

"You're a quick study, lad. I'd say you'll be a good instructor," he said handing the rifle back. "Practice shooting it on your way. Get acquainted with it."

"Thanks," Hardy said, "Weather permitting, I'll be showing them how to use this in less than two weeks."

"Vive Los Sandinistas," George said. He opened the truck door and climbed behind the steering wheel, started the engine and slowly crept away from the dock.

"Patria libre o morir," Hardy said, "Freedom or death!"

"Hardy," Gillies called out from the bridge, "weather's coming in from the east, it's gonna get stinky. Cast off the rear line, will ya? Time to shove off."

Hardy jumped onto the deck, rifle slung over his shoulder, removed the stern line and tossed it onto the dock. He felt the deck vibrate as his brother put *Kinchyle* into gear. He climbed the stairs to the bridge and watched as the boat moved toward the harbor channel buoy. Rounding the buoy and heading to the open ocean, a U.S. Coast Guard cutter appeared at the mouth of the harbor. Gillies waved as they passed in mid channel, while Hardy held his breath and watched as a crewmember waved back.

"Don't worry, Hardy," Gillies said. "They know me, and for all practical purposes we're legal."

Hardy looked out into the darkness as Gillies set the Loran coordinates. "Vessel name?" Gillies asked.

"SS *El Capitan*," Hardy replied. "Panamanian flag."

"Okay," Gillies said, reaching up and turning the VHF channel to 9. "We'll be on site in about two hours, just before seven. Sure wish the weather would accommodate. They're calling for five-foot seas, 15 to 25 knots, not the best conditions, but I think we'll be able to pull a couple of strings after the transfer, pay the fuel."

"I did offer, Gillies," Hardy said.

"I know little brother, but I didn't ask you too. For all the years we've been brothers this is the first time in more than I can remember, if

240

ever, that we collaborated on anything together. I just didn't think we'd be running guns. If Pop only knew."

"But he won't will he?"

"No he won't. What he doesn't know won't hurt him. You know he did help me buy this boat, but he's all paid back."

"He told me," Hardy said.

Hardy thought about Gillies refusing to be paid for his help and the envelope containing $7,500 that he stuffed into his brother's overalls. He figured his brother would find the money when he put them on, just about the time *El Capitan* would be lost on the horizon.

"Right on time," Gillies said. "Sun is coming up and there she is." He reached up and grabbed the VHF mike.

"SS *El Capitan*, this is *Kinchyle* four nine- nine-niner, do you read me, come back."

He waited 10 seconds and repeated, "*El Capitan* do you read me, come back."

"SS *El Capitan*," a voice blared with a British accent, "read you load and clear, this is the captain speaking, over."

"Switching to channel 68, come back," Gillies replied.

"Sixty-eight, over," the captain replied.

"We've got a Brit, Hardy, whad'ya know," Gillies said.

"Seems like we do," Hardy said.

"Bearing east south east, 120 degrees," the captain's voice called out. "Let's pair up and see how we do, over."

"Roger that," Gillies replied, "Come back."

"We've done this before, very important to keep on course, pretty sloppy out here, over," the captain replied.

"Twice the tonnage, Hardy," Gillies said as he lowered his speed.

241

"Don't want to rub up against that."

They watched as the *El Capitan*'s crew put three large fenders made from multiple truck tires over the starboard side.

"*Kinchyle*, do you read me, over," radioed the *El Capitan*.

"I read you, come back," Gillies replied.

"Steady on course, move in, increase speed," the captain relayed.

"Here goes nothing," Gillies said as he bumped up the speed.

"You and Arthur get on deck and ready the lines."

Hardy's adrenaline spiked as he swung his backpack over his shoulder and left the bridge. The *Kinchyle* moved closer to the *El Capitan*, dipping into a swell, welling up and sending water spouting as they came together.

"Jesus Christ," Gillies muttered.

"*Kinchyle, Kinchyle*, ready for lines, spring line first, over."

"Aye, captain," Gillies replied.

"How many pallets, weight, over?"

"Eleven, 750 pounds each, with the last one about a thousand, come back."

"Right, spring line secured, cargo crane operational, over."

"Heads up, men, cargo hook coming over!" Gillies cried through the speaker.

"Ease back on your speed *Kinchyle*!" the captain barked.

"Aye, captain, holding steady," Gillies replied.

Hardy grabbed the rope attached to the hook as it swung over his head. He worked in tandem with Arthur, spikes of water bursting between the boats raining down upon them. When they reached the ammunition, Hardy swung his backpack and rifle over his shoulder, fastened the hook around the chains and climbed on top of the crate. He

242

looked up at the bridge and shouted out, "Gillies!" With one hand clutching the cable and the other hand with a thumb up, he gave his brother a wide mouth open grin along with a yelp. The crate lifted off the deck of the *Kinchyle* as the boats came together once more, sending a plume of water over Hardy as he was swung onto the *El Capitan* deck.

"God, Hardy!" Gillies muttered, "You crazy bastard, and you and your fear of fucking heights!"

Arthur let go the lines holding the boats fast together and joined Gillies on the bridge.

"Great job, Arthur," Gillies said, as the Kinchyle fell off to the south.

"*Kinchyle, Kinchyle*," came over the radio, "Well done, over."

"Have a good trip and Godspeed," Gillies replied. "Tell my brother to come home safe, *Kinchyle* over and out."

Gillies turned the *Kinchyle* to the south and set course to Georges Banks.

"Get some rest Arthur, we'll reach our trawls in two hours."

As *El Capitan*'s engines propelled Hardy and the weapons toward Nicaragua, Gillies set the automatic pilot for Gilbert Canyon and reached for his overalls. As he pulled them on over his long underwear, he felt a bulge in his left rear pocket. "What in hell?" he thought.

"Well, I'll be a son of a bitch!" he said, opening up the envelope stuffed with hundred-dollar bills. He looked out the cabin window and scanned the ocean, thinking about his brother and his determination to help the Nicaraguan revolutionaries.

"God damn you, Hardy," he muttered. "You never listen. but Take care of yourself little brother, I know we'll see you again!"

Chapter 38

"Gillies!" Hardy yelled. "The fucking Coast Guard has turned, they're coming after us for Chrissakes! They're shooting at us!"

Hardy awoke to a loud rapping on the cabin door, his shirt drenched in sweat, a bad dream, he realized.

"Yes?" he asked.

"The captain wants you to know we're within range," came a voice from the other side of the door.

"Alright," Hardy replied, swinging his legs out over his bunk. "I'll be right there."

Gaining the bridge, Hardy looked out the forward windows into darkness.

"We're at half speed," the captain said. We'll be at the coordinates around 8 o'clock."

"That's good, it'll give them enough time."

Hardy reached for the radio mike and set the dial to channel 56.

"Guardabarranco, Guardabarranco, over," he waited two minutes and repeated, "Guardabarranco, come back, over."

"You think they're out there?" the captain asked.

"I do, but you never know, something may have happened."

"If we miss this, you know I can't keep the cargo."

"I know. They'll be here."

"Okay, I'll slow to five knots."

Hardy continued to hail, "Guardabarranco, Guardabarranco, come back."

Where the hell is Herman, he wondered. He stepped out onto the deck and looked out past the *El Capitan*'s running lights into a starlit sky, watching, waiting for any sign of the boats.

"Well, I'll be a son of a bitch!" the captain shouted, "Looks like they've found us, MacBean! There must be a dozen or more coming at us."

Hardy looked over at the radar screen and watched as the boats streamed toward them in a line stretching over a half mile.

"Should be at least 20 of em."

"Right on time," the captain said, slowing to an idle, throwing the ships engines into neutral.

"Yes sir, I knew they would come," Hardy replied, and he followed the captain down to the deck.

"Twenty panga's in all, about 400 pounds of cargo for each one."

"Is that all they'll hold?"

"The panga is built for speed when you need it," Hardy replied.

"Four hundred pounds is a lot of weight to carry, and I'll be joining the last one for the ride in."

"All men on deck," the captain called out as the first boat came along the port side.

Hardy pulled the tarp off the cargo as the men lined up ready to hand the boxes down into the boats.

"Twenty five boxes to a boat," Hardy ordered, looking down into the first panga, instantly recognizing the smile looking up at him.

"Herman!" Hardy exclaimed. "Lo que llevo al hombre tanto tiempo?

"We got here as soon as we could," Herman called up to him. Patrols are out."

"Twenty-five boxes for each boat Herman," Hardy called back. "Two rifles to a box, plus 40 rounds of ammunition in each box. Tents, clothing and medical supplies coming your way."

"Yes sir, Commandante Beano," Herman shouted out.

"What the hell did you say Herman?" Hardy asked handing down the first box.

"What do you mean, Hardy?" Herman replied with a grin.

"Beano!"

"When you left Nicaragua after the earthquake, my father was asked if he knew an Englishman by the name of El Beano. I never thought about it, but then I realized it must be you. Am I right?"

"I guess you can say that, Herman, but I'm no Englishman!"

"I know, I know, and my father said he had no idea anyway."

His boat fully loaded, he looked up at Hardy and made the victory sign.

"I will see you on the Costa Rican side of the river El Beano!" he said starting his motor and pulling away from the ship.

Two hours passed before the last panga slid alongside the *El Capitan*. Hardy shined his light down on the top of a green camouflage bush hat. He thought he saw what appeared to be a woman's hands tying up to the ship.

"I guess I'll be riding with you," he called down to the boat.

"I guess so Commandante Beano!" the woman's voice exclaimed.

"Good God, is that you, Tanja?"

"It most certainly is," she said, laughing, removing her hat, and showing her closely cropped hair.

"I can see Herman shared his little secret?

"No, not really, I don't know what it's about, just that he called you Beano!"

"When did you join up?"

"The day after my sister's funeral."

"Well, I'll be damned," Hardy said, handing down his duffle bag.

"Yo te ayudo a guarder las cajas."

"Gracias, Hardy, I could use the help." Tanja said with a big smile.

"How are your mother and father?" He asked handing her the first box.

"I do not know. I have not seen them since the funeral. They know I am with Herman."

"I thought you were in law school. Will you return when this is over?"

"I do not know. It depends on whether or not we are victorious. I am a Sandinista first; I am equal with the men. A law degree from the university does not give me this equality. The laws are what Somoza makes them, and his family has made the laws for more than 40 years. Women are expected to remain subservient to males in Somoza's Nicaragua. After we are victorious, equality will be established between all the men and women of Nicaragua. Until women are accepted as equals, the study of law in Nicaragua is meaningless. I am the commandante of this battalion and chose to be the last boat. When I knew you were going to come I appointed Herman lead boat. Did you know that Herman also smuggled guns?"

"No, but I knew he was a scout leader and took boy scouts into the mountains.

"Yes, the truck he used was equipped with secret panels behind the cab underneath the seats. It was a very effective way to hide the rifles until one day a soldier on a routine inspection stopped him. When the soldier discovered the rifles, Herman cut his throat and hid his body in a ditch. He left the boys off in Managua and joined us here in Costa Rica."

"That's the last box, MacBean. And you may need this," the captain said, lowering Hardy's rifle into his hands. "Good luck, and remember I promised your brother you would return home safe."

"Thanks, captain, adios!" Hardy exclaimed, pushing the boat away from the *El Capitan*.

He sat in the panga bow, closing his eyes with fatigue, breathing in the smells of the mainland as they sped toward the coast and the mouth of the San Juan River. "Incredible," he thought, "Comandante Tanja!" He began to sink into sleep, jerking awake each time he felt his body slump forward. His eyes opened wide as the engine abruptly quit. He turned and watched as Tanja reached back and pulled on the engine cover, lifting the prop from the water. She pointed ahead at the lights sparkling in the distance.

"Greytown" she said quietly, "We paddle from here until we pass by the town. You have a paddle under your seat, Hardy, use it."

Hardy pulled the paddle forward and joined in with broad strokes.

"You're quite strong," he said.

"Yes, I was always the strong one. Maria was the pretty one, the princess. She was our father's favorite."

"You are as beautiful," Hardy said, thinking about Maria's beauty and how he had been taken by it. "I know your father thinks so, too."

"Enough talk, Hardy, I saw the way you looked at my sister."

They paddled steadily toward the lights along the southern bank of the San Juan as it wrapped its way past Greytown. They could see clearly the Guardia Nacional barracks at the bottom of the old fort.

Tanja whispered to Hardy, pointing out a guard asleep against the barracks wall. He watched as another puffed on his cigar, the burning tip glowing brightly with clouds of smoke rising into the corner light. Faint Afro-Caribbean dance music played and the smell of bacon drifted across the water. Hardy's stomach growled with hunger.

"Jesus Tanja, we're getting pretty close, too God damned close."

"We'll be by them soon enough. They think we're night fishermen. We blend in with the darkness, Hardy. We will use the engine again when the lights fade. Keep paddling, be at the ready."

"I am as ready as I'll ever be. The mosquitoes are unmerciful."

The lights from Greytown fell away as the panga clung to the Costa Rican side of the riverbank.

"Okay," Tanja whispered, "time to use the engine." She pulled the engine cover forward and released the prop back into the water. "The morning light is coming," she whispered. "We will pull into the next lagoon and wait out the day. The patrol boats will be out soon but they always head back to the fort when darkness falls. We have another 50 kilometers to base camp, about two and a half hours."

She started the engine and threw it into gear, slowly bringing the panga up to full speed. Hardy looked ahead as the night fell into day, watching as the birds flew up from nearby trees, startled by the noise from the engine. They sped along until full daylight when Tanja cut the engine and steered toward the riverbank.

"Watch out, keep your head down!" she commanded as the bow plied through what appeared to be an overhanging bush, gliding into an open lagoon completely hidden from the river.

"Secret place?" Hardy called back.

"One of them," Tanja said, as the panga rested up against the sandy bank.

"Where did you put the tent?"

"Here it is," she said, throwing a canvas cylinder from the boat.

"What kind of tent is that?" she asked

"It's a U.S. Army geodesic tent made for the Vietnam War, camouflaged with netting. Where do you want it?"

"Anywhere will do," Tanja replied as she tied the boat to a tree.

He rolled out the tent, swatting at mosquitoes, put four poles together and threaded them through loops spread out on the tent floor. He stood up and pulled on the poles where they joined, snapping the roof up into place. Drawing down the front zipper, he started to enter the tent when Tanja pushed him from behind.

"Move over, I'm coming in," she exclaimed, handing him a container of cold guayo pinto and a canteen filled with water, "I'm being bitten alive!"

"Thanks, I'm starved, "he said, sitting back and opening the container.

She smiled, looking up into his eyes. Hardy glanced at her ample breasts filling her open shirt. He finished eating and removed his boots and pants and lay back on the tent floor, using his pants as a pillow.

"Seems like it's going to be a hot one," he said.

He closed his eyes and breathed deeply, quickly falling fast asleep. Tanja put down her empty bowl and drank from the canteen. She lay down next to him and closed her eyes. The morning sun began to rise along with the temperature. The air was still.

250

She sat up and removed her boots and pants, the temperature continued to climb as she listened to Hardy snore. She removed her T-shirt and lay on her side naked. She watched Hardy's hands and legs twitch as he slept. She watched his mouth move listening to him murmur in his dream. She wanted him, but thought he would say no if she asked. She reached into his boxers, gently squeezing. He grew hard. She continued to stroke him, rising onto her knees, straddling him, and then taking him in. He awoke startled, his eyes looking up, his hands rising to cup her breasts, rubbing her nipples with his thumbs, and then lowering them to rest on her hips as she rocked back and forth, keeping her eyes on his face.

"I thought I would wake you," she said, stopping in mid stride, bending over, and pushing her tongue deep into his mouth.

He looked at her nakedness as she arched her back. Her hips moving rhythmically up and down, faster with each move, her nipples erect.

"You're beautiful," he said.

"You really think so?"

"Yes, I do. We shouldn't be."

"A little late for that, Hardy. Who's going to know? We're in a tent in the jungle, miles away from anyone. I want you. I've wanted you since the day we first met."

He put his hand on her arm, pushing her over onto her back, moving over her without withdrawing. He slid his arms under her legs, her knees bending, and began a slow even rhythm. She called out his name, over and over, moaning, until they both simultaneously reached climax. Hardy exhaled a long held breath, collapsing alongside her.

"I know, that's who," he said, breathing heavily, rolling off to the side.

Tanja lay with her head resting in the crook of his arm, listening to a toucan call in the trees overhead, followed by a distant roar of a mantled howler. She felt a burning, but also exhilaration. Hardy's breathing was even as he slept. She moved her hand, squeezing lightly as she had done before. She continued to stroke him. It thickened and became hard. Once more she got on her knees and straddled him. She began with slow shallow strokes, with her first deep thrust waking him from his slumber. She looked at his face moving her hips in a circular motion.

"Do you like that?" she whispered.

Yes, It's wonderful," he said as he pulled her down and turned her onto her back, continuing to make love, lowering his lips to her breasts, sucking her nipples until they grew hard.

She felt suspended in time as Hardy moved her into different positions without withdrawing.

"Hardy, please, please finish with me, I am done."

He turned her onto her stomach and spread her legs with her knees bent, pulling her thighs back toward him in quick motion, increasing his speed, skin slapping together. She cried out his name repeatedly. He fell away from her, as she lay still, exhausted.

"You okay?" he asked, his heavy breathing beginning to diminish.

"Yes, okay. I thought you would never finish."

"I'm sorry, I always go longer the second time."

"I'll remember that, and I'll remember this time. Soon we will leave and join up with the others and I don't think we will make love again before you go."

"Why not?"

"There will be no time. The Mennonites will be there when we arrive."

"The Mennonites?"

"Yes, they provide us with supplies. They take good care of us and they will take you to San Jose."

"I thought I was going to teach you how to take the rifles apart and clean them."

"No need, Hardy, we already know how to do that. We want you out of harm's way. You are more important to us alive than dead."

"I guess its Scotland for me then."

He thought of Darcy for the first time since he had been with Tanja, wondering what he would do, or what he wouldn't do. He didn't know when or how he could tell her. He didn't think his marriage would survive if he did.

"Don't worry about it," Tanja said, seeing the concern on his face. "It was meant to happen between us, but that is as far as it goes. You are married, remember?"

"Thanks for reminding me, but as far as being meant to happen, I don't think so. More like you made it happen, and I'm weak when it comes to beautiful women Tanja. You probably already knew that."

"I will never forget you, Hardy. You helped us when we needed it most. We will give Somoza a taste of his own medicine thanks to you."

She turned her head and listened to an engine whine in the distance.

"They are coming down the river, time for us to pack up. Herman will be anxious."

They dressed and collapsed the tent, stowing it away in the boat, waiting until the Guardia patrol passed by and the sound of the engines became faint.

Part 10

Life and Death

Chapter 39

"Hello, this is Hardy MacBean, may I speak with Mr. Onassis please?"

"Just one moment, please," the woman's voice said.

Hardy looked out from the Miami International concourse. His flight to Glasgow posted 4:15 pm departure, gate 16.

"Hello, Hardy, this is Jackie Onassis. How are you?

"I'm fine Jackie, thank you."

"I am so sorry to tell you Hardy, Ari passed away March 15."

Silence ensued as Hardy digested the news. "The day of the transfer from the *Kinchyle* to the *El Capitan*," he thought, "my birthday."

"I know you were of special interest to Ari, and I can tell you that he mentioned your name more than once not long before his death, something about your passion to help the less fortunate."

Hardy let the words sink in.

"Are you there, Hardy?"

"Yes, I am," his voice trailing off. "I'm so sorry to hear the news. He was a good friend and I will miss him."

"Take care, Hardy, thank you for your call," she said, and the line went silent.

He wished he could have spoken to him one more time, to thank him for his help. He wanted to tell him how the captain and crew all made the trip a success. He felt empty, his passion dissipating. He was ready to go home. Nicaragua began to fade from his consciousness as the reality of his return to life in Scotland came into focus.

Chapter 40

What are we going to name our baby if she's a girl?"

"I don't know, Darcy, how about Maria, Maria MacBean."

"That has a nice ring to it Hardy," Darcy exclaimed, remembering Maria. "Your mother and father will be at the airport at 4 o'clock, Hardy. You best get going. Their room is ready, bed is made."

"Thanks, sweetie, I appreciate it. You know Mum couldn't bear missing her first grandchild being born. I hope it's on time."

"Don't worry, I'm over ready, maybe tonight!"

"Wait a few days please, we'll be able to celebrate her birthday along with Christmas."

"I knew you would say that, Hardy, always a method to your madness. Two birds with one stone!"

"No, it's not that, I'd like her to be born at Dalcross."

"Well it's a good thing Winwood has made arrangements with the community midwife, so I guess I'm covered. Why do you keep calling it a her?"

"Because I believe that our neighborly Greek lady knows what she's talking about. You are rather round about and she did say if it was a boy your tummy would be shaped more like a bullet."

"Round about am I? Hardy, you bugger!" she exclaimed, laughing.

"Yes sort of."

"Do you still find me attractive?"

"Of course I do, Darcy!" he exclaimed, hoping that would be the end of it. He thought about the many months with no sex and his time with Tanja. The guilt seeped into his conscience as he stood up from his chair. He knew it would follow him until he either told Darcy or she found out on her own.

"I'll be back soon," he said, throwing on his coat. "Hopefully, customs won't take much time. Pop will make sure of that."

He wondered what his father would say to him. This was the first time they would see one another since he left New Bedford bound for Nicaragua. He had spoken with his mother over the phone about travelling to Scotland for Christmas and the baby's due date, but his father had remained aloof, uncommunicative. He knew his brother had spoken with him about his trip to Nicaragua, but he had yet to hear about it. He would just have to wait and see.

"Hardy!" his mother shrieked as she emerged from customs. He watched his mother come toward him as his father labored behind, carrying two large suitcases.

"Hello, Mum!" Hardy called out. "It looks like you're prepared to stay for the month!"

"I will if I have to," she called back. "I wouldn't miss it for the world!"

"You won't miss a thing, Mum," Hardy replied as he embraced her. "We've decided to head up to Dalcross tomorrow so Darcy can get acquainted with the midwife."

"No hospital?" his mother asked.

"No, no hospital, after all, Mum, you didn't need one."

"Well, we certainly did so, Hardy!"

"I know, but Darcy is full term and we shouldn't have any problems. She's well up on it, and she is a doctor after all," he said, "and if we do need a hospital, we can always run into Inverness."

"Okay, if you say so," his mother replied.

"Let me take your bags, Pop," Hardy said, reaching out and shaking his father's hand.

"Thanks, Hardy. Great to see you son, your mum is driving me mad."

It began to snow as Hardy drove through the Dalcross gates and crept up the drive toward the castle. Uncle Gillies swung the entrance door wide as the Volvo station wagon came to a stop.

"Wonderful, finally!" Gillies shouted out, hugging Mary and then Darcy as they emerged from the car. Winwood appeared and pushed Gillies aside.

"Why, Darcy," she exclaimed, "Look at you!"

"I know, I know, Hardy won't let me forget for a second!"

"We'll take care of Hardy, you can count on it," Winwood said. "Now come in out of the cold. Young Gillies is in bed. Poor little one has a cold. He came down with it yesterday. He's got quite a thirst and a bit of the backdoor-trot. We best keep him well away from you until he's feeling better."

"I'm so sorry to hear it," Darcy replied. "I hope he feels better soon."

"Don't you worry, he's pretty keen on Christmas and he thinks that Santa is giving him a shotgun now that he's reached the advanced age of nine. His father let him shoot his old .410 this fall and damned if he didn't bring down a grouse."

"That he did," Gillies exclaimed, "He's a natural."

"Early dinner tonight. Please make yourselves comfortable. Same rooms as always. I'll call you when it's ready," Winwood said.

"How is little Gillies breathing?" Darcy asked.

"He's stuffed up, Darcy."

"Are his hands cold?"

"Yes, they are. I have him under two quilts."

"Has he complained about pain in his legs?"

"He did say his legs ached," Winwood replied, "Should we be worried?".

"I think you should take him to hospital," Darcy exclaimed, her voice measured but firm. "I don't want to upset you, but he may need medical attention."

"I'll go up and check on him, Darcy. I'm sure he will be okay."

Hardy walked into the great hall carrying two suitcases and headed for the stairs. As he began the climb to the third floor, Winwood descended the stairs in a panic.

"I can't wake him, he's barely breathing!" she shrieked. "Gillies, get the car!"

"What do you need?" Hardy asked. "I can take you!"

"All right! Gillies, come up and carry your son down!"

"What's the matter?" Gillies asked as he appeared from the kitchen.

"I can't wake your son, he is unconscious! Come quickly!"

"Get my bag, Hardy, my stethoscope!" Darcy exclaimed.

Gillies brought his son down and laid him on the couch. Darcy listened to his breathing.

"No time to waste."

"What hospital? I'll call ahead," William broke in. "I'll alert the police as well."

"Raigmore!" Winwood exclaimed as they ran out the door to the car. Hardy floored the volvo out the drive toward Inverness.

"Hold on, we'll be there soon!" he exclaimed.

"For Gods' sake William, pacing isn't going to help," Mary said. "I'll go back up and look in on Darcy."

As she reached the second story landing, she could here Darcy call out.

"What is happening?" Mary shouted as she walked into the room.

"I'm in pain mum."

"Has your water broken?" Mary asked.

"No, not yet!"

"No need to worry, Darcy. You've got a ways to go. Now lay back on the bed," Mary said, propping pillows behind Darcy's head. "I'll make a call to the midwife and tell her to hurry along. Don't worry, I'll be right back."

Hardy's car squealed to a stop at the Raigmore Hospital emergency entrance. Gillies burst from the rear side door with his son cradled in his arms as Winwood sprang from the passenger seat and started running toward the entrance. A doctor, along with three medical personnel, laid Gillies on a gurney and wheeled him to the emergency room door with Gillies and Winwood following close behind.

"How long has he been like this?" the doctor asked in a thick Hebridean accent.

"We don't know," Winwood said. "I put him to bed at 2 this afternoon and when I went to check on him at 4 o'clock he was unresponsive.

"Alright," the doctor said. "His breathing is labored and his blood pressure is very low. We will put him on an intravenous course of penicillin and hope for the best. All symptoms point to infantile bacterial meningitis, but we will perform the necessary blood tests to confirm."

"Is that bad?" Winwood and Gillies asked in unison.

"It can be," the doctor replied. "It depends on how quickly he responds to the antibiotic. We can only wait and see."

"Can we stay with our son?" Winwood asked.

"Why, yes, but it may be a long night," the doctor replied."

"Nurse?" Hardy questioned the woman behind the front desk, "Can you tell me how Gillies MacBean is coming along."

"And who are you?" the woman asked.

"I'm his cousin, Hardy MacBean. Could I speak with my uncle, please?"

"Certainly, let me see where they are. Just a moment, please," she replied.

"Here they are, use the phone on the counter and dial 103."

Hardy picked up the phone and dialed 103.

"Yes?" Gillies answered.

"Uncle, it's me, Hardy."

"Oh yes, Hardy" his voice growing quiet.

"How is Gillies doing?"

"We don't know, Hardy. They have him on penicillin and now oxygen. We just don't know."

"Alright," Hardy said. "I'll be returning to Dalcross then. Do you need anything back?"

"We'll call you, or you call us if you need us. We will be here until Gillies wakes.

"And please tell Maggie not to worry about her little brother," Hardy heard Winwood say.

He drove the nine miles back to Dalcross, slowing through the wisps of fog forming in the dips of the road. It was almost 9 o'clock when he turned through the castle gates and parked next to a car he didn't recognize.

"The midwife is here Hardy, she has been here since 5 o'clock," his mother said meeting him at the door. "Darcy started labor just after you rushed out the door."

"Why didn't you call me?"

"We didn't want to worry you, running off the road, speeding."

"How's she doing?" he asked, heading toward the stairs.

"The midwife is with her. She's uncomfortable, contractions are fairly constant."

Hardy could hear Darcy's moan as he climbed to the third floor.

"Hello, sweetie," he said, entering the room.

"God, Hardy, where have you been?"

"I've been in hospital."

"All this time?"

"Yes, Gillies is in a coma."

The midwife placed a wet hand towel across Darcy's forehead and looked up at Hardy.

"I'm Hardy MacBean," he said.

"Karen Kennedy," she replied, leaning over Darcy and placing her stethoscope over her belly button. She stood and motioned Hardy to the door.

"Where are you going," Darcy called out.

262

"I'd like to have a word with your husband."

"I'm a doctor for god's sake, if there is any word it will be right here in front of me."

"The heartbeat is in the wrong place."

"What do you mean, wrong place?" Hardy asked as Darcy cried out in pain.

"It's a breech, the child is foot first There's nothing I can do," Kennedy said calmly. "We need to get her to the hospital, and quickly. Help me get her up. Any hospital you prefer?"

"Raigmore," Hardy replied.

"I will call ahead and sign her in. Phone?"

"Downstairs in the hall."

He could hear the midwife speaking on the phone as they descended to the great room.

"Mid-wife Kennedy here, I'm coming in with a patient. We have a breech birth."

I'm so sorry," Mary MacBean said, slipping her hand under Darcy's arm and helping her walk to the car. "Everything will be okay, Darcy."

Maggie watched as Darcy winced in pain. William put his hand on Hardy's shoulder.

"Do you want me to come?"

"No thanks, Pop, stay here and hold down the fort," Hardy replied, closing the rear door to the car and getting in behind the wheel.

"At least I know my way to Raigmore," Hardy said, starting the engine.

William and Mary stood in the doorway with Mary clasping her hands around Maggie's waist, watching Hardy drive off with Darcy and the midwife sitting in the rear seat.

"God, what a mess," Hardy thought as he drove up the road to the hospital.

"Arrived at 10:45," the doctor said walking toward him. "You have a beautiful eight-pound girl. Your wife came through with flying colors. You can go in now."

Hardy shook the doctor's hand, his emotions welling. He opened the door and looked in at Darcy. Her eyes were closed. A nurse stood next to her, holding his daughter. Darcy opened her eyes and watched Hardy take their baby into his arms.

"A girl, Mr. MacBean," the nurse said.

"Yes," Hardy replied.

"You were right Hardy," Darcy said softly, recovering from the anesthesia.

"Maria?"

"Yes, Maria," she said.

Hardy entered the elevator and descended to the first floor. When the door opened, he saw Gillies and Winwood sitting on a bench across from him. They did not see him at first, but the distress he saw on their faces was unmistakable.

"Uncle Gillies," he said looking into his uncle's tear stained face, "What has happened?"

"He's gone," Winwood sobbed. "Our little Gillies is gone."

His uncle was speechless, something Hardy had never witnessed.

"What can I do?"

"I guess we will go back to Dalcross and tell Maggie," Winwood said. "We can do nothing more here."

Gillies appeared bewildered.

"Come on Gillies, let's go home."

Not a word was spoken on the drive back to Dalcross.

"How is Darcy?" Winwood asked softly when they arrived.

"She's okay. She's in hospital, a cesarean. We had a girl."

"When?" Winwood asked.

"Ten forty-five."

There was complete silence until the car came to a full stop.

"Little Gillies passed away about the same time." Winwood said. "I'm so sorry we're in such a state, Hardy. Do you have a name yet?"

"Maria."

"Wonderful name," Winwood said. "We'll make ready for Darcy and Maria's arrival."

"No need."

"I have a need, Hardy," Winwood replied, "I have a need."

William MacBean waited for Hardy to park his car. Glasgow International Airport was busy with holiday travelers and Mary had joined in a long line to check their baggage.

"I'm sorry Darcy couldn't see you off."

"She has her hands full, Hardy," William said. "New babies take a lot of getting used to. I know your mother and I were a bit overwhelmed when Gillies came along. It was easier with Eliza and then you. But on another subject…"

Hardy felt that ominous feeling when his father entered into a discussion with "But on another subject." He braced himself for what he felt sure was coming.

"You know, this Nicaraguan conflict," William continued. "I know about the guns, Hardy. I never thought a son of mine would get involved in a revolution. You certainly have shown your mettle."

"Pop, it's not so much that, it's complicated."

"Life is complicated, a long road. You make your own choices Hardy."

"They asked and I said I would help. I kept my word. I haven't spoken with them in nine months and I have no idea how it's going."

"It's not going well for them, Hardy," Somoza declared a state of siege and has killed thousands. He is dropping bombs and napalm indiscriminately on mountain villages and killing radical students and Catholic activists in the cities, shooting many of them at point blank range. The Ford administration is distancing itself from Somoza and has opened contacts with the opposition. We don't know where this is going, but we also have an election coming up this year and I don't think the voters will return Ford to the White House.

Chapter 41

"Mackenzie's," the secretary answered.

"Hardy MacBean, please."

"Just a moment, I'll ring him."

"Hello, Hardy here."

"Hardy, you haven't forgotten, have you?" Darcy asked.

"Maria getting excited? He questioned. "Let me see, excited for Christmas?"

"Yes, that, too," Darcy said feigning exasperation. "Third birthday is a big deal Hardy. I know your mother always managed to destroy your cake, but that isn't going to happen on my watch."

"That she did, timing is everything. Of course I didn't forget Maria's birthday. And I do have a present!"

"See that you do, Hardy, you incorrigible rascal! Maria has been helping me with the cake, eight layers and lots of chocolate."

"Sounds terrific. I'll be home soon. Have you packed for Dalcross?"

"I laid out some clothes for you to choose from. Got to go, Hardy, Maria is beginning to wear chocolate! Hurry, Goodbye!"

Hardy finished with his inventory and stood up from his desk.

"Call on line four."

Standing, Hardy picked up the phone and heard Winwood's voice.

"Hardy," she said, her voice breaking.

"Winwood, what is wrong?"

"Gillies is dead, a massive heart attack, Hardy. He just had his physical and the doctor said he was fine. I just don't understand. We're a mess. Maggie and I can't stop crying. I know I must be strong, but we need you here Hardy."

"Of course Winwood, I will be there in the morning. Have you told Pop?"

"Yes, William and Mary are coming over on the first flight out."

"I was told your brother and sister will be along soon after."

"I'm so sorry I have to bother you, Hardy. I have no one else to turn to."

"That's what I'm here for Winwood, I love you. Gillies was my best friend, my second father," he said haltingly. "I can't believe he's gone. I am so sorry, I'll see you soon."

"Thank you, Hardy, I'll see you tomorrow then."

Hardy hung up the phone. "Sixty five," he thought. "Too young to die."

The family gathered around the long table in the great hall. There were nine of them in all. William, Hardy and Hardy's brother Gillies wore their kilts and the women, including Maggie, wore long skirts made from the MacBean tartan. Maria wore a small pleated skirt with bib and shoulder straps her grandmother made for her birthday. It was just past noon when the family solicitor began to recite Gillies last will and testament:

"I, Gillies MacBean VIII," he began, "leave my wife Winwood Grant MacBean, the use of the Dalcross estate farmhouse for the rest of her natural life, with monies from the general fund in the amount of 18,000 pounds sterling per year. Said monies to be used by her to support herself and our daughter Margaret until such time Margaret leaves Dalcross to attend university. At that time, the sum will be reduced to 15,000 pounds sterling, with the residual 3,000 pounds to be given over to Margaret until such university education is remedied. Further to the financial well-being of our daughter, I bequeath to Margaret the sum of thirty thousand pounds sterling to be held in trust by our solicitor Kendall and Forbes, and invested in interest bearing notes of which interest may be distributed to Margaret for any purpose related to her present or future condition."

Winwood looked forward, eyes unblinking, gripping Margaret's hand tightly as if she could never let go. A tear rolled down her face.

"Finally," the solicitor droned, "the express wishes of Gillies MacBean VIII, Chief of Clan MacBean, Laird of Dalcross, as written the fifth day of March 1976: At my death, or when I am no longer able to perform my duties as Laird of Dalcross, Chief of Clan MacBean, I bequeath my titles and the Dalcross properties to my brother William. If he should precede me, then these titles will hand down to the oldest living male, either, in direct succession or distant relative."

There was silence in the room as the solicitor's eyebrows raised above his spectacles.

"And I am to understand," the solicitor continued, "That after careful deliberation, you, William, and your son, Gillies have relinquished all rights to these titles and responsibilities?"

"We do," they said in unison.

"And thus you grant, and give these titles and responsibilities freely to your son and brother William Hardy MacBean?" he questioned.

"We do," they said in unison.

"I would like to add," William said, "that my son Gillies and I have our lives in America. I have lived longer in the United States than I have Scotland. Hardy has lived and breathed Dalcross since he was a young boy, and we believe that his grandfather and his uncle through association groomed him for this eventuality. Although none of us expected that the stewardship of Dalcross and the representation of the family within the Clan Chattan Confederation would be his one day, Hardy is definitely the right man for the job."

"And now Hardy," the solicitor began, "Do you accept the responsibilities and title set forth under your own free will?"

"I do."

"In that case," the solicitor continued, "according to your Uncle Gillies wishes, I now appoint you, William Hardy MacBean, The MacBean of MacBean, Laird of Dalcross. And now this concludes my obligation."

He stood and shook Hardy's hand.

"Congratulations Hardy, I know your uncle would be satisfied with your appointment. He always spoke well of you and held you dear to his heart. Please come and see us when you are settled. I can see my own way out, thank you."

Duncan Forbes snapped his briefcase shut. Hardy stood behind Winwood's chair and put his hand on her shoulder. She turned, placing her hand over his and stood up. They embraced, tears streaming down her face.

"When will you come?" she asked, her voice shaking.

"Not for a bit. Darcy needs to give notice and she plans to find a position here in Inverness. I can work from wherever I am, so I should be ready to move as soon as I pack. Darcy and I hope and expect you to stay on with us here. We don't want you to move out now or ever. There is plenty of room for us all and we'd be lonely without you. We also hope that Maggie will take Maria under her wing."

"Don't worry about Maggie, from the looks of it, she already has done so."

They hugged again and Darcy stepped between them, pulling Winwood into her arms.

"You'll get through this Winwood," she said looking up at Hardy. "I promise, and we'll be here to help you."

"The pipers have arrived along with our guests," Hardy said. "Time to take our seats, everyone."

The funeral was very short, with no clergy present. William stood up and recollected his childhood with his brother, the loss of a mother they never knew, and a father who relied on the Dalcross staff to bring them up until they were both sent off to boarding school. He recounted how his brother always looked after him at school, and when necessary fought off a bully or two.

Hardy stood when his father had finished and began to recollect the years that he had enjoyed with his uncle.

"Gillies taught me about all things connected to Dalcross," he began, "and a few that weren't." A knowing laughter arose from the crowd. "There was never a truer friend, confidant or mentor as Gillies was to me. And as my ancestors were want to do before me, I raise my voice and salute him with our family motto and battle cry. Kinchyle!"

The Clan Chattan Chiefs walked forward, the same men who had recognized Gillies MacBean as the MacBean of MacBean six years before. They stood shoulder to shoulder, coming to attention and saluting in unison, holding their salute as Hardy's brother stood along the casket and played the lone piper funeral march 'Flower of Scotland'. One by one the chiefs tapped the casket once, bidding their friend farewell, nodding their heads and acknowledging Hardy's ascension and acceptance into the confederation. Hardy felt the history of his family and country weigh upon him. He realized at the age of 29, he was the youngest of the chiefs by at least 20 years.

"It wasn't too many years ago," he addressed the gathering, "when many of you attended my grandfather's funeral. At the time my uncle made sure that we would provide the best food and libation that ever was witnessed in the County of Inverness. We now honor Gillies memory as we did his father before him. Please join us. I am sure you will not be disappointed."

A cheer rose from the crowd and they stood and followed the MacBean family into the great hall as the Clan Chattan pipers struck up *Scotland the Brave*.

Chapter 42

"Hello, Dalcross Castle, Winwood speaking."

"Winwood," Darcy gushed, "I'm on break. Is Hardy available?"

"Is anything wrong?"

"No, nothing wrong. Get Hardy to turn on the BBC!"

"He's in the kitchen garden with the girls, hold on."

Winwood turned the radio dial to BBC and called out.

"Hardy, Darcy is on the phone, something about the BBC, come quickly."

"What's going on?" Hardy asked as he came through the kitchen door.

"Darcy said to listen," Winwood replied, turning up the volume.

"This is Martin Bell reporting: July 17, 1979. Fighters of the left-wing Sandinista National Liberation Front have overthrown the regime in the Central American republic of Nicaragua and taken the capital, Managua. The notorious U.S.-trained National Guard has crumbled and its surviving commanders are negotiating surrender.

In the last six weeks, Sandinista fighters have gained control of 27 cities around the capital, as well as the southern part of Nicaragua that borders Costa Rica. President Anastasio Somoza Debayle, third member of the Somoza dynasty to rule Nicaragua since 1937, has fled to the United

States. This evening he abandoned the battle-torn capital with about 45 other people in five planes that landed at Homestead US Air Force Base near Miami, Florida. Earlier, he presented his resignation to the Congress and handed power over to the chairman of the lower house, Francisco Urcuyo, who is now caretaker president. Mr. Urcuyo has declared the Sandinistas will have no part in his new government and demanded they lay down their arms. But the Sandinista-backed provisional government, currently based in the city of Leon, is expected to force Mr. Urcuyo to resign. The Sandinistas, named after Nicaraguan resistance leader Augusto Cesar Sandino, was set up in 1962 by Carlos Fonseca Amador, Silvio Mayorga and Thomas Borge. For the last seven years, they have waged a civil war against the Somoza government. Fighting has been at its most intense in the last two months and thousands have been killed and about half a million left homeless. Last year, the assassination of the leader of the opposition Democratic Liberation Union, Pedro Joaquin Chamorro, triggered a general strike and brought together moderates, the Roman Catholic Church and the Sandinistas in a united front against Somoza. The Americans have long supported the Somoza regime but realizing that the Sandinista rebels had the upper hand in the war, U.S. officials have spent the last few weeks trying to persuade President Somoza to step down, assuring him that his Liberal Party and the National Guard would survive."

"Just like when they left Saigon," Hardy muttered. "Empty promises."

"Last week," Bell continued, "William Bowdler, a special American envoy, began talks with members of the provisional government asking them to enlarge the junta by including representatives of the National Guard and Liberal Party. His request was denied."

"This is Martin Bell reporting for the BBC."

"Finally over," Hardy said as he left the kitchen and returned to the garden. He listened to the children laughing as they picked strawberries.

"Girls, girls, make sure they go into the bucket, not in your mouth. Winwood is using them for desert tonight." He heard a car pull up the drive and briefly stop before turning around to leave. Must be the mail carrier, he thought.

"Hardy," Winwood called out, opening the screen door from the kitchen, "you've got mail. It's postmarked San Jose, Costa Rica."

Hardy looked over at Maria, her face stained red from strawberries. He wondered who could have written him from Costa Rica. Maybe young Herman was writing him about the war. Maybe it was Tanja, he thought. He turned and walked through the kitchen door.

"It's on the table," Winwood said.

Hardy looked at the neat cursive and recognized it was the elder Herman's handwriting. Opening the letter, he wondered why Herman was in Costa Rica.

July 1, 1979

My Dear Hardy,

I am writing to you from Costa Rica. My wife and I fled Managua June 27 when Somoza's air force bombed Managua's eastern neighborhoods. I am so sorry to report that both our son Herman and our niece Tanja were killed on the night we escaped to Costa Rica. We have received this sad news today. A bomb was dropped on San Jeronimo Park while they were in charge of the evacuation and we are told that they died instantly.

274

My wife and I are terribly grief stricken by the loss of our brave son and niece and hope that we will be home soon to give them a proper burial. My son told me before he died that if anything happened to him or Tanja, there was something you must know. He wanted me to tell you that Tanja gave birth to your son February 1, 1976. She named him William Hardy after you and he lives with Frederick and Avira in Granada. I will let you know our plans when we return to Managua. The Sandinistas now hold every major city except Managua. The Nicaraguan people have suffered greatly, but they are resilient and we hope that we shall soon be victorious. We wished that Herman and Tanja would be with us to celebrate the coming victory, but they will forever dwell among the hero's' of Nicaraguan independence.

God bless you, Herman

Hardy folded the letter, put it back in the envelope, and stuffed it into his pants pocket.

"Good news?" Winwood asked.

"Just news," Hardy said, his voice trembling, his eyes filling with tears. He got up from the table and left the kitchen, heading off toward the barn and the woods beyond.

"Winwood said you received a letter from Costa Rica today. Was it important?"

"It was."

"Who was it from?"

"Herman. He said that his son and niece were both killed."

"That's terrible Hardy."

"Yes it is. I'm afraid there is more."

"What?"

275

"I have a son."

"What!" Darcy exclaimed, her eyes filling with tears.

"I'm sorry Darcy, I just found out."

"Who is the mother?"

"Herman's niece, Tanja."

"God Hardy, were you ever going to tell me?"

"I tried, I couldn't, I just found out about the boy today."

"You couldn't? How could you not Hardy?"

"I don't know, I wanted to, I knew how terribly it would go, how upset you would be. I am so sorry Darcy."

"God Hardy, what are you going to do now?

They sat in silence, neither one looking at each other.

"You bastard," Darcy exclaimed as she stood up and left the room.

Part 11

"Venganza"

Chapter 43

"Thanks for giving me a ride, Herman, I appreciate it," Hardy said.

"You are very welcome, Hardy. You look well. Five years is a long time. We also look forward to seeing our grandnephew. Frederick tells me he speaks Spanish, German and English now, sometimes jumbled in the same sentence."

"And he just turned four last February," Henrietta broke in. "He is such a handsome boy. Frederick and Avira love him so. He is the son they never had. Their daughter, Marlina, is helping out. She has been back in country since Somoza fled. She told us that she remembered meeting you briefly in London at the Nicaraguan Consulate."

"Yes," Hardy said. "She introduced me to your husband many years ago, I think eight years now."

"Yes," Herman said. "I remember your first visit, our trip around the country, the earthquake. It was a good trip except for the time in Matagalpa and the earthquake of course. Maybe I can find lumber for you again. The mill in Granada is no longer. It was destroyed during the war. It's a wonder my brother was not harmed. He says that someday William Hardy will own the ranch, but until then his aunt will take care of it for him."

"Is she married?"

"No, no marriage, she is too busy. But she is only 27."

"She has plenty of time to get married," Henrietta joined in. "But first, she must take care of the family. She is the only one we have now other than William Hardy. How old are you now Hardy?"

"Thirty one last March."

"That is a good age, are you still married?"

"Yes, I have a daughter that is two months older than William Hardy."

"What is her name?"

"Maria."

They drove in silence until they reached the hacienda gate.

"I never get tired of the view across the lake," Herman said. "It always feels like home to me."

"Darcy and I had a wonderful sail," Hardy said, his voice showing no emotion.

Herman drove into the courtyard and hit the horn twice. His brother Frederick sat in a rocking chair on the porch, pushing a hammock back and forth. Marlina appeared on the porch and scooped up a young child from the hammock.

"There he is, little William Hardy!" Henrietta exclaimed.

Marlina held him close as his head rested on her shoulder. She bent down and said something to her father before disappearing into the house

"Welcome to our hacienda, Hardy MacBean," Frederick said standing up, "I was hoping you would come."

"It has been a long time, Don Frederick," Hardy said, climbing the front steps, reaching out his hand.

"It is good to see you, Hardy," he said, clasping Hardy's hand. "Marlina has taken the boy to clean him up and change him. It's not every day a boy gets to meet his father for the first time."

"About that," Hardy began, "I am sorry, Don Frederick. It is not how I had planned."

"Nothing to be sorry about, Hardy, Your son gives us great joy. He looks much like his mother. He reminds us of her. Someday he will be the man of the house and he will own all of Rancho de Vogel. Even at four years old he is multilingual."

"Herman told me."

Marlina and Avira entered the porch along side William Hardy, each holding a hand. He marched, unknowingly, toward his father. He wore a white short-sleeved shirt and a pair of short lederhosen with a halter showing a design of an embroidered bull. Hardy got down on his knee and watched as his son walked toward him.

"How do you do, William Hardy," he said softly as his son stopped less than a foot away.

"Say hello," Avira prodded.

"Hola," he said, without hesitation, reaching out his hand.

Hardy took his hand and shook it once, holding it, unwilling to let go.

"A very handsome boy," he said, feeling out of place.

"Let us go where we can speak privately," Frederick interrupted. "Herman and Henrietta do not want to see us, they want to see William Hardy."

Hardy let go of his son's hand and stood up, following Frederick into his library. He stood as Frederick sat behind his desk.

"Have you decided to represent us?" Frederick asked, rigid in his chair, looking off across the lake.

"Yes I have."

"I thought it would be good for you to see your son before you go."

"Thank you, Don Frederick, I appreciate that very much. He looks like his mother; his hair has the same color with red highlights. I am so sorry he will never know her. If there is anything I can do for you or William, I want you to promise me that you will ask."

"Don't worry, Hardy, you will hear from me or Marlina about the boy. We take pictures of him all the time. He speaks in three languages, Spanish, German and English. We teach him a little each day. He is very bright.

About this business, tomorrow morning my brother will take you to the airport. My friend Tomas has it all arranged. He will meet you and the others before you fly out and provide you and your team with the weapons. He will address you as Comandante Beano. There are seven on your team and two are already in place. "Tachito," he is the snake, and that is why this is called "Operation Reptile," Frederick continued. "We will show him no mercy. We will cut off his head and avenge the thousands of our countrymen and woman who have died by his hand and the hands of his Guardia Nacional. With your help, we will send him straight to hell.

Chapter 44

Hardy opened his door and thanked Herman for the ride.

"Vaya con dios, Hardy," Herman said.

"Gracias, Herman. Decir una oracion por me."

"I will," Herman said and he put his car into first gear. He gave Hardy a salute and drove off the military's landing field adjacent to the Mercedes International Airport.

Two men and three women stood on the tarmac next to a Hawker Siddeley turbojet, one of them in military fatigues, the others in street clothing.

"Comandante Beano," the man in military dress said. "Welcome, I am Tomas."

Hardy looked at the man, who was of short stature and wore aviator glasses.

"Thank you, sir," Hardy replied, shaking the man's hand.

"These are your comrades," he said, waving his arm in an arc.

"This is Capitan Santiago," he pointed to a young man with scruffy hair and a blond beard. "And the women," gesturing to each of them in succession, "Comandante Uno, Comandante M, and Teresa."

Hardy smiled, extending his hand to each one in succession. They did not smile or speak as he shook their hands. They couldn't look more serious, he thought, but this was serious business, a gathering of assassins, together for one purpose only.

"Now we can begin," Tomas exclaimed. "Your team members Ramon and Oswaldo are waiting for your arrival in Paraguay. They will meet you at a small landing strip and take you into Asuncion by van. It is all well planned. They have watched Somoza for five months. The weather is good. You should have no problem. Your flight will take seven hours with one stopover for fuel. Your pilots are well trained. Both are former captains with Taca airlines. Remember, you have until 1 o'clock tomorrow afternoon to return to the aircraft. The pilots will not wait. If you miss the flight you are on your own. Is this understood?"

The question was answered with silence.

"Buenos," Tomas said. "We have stowed the following weapons aboard the plane. Two Uzi machine guns, courtesy of the Israelis, the last to supply Somoza with weapons. We find as Somoza did that they work well in close battle. Two AK-47 assault rifles, two automatic pistols and one RPG-7 rocket launcher, including four anti-tank grenades and two rockets, all supplied to us by our Soviet friends. Capitan Santiago is familiar with the rocket launcher. The rest of you know what to do." He then reached out his hand to each of them and repeated, "Vaya con dios."

Hardy watched as a military jeep sped across the runway and stopped in front of them. With a brief smile, Tomas held up his right hand, waved once, turned, climbed into the jeep and drove away in great haste.

"We will be leaving within the hour," one of the pilots called out from the cabin door.

Hardy boarded with the others and took the first window seat to his left. Capitan Santiago followed and abruptly sat down next to him as the pilots voice came over the speaker.

"This is the captain speaking, la bienvenida a bordo. Our arrival is scheduled for sunrise tomorrow after a brief layover in Bolivia. Fasten your seatbelts, please."

"Do you mind?" Santiago asked, turning to Hardy.

"No, por favor," Hardy gestured with his hands.

"Buenos," Santiago said. "You are famous Comandante Beano."

"I am?"

"Si, we all agreed that you would join us."

"What?"

"We voted. We all know what you did for us when no one else would. The rifles you brought to us that kept our revolution alive. You gave us hope when we needed it most. We suffered defeat, but then we achieved victory."

"We must complete our task," Santiago continued, "for those who are no longer with us, for those who have lost their sisters, brothers, wives, husbands and children, especially the children, all murdered. We signed up for this mission, as you have. You are now one of us."

Santiago stood up and moved to the back of the plane. Hardy looked out the window as the turbo props ignited and the plane began to move. He closed his eyes and thought about his daughter and his newfound son. He thought about his meeting with Duncan Forbes the week before and the concern Forbes showed when he handed him a letter with instructions to open if he didn't return.

"Fasten your seat belts, prepare for landing," the captain's voice exclaimed over the cabin speaker.

Dawn was breaking and Hardy woke from a restless sleep, his chest wet with sweat. He looked out his window into the early morning light at a blood red sky. "Red sky in the morning, sailor take warning," ominous he thought. No landing field in sight, he looked down upon a long straight road running through endless fields of green.

"Hold on, this will be a rough landing," the pilot warned, "brace yourselves."

Hardy kept searching for a landing field as the jet descended. He soon realized the road was the landing strip. They landed with such force they bounced once before making full contact. The pilot immediately reversed engines, sending up billows of dust behind them.

"Jesus," Hardy said, looking at two of the women sitting across from him.

The jet taxied and came to a stop adjacent to a small farmhouse that faced the road with a long shed behind it. The pilot turned in the direction of the shed and maneuvered around the back, out of view. As the engines shut down, a white Chevy cargo van carrying two men drove up and parked alongside. Hardy watched as the driver left the van. He was about five foot eight, 175 pounds, balding head with dark brown hair and a brown goatee. The pilot opened the door and lowered the stairs.

"Buenos camaradas de la manana, estoy Ramon," he said as he entered the cabin.

"Reunamonos las armas?"

Santiago stood up and pulled a metal trunk from the rear of the plane.

"Ah, the weapons," Ramon said. He opened the lid and began to hand out the inventory.

He looked at Hardy and held out an Uzi. He then held up the RPG-7 rocket launcher.

"You have had practice, Santiago?" Ramon asked handing it over. He then gave two automatic pistols and one AK-47 to the women.

"Vámonos!" he commanded.

Ramon swung the remaining AK-47 and Uzi over his shoulder and led them to the van. A second man appeared and opened the van's back doors. Hardy and his crew got in and sat huddled on the floor while the man closed the doors behind them.

"This is Oswaldo," Ramon called out as he joined him in the front seat.

The bumpy ride to Asuncion was uneventful and within the hour they parked on Avenida de Espana about 300 feet up the street from No. 433, the gated house belonging to Anastasio Somoza Debayle.

No one had spoken during the trip and there were no windows in the van for them to see the countryside. It was 10 minutes before 7 when they arrived, and they remained sitting for three hours while the heat in the van became unbearable. The sweat rolled off Hardy as the stench from the team became increasingly oppressive. Oswaldo stood outside Somoza's gate equipped with a satchel of newspapers, completing his disguise as a paperboy, a task he had performed daily for months.

"Oswaldo will signal us when Somoza is leaving his estate. If all is normal, they will leave around 10 o'clock. And you, Santiago, get ready with the rocket launcher. Remember, we want to hit the Mercedes broadside. The rest of you will cover. Let us hope that the police are sleeping.

Hardy gripped his Uzi, his hands sweating. Ten o'clock came. Nothing, Oswaldo stood like a sentinel, newspaper in hand. Five after 10, the silence in the van was deafening. Eight after 10, six sets of eyes peered intently through the van's windshield.

"Don't worry," Ramon said, "he has been leaving his house at 10 o'clock every morning or close to it for six months."

Ten after 10, Oswaldo's arm went up, waving the newspaper in the air, signaling the kill. Hardy's heart skipped a beat. The commandos spilled from the van at Ramon's command as Somoza's car appeared at the curbside. Oswaldo handed a newspaper through the rear window and quickly walked away.

"Santiago!" Ramon shouted, "Fire!"

Santiago aimed and pulled the trigger, nothing, a misfire. Ramon could see alarm on Somoza's chauffer's face and quickly aimed his AK-47, letting out a burst of fire, striking him in the face and body. The Mercedes came to an abrupt stop. The chauffer slumped from the wheel.

"Now, Santiago, now! Fire! Fuego dios Maldita Sea!" Ramon barked.

Hardy watched the bewilderment cross Santiago's face as he took the rocket launcher from his hands and quickly reloaded. He fell to one knee, aimed and pulled the trigger without hesitation, shouting out "KINCHYLE" in a deep guttural voice as the rocket made a direct hit, exploding the Mercedes, blowing off the roof, and leaving the incineration of its occupants total and complete. Five commandos quickly loaded into the van, with Oswaldo racing to join them. Santiago ran madly toward the Mercedes, yelling back to them.

"I must see Somoza's dead body with my own eyes."

Oswaldo raced by him, running for the van, shouting out to Santiago.

"He is dead, he is dead! Come with us Santiago, quickly! He is dead!"

"Santiago get into the van, we must go," Ramon called out.

Santiago continued to run. He would not listen. Blaring sirens were heard in the distance as they watched police cars fast approaching with lights flashing.

"Mierda!" Ramon exclaimed as Oswaldo jumped into the van.

He stomped on the gas pedal and sped east toward freedom, leaving Santiago behind. Hardy looked out the rear door window and watched as the police converged upon Somoza's destroyed Mercedes. Santiago fell to his knees with his hands in the air.

Chapter 45

Six of the original seven commandos landed in Managua and went their separate ways. Hardy climbed aboard an early morning flight to Miami and watched Nicaragua fade into the distance. He was on his way home.

EPILOGUE

The Paraguayan media reported that Somoza had been assassinated, his body so unrecognizable that he could only be identified by forensics through his feet. Capitan Santiago was never heard from again.

In January 1981, four months to the day after the assassination, the United States suspended all aid to Nicaragua. The Carter-era financial commitments were fully terminated by the Reagan administration in April 1981.

Hardy MacBean returned to his life in Scotland and soon entered politics, spending much of his time in Edinburgh. He would learn through his father that CIA officials and former Somoza National Guard leaders held a series of meetings in Guatemala City from August to October 1981. Together they would fund and establish a force of 500 anti-Sandinista fighters who would be known as the Contras.

Made in the USA
Middletown, DE
09 January 2020

82611868R00166